"I'M BEGINNING TO REALIZE THAT I'M ON THE WRONG SIDE."

White Frog, the Cheyenne chief, reached up, put his hands on the taller man's shoulders.

"You are part Indian and part Whiteman, Soldier Wolf. Your blood is Indian, though your people are different from mine. But you have lived your life among these Whitemen and have gone to their school. Medicine Calf was the same. He has had to live in both worlds—he is one of us, but he is one of them also. When the time to fight comes, you will have to choose."

White Frog's words echoed and reechoed through Soldier Wolf's brain . . . *part Indian and part Whiteman.* Not even White Frog realized what utter truth he had spoken. *Don't know for sure just what the hell I am. Cherokee father, White mother. Should never have come out here, didn't know about freedom until I saw the mountains, the long white wall of the mountains, until I heard the coyotes and wolves howling, until I took that scalp . . .*

Soldier Wolf

Bill Hotchkiss

BANTAM BOOKS
TORONTO · NEW YORK · LONDON · SYDNEY

SOLDIER WOLF

A Bantam Book / September 1982

ISBN 0-553-20896-9

Published simultaneously in the United States and Canada

Bantam Books are published by Bantam Books, Inc. Its trademark, consisting of the words "Bantam Books" and the portrayal of a rooster, is Registered in U.S. Patent and Trademark Office and in other countries. Marca Registrada. Bantam Books, Inc., 666 Fifth Avenue, New York, New York 10103.

PRINTED IN THE UNITED STATES OF AMERICA

O 0 9 8 7 6 5 4 3 2 1

For my good friend
Don Jordan (K'os Naahaabii),
the unindicted coauthor of this volume,
from whose fertile imagination
the figures of Soldier Wolf
and the Goths emerged.

Chapter One

The Cherokee Sequoia was a cripple, but his mind was not crippled. He saw that the Whitemen made markings on paper to record all that they did, and in these markings, he came to believe, lay the secret to their power. With this in mind, Sequoia began in the early 1820's to devise an alphabet for the Indian peoples, a system of signs based on syllables and word roots. Armed with Sequoia's alphabet, the Cherokees soon had schools, mills, churches, and efficiently operating farms, as well as a governmental system consisting of legislative, judicial, and executive branches. Within a few short years they had become a civilized Nation. Even after Congress had passed the Removal Act, and the Cherokees and other Southeast peoples had been forced to march to Oklahoma over the Trail of Tears, the survivors were able to establish new schools for both men and women and to publish a newspaper in both English and Cherokee. Sequoia himself died in obscurity, in Mexico, in 1843. A relative handful of Cherokees avoided deportation and remained in North Carolina, among the folds of the Great Smokies, on lands the Whitemen did not want.

Lester Harriman, head clerk of the Bureau of Indian Affairs, struck a match and lit the loosely tamped grains of burley tobacco in his favorite pipe, puffed two or three times, and stared out through the gray panes of window glass to the cobbled Washington street outside. A wet snow was falling this first week in December, half-sticking, half-melting, and the iron-belted wheels of a coach and four, passing by, spun up trails of slush behind them.

Harriman glanced at the stacks of papers on his desk, puffed disconsolately at his pipe, and idly rearranged the papers. He opened the center drawer, withdrew an envelope, took out the letter within, and read it over for perhaps the hundredth time since he had written it.

His letter of resignation. Only the effective date had not yet been penned in.

Harriman glanced across to the other desk in the office, the desk of his son, Daniel, who was engrossed in the reading of a report concerning one Edward Cramdon, a former BIA agent to the Cheyennes, a man who had turned renegade and who, with a band of half-breeds and Spaniards and men wanted by various local authorities, had now engaged in a profitable trade consisting of general thievery, attacking wagon trains and Indian villages alike. Cramdon, Harriman reflected, had in effect been grub-staked by the federal government—having misappropriated funds and supplies.

This problem and many others from half a continent away came inevitably to Harriman's desk, where he, through judicious action, was expected to resolve them.

Harriman puffed on the pipe, biting down on the stem, and squinted at his son.

Like father, like son, Harriman thought, and then glanced once more at his letter of resignation.

Lester Harriman's career with the BIA had been a long one, and over the years his sympathies had fallen ever more with the Indian peoples—for in his mind these peoples over whom he held judicial authority seemed far more sinned against than sinning. But for all the situations he had somehow managed to ameliorate, the problems seemed nevertheless always to increase, both in number and in intensity. And now, he feared, with the United States having reached out to the far Pacific Ocean, and with floods of emigrants moving constantly westward to the gold fields and the silver fields and the rich farmlands along the Pacific rim, and with plans afoot to span the continent with rails, the last great domain of the Indian peoples appeared doomed. Trouble was brewing everywhere.

Now, with the election of Lincoln, and the Union itself on the verge of dissolution, it was time to leave the nearly thankless task of attempting to administer justice to the aboriginal American peoples—to leave the task to younger men, such as his own son, Daniel, already well-established within the hegemony of the Bureau.

Lester Harriman knew, as did everyone else in Washington, D.C., that within a few days a convention ordered by the South Carolina legislature would meet. The issue was one of great import to the Union itself. Should South Carolina secede? Certainly, if South Carolina struck out for independence, the other slave states would follow. And the result of that would be either two separate nations, in all likelihood, or a war between North and South.

Douglas, defeated in the election but consummately loyal to the Union, was already in the South, speaking out against secession—and, from reports, was being greeted by fusillades of eggs and vegetables.

Harriman had just slipped the folded letter back into its envelope and had closed the desk drawer when he became aware of a repeated and heavy thumping sound in the outside office.

Daniel looked up from the report and said, "What the hell?"

The father and the son rose at once, moved rapidly to the door, and exited into Kramer's waiting room outside.

The little assistant's feet were at least eighteen inches above the polished oak floor, and his shoulders were pinned against the papered wall. The face was red, and the eyes were wide. He was being held there by the collar of his white shirt.

The man holding him up with one hand was huge, well over six feet in height, and broad through the shoulders. He wore a blue soldier's uniform, and there were yellow sergeant's stripes on the shoulder. Strangely enough, he wore a turban, purple and yellow. He was laughing loudly. And in his other hand was a pistol.

Kramer, words having deserted him, could only squeal with terror.

"Put that man down!" Lester Harriman ordered. "What the hell's going on here?"

The turban-wearing sergeant stepped back, and Kramer slid down the wall, crumpling to his knees.

"We'll have you court-martialed for this, sergeant!" Daniel Harriman shouted. "How dare you!"

The man in the turban grinned. "I'm looking for Lester Harriman," he said, "and this civilian doesn't seem to understand my words. Is one of you Harriman?"

"We're both Harrimans," the father said. "Who are you, young man?"

"Guess I don't need the pistol anymore, then," he said, returning the weapon to its holster and extending his hand. "My name's Soldier Wolf—Sergeant Jerry Soldier Wolf, gentlemen. I was told you wished to see me. . . ."

"Soldier Wolf? Oh, yes, yes," the senior Harriman said. "You come highly recommended, young man—but this sort of thing . . . Hardly the actions of a gentleman, hardly the actions of a noncommissioned officer!"

"Civilian, sir, as of tomorrow. My enlistment's up." Soldier Wolf grinned. "What did you wish to see me about, gentlemen?"

"Apparently there's been a mistake," Daniel Harriman said, glancing at his father, the eyes narrow, searching.

"Possibly so," Soldier Wolf said.

But the senior Harriman thrust his hand forward, clasped Soldier Wolf's bearlike paw, shook it. "Present appearances to the contrary," he said, "I've never yet been disappointed in one of Colonel Brownell's recommendations—and he thinks highly of you, young man. But is it necessary to brutalize my subordinate?"

Kramer, in the meanwhile, had picked himself up from the floor, had stared questioningly at first one, then the other of the Harrimans, and at a nod from Daniel had left the foyer.

"Lost my temper, I guess," Soldier Wolf said, not apologizing. "I've got things to do—I came here only because the colonel asked me to. But no man's going to insult me without paying a price for it, and that little—"

"All right, all right," Lester Harriman said. "Sometimes Kramer struts a bit too much. That's true. Jerry, is it? We've an offer for you, one that may interest you."

"Yes, sir. Jerry. Jerry Soldier Wolf. An offer?"

"Brownell sent over your file this morning. Mr. Soldier Wolf, this is my son, Daniel. We've both read through your papers. Interesting, very interesting."

The younger Harriman now extended his hand. The two men shook, and Harriman the elder gestured toward the inner office.

Soldier Wolf, more than a little puzzled and still annoyed by the whole business, shrugged his shoulders and followed the two civilian officials, took the chair offered him, and sat down, glancing from one Harriman to the other.

"You're Cherokee?" Daniel asked.

Soldier Wolf nodded. "Half-breed, actually," he said. "A blue-eyed Injun. My mother is White, my pa's Cherokee."

"And you were raised in North Carolina, I believe. A graduate of the college at Chapel Hill?"

"Guilty of both counts." Soldier Wolf nodded. "When your people sent my people to Oklahoma on the Trail of Tears, a few of us avoided the roundup. My pa led us back into the Smokies. A few hundred of us in all, and we've managed a good life there. Pa's got a little farm on a creek called Raven's Fork, just below Newfound Gap and Eagle Rock. I grew up there, got interested in books, and a Baptist missionary took a liking to me and secured a scholarship for me at Chapel Hill. I'm an outside insider, you might say, the victim of two cultures and the master of neither. From there to the U.S. Army, and from there to your office. In short, gentlemen, the story of the life of one Jerry Soldier Wolf."

The Harrimans looked at each other, then back to Soldier Wolf.

"Brownell says you've a reputation as a box-fighter," the elder Harriman suggested.

"Guilty of that, too, sir. A half-breed in a Whiteman's world had best learn to defend himself."

"Well, you're big enough." Lester Harriman chuckled, reaching for his pipe, refilling it with burley, and lighting it.

"All right, then," Daniel Harriman said. "We're prepared to offer you a job, Mr. Soldier Wolf. A job that should be suited to you, one that carries with it some very real risk. We need a BIA agent to the Cheyenne peoples out in Colorado Territory. Double your military salary, and expenses to boot."

"I don't understand," Soldier Wolf said, shaking his head.

Lester Harriman stared momentarily at the traditional Cherokee turban, glanced at his son, and then explained: "The assignment will be with a group called the People of the Valley," he said. "They're Cheyennes living in the Rocky Mountains, northwest of Bent's Fort, almost due west of a settlement called Colorado City, near the headwaters of the North Platte. We had a man out there named Edward Cramdon—"

"Had?" Soldier Wolf asked.

"Yes. He's still there somewhere, but no longer with the Bureau. This Cramdon was a political appointment four years back. He's misappropriated agency funds and has turned renegade. We sent two agents out there last year to assess the situation, and both ended up getting killed—Cramdon and his boys, as best we can tell."

"He's got an army of outlaws with him," Daniel put in.

"That's it exactly," Lester agreed. "And he's become virtually a law unto himself. Six months ago he tore up Colorado City. He's hit wagon trains and Indian villages. Cheyennes, Arapahos, Pawnees—they get blamed for the wagon-train problems. Cramdon's men come in dressed like Indians, and I guess some of them are."

"So what would you want me to do?" Soldier Wolf asked.

"It's simple, my boy," Lester Harriman said. "All you have to do is to enlist the loyalties of the Cheyenne people. You're Indian, and you may be able to succeed where the others failed. Then you get your Cheyenne friends to cooperate with one another, and you bring Cramdon and his henchmen in—to Whiteman's justice."

"Why, hell," Soldier Wolf said, starting to rise, "any child could do that. Best you find yourself a White boy. This nigger's heading back to Raven's Fork. I'm going to help my pa with dirt farming and watch the Union fly into pieces. . . ."

"Mr. Soldier Wolf," Lester Harriman said in the way of a man quite used to wielding authority, "we need *you*—not someone else. That's why I sent for you. As to the fate of the Union, God only knows, and His will shall prevail. But dissolution or not, the westward movement is not going to stop, not while there's gold and silver and farmland and cattle range out there. The Cheyennes and the other Plains peoples cannot stand in the face of the monolith that bears down upon them. The Trail of Tears and all the other relocations have been utter abominations, and Daniel and I have resisted and continue to resist such things, even as we deplore them. But without help, we are ineffectual. The assignment we've proposed to you is vital, and its successful accomplishment will save many lives. You are Indian, Soldier Wolf. Cheyenne or Cherokee or White, all have a right to fair treatment and to justice. But we must cooperate. We are on your side. Are you willing to be on ours?"

The current of words roiled about Soldier Wolf, and he sat down once more, studied the two men for long moments.

Finally he grinned, gestured with his big hands. "You could talk the false teeth out of a brush wolf," he said. "All right. I guess this dumb Injun's been had. So lay it out for me. I guess I'm your man."

The conversation went on for some time. At length papers were produced, were filled out, and Jerry Soldier Wolf found himself affixing his signature in several places. Soldier Wolf was invited to a social gathering of BIA officials and their wives, meeting that evening for the purpose of listening to Commissioner Greenwood's projections of what his career professionals, such men as the Harrimans, might expect under any new commissioner whom President-elect Lincoln might appoint within the next month or so. But the tone, Soldier Wolf was assured, would be festive, complete with ballroom dancing and excellent conversation, as well as an abundance of good food and fine liquors and wines. Soldier Wolf wished to decline the invitation, but Lester Harriman was insistent, and Jerry finally succumbed to his new employer's protestations.

After a final round of handshakes, Soldier Wolf exited the Bureau of Indian Affairs offices and walked out into the chilly half-snow, half-rain of the Washington afternoon. He drew his military-issue overcoat about him, gritted his teeth against a sudden gust of wind, and strode quickly along Nineteenth Street to its junction with Constitution Avenue.

A horse-drawn omnibus came clattering and creaking down the avenue, and Jerry hailed the driver, a big fellow smoking a pipe and wearing an old battered felt hat and wrapped in a black slicker.

"Climb aboard, lad!" the driver shouted as the omnibus slowed.

Soldier Wolf grasped the safety rail and vaulted up onto the running board, climbed inside, worked his way down the aisle, and took a seat by a window. The omnibus moved on, the interior blue with pipe smoke and the air filled with careless, good-natured chatter. Across from him sat two men who spoke with heavy Southern accents, one White and one Black—a proper Virginian and Negro man slave, Soldier Wolf conjectured. Across the aisle and one tier back were two other men, plainly dressed, both of them staring intently at the Virginian and his slave.

Abolitionists, Soldier Wolf thought.

The omnibus was nearly full—businessmen, women, a few children. And the spaces above the windows were filled with advertising cards and one or two Christmas decorations.

On the ash paneling next to which Jerry sat, someone had scrawled the single word "SECESSION."

The Great American Democracy in all its glory, all its contradiction—Soldier Wolf felt, at that moment, unsure whether he wanted to laugh or to cry. He shrugged, stared out the window, the glass misted around its edges.

Across the open field of the Ellipse, he could see the White House. He thought about James Buchanan, the defeated incumbent, one who had come into office four years earlier after a close but resounding victory over John Frémont, the explorer, and Millard Fillmore. The man had risen on the great wheel, and now the great wheel was spinning down—and the nation he led was ready to burst into fragments. In a little over two months, the tall, gaunt man from Illinois would take over the reins of American governance, but whether a single nation would remain by that time was highly doubtful.

Soldier Wolf shook his head, thought again about his new job. He still wasn't used to the idea, probably wouldn't be for some time. Things were changing too rapidly, but in such times, all a man could do was to drift with the current, not fight it. Many times the lure of the lands to the west had sung in his ears, but always the prospect had seemed dim, distant. Now he had a federal appointment to go there, to see it all for himself—even though by the time he arrived in the high plains and the mountains of the Jefferson Territory, the very agency which had just employed him, for all he knew, might well have passed into nonexistence.

No point in worrying about it, I guess, he thought, and continued staring out through the partially misted pane of glass.

The omnibus clattered on down Constitution Avenue, with people getting on, people getting off, past government buildings, past the Capitol Building and the Supreme Court, and on toward the Anacostia River, the big Irish driver singing loudly now, shouting to the Clydesdales in harness, whistling, snapping the guy reins.

At the river, Soldier Wolf got off, walked upstream through the wooded area beside the water. Snow was falling now, and the whiteness was sticking to leafless trees and winter-dead grasses, covering even the well-defined track of the footpath. Soldier Wolf stared up into the white downfall, felt the snowflakes touch at his face, stick to his eyebrows.

He walked to the water's edge, brushed the wet snow off a ledge of stone, sat down, and gazed across the gray-blue current of the river, flowing now with the outgoing tide, gliding on down to the Washington Channel and the much greater flow of the Potomac, that river merging, in turn, with the broad waters of Chesapeake Bay, some miles to the south, with Maryland on the one side, Virginia on the other, the channel dividing the nation itself, the slave states from the states that were called *free*, whatever thing the word meant.

What did the term signify with regard to his own race? And what *was* his own race? The original Americans, the tribes scattered, some vanished, some on reservations, some, like the Cherokee people, having themselves become civilized and even prosperous and yet having been herded westward to the so-called Indian territory of Oklahoma, other tribes yet wild, the peoples of the far plains, the Cheyennes, to whom he would go as a government agent, and for what purpose? However good the intentions of such men as the Harrimans, Soldier Wolf knew well enough what the ultimate outcome would be. The Cheyennes and the others, their numbers diminished through disease and massacre, would be forced at last onto lands that the Whites felt, at least for the time being, they did not want.

Hard to imagine what the future held—now, in particular, with the Union threatening to dissolve, to fly into pieces.

The nation is forming itself, Soldier Wolf thought, and yet it has no idea what it wishes to be. . . .

Soldier Wolf stared out at the gray water, bits of driftwood, a half-submerged wooden barrel, the remnants of a log-and-board raft floating close to shore, the planking covered with snow, an upright spar fashioned from a branch, a yellow scrap of rag hanging limp and damp from the top. Soldier Wolf withdrew his Marston revolver, a Navy-issue weapon actually, one that he had acquired a year earlier in a poker game when he had been in New York City on leave, a highly satisfactory piece, it seemed to him, with walnut grips and a roll-engraved Whitney cylinder. The weapon felt good in the hand—the weight, the balance, just right. He checked the loads, aimed at the yellow rag, clucked his tongue, and started to return the pistol to its holster—stopped in mid-motion, drew down once more upon the little yellow flag atop the twisted branch, and fired.

The shot echoed out over the swirling gray water, and the yellow cloth jumped, the branch stem snapping over, hanging by shattered fibers of wood. Soldier Wolf fired a second time, and the little banner leaped upward, fell, splashed soundlessly into the running flood.

The good smell of gunpowder, and a trickle of smoke curling upward from the barrel of the Marston.

Jerry Soldier Wolf returned the pistol to its holster, withdrew a cigar from his jacket's inside pocket, bit off the end of the cheroot, touched his tongue to the drawing end, clamped the tobacco between his teeth. He struck a match, lit up, and savored the rich taste of the smoke.

The snow continued to fall, and the river continued to run. Across the stream, the wooded land rose gently to District Heights: buildings, houses here and there, smoke rising from chimneys, hardly visible in the snowfall. The smoothly contoured folds of Maryland, beyond the limits of the District of Columbia—the land and the nation itself, sleepy now, quiet, seemingly peaceful this winter day.

Soldier Wolf thought of the mountains some forty miles due west of the Capital City, the Blue Ridge and the Massanutten beyond that, and the Shenandoahs beyond that—the long, parallel ridges of the Appalachians, their crests running southwest to northeast, dividing the land, the seaboard from the interior, tying the Southern states to the Northern—a grand unity of coast and waterway and ridge and valley, the rhythms, the undulations of the land, the towns and farms and forests, hardwoods and a sprinkling of conifers higher up, streams that sang down out of their canyons and through their little valleys, on to join the Potomac, the Susquehanna, north and westward to the Ohio and on into the interior, south and eastward to the piedmont, the fall line, the low plains—Roanoke, Cape Fear, Catawba, Congaree, Saluda, Savannah. . . .

The lands of the Whiteman, North and South—formerly the lands of his own peoples, the Cherokees, Croatans, Chickasaws, Creeks, even the Robinson County Indians, light-skinned, light-haired, gray-eyed, speakers of a strange sort of English, but Indian nonetheless.

The Trail of Tears.

A land, a world undergoing immense changes, the transformation of the beautiful land to a land of neo-Europeans, roads, bridges, ferries, the boisterous and emerging cities, small farms, the wilderness dwindling, growning tame under the hand of the Whiteman, a new nation, a nation whose independence had been earned less than a century earlier, a nation that had sprawled westward to the far Pacific Ocean, a nation already grown complacent and corrupt and yet a giant which, even as it awoke and began to define itself and its ultimate destiny, was on the very brink of internecine war. One nation or two? And if two, then why not three or four or half a dozen?

Soldier Wolf thought about Abraham Lincoln, the President-elect, the unknown man, the backwoodsman who had won a great election but in winning had probably lost the country which had chosen him.

Soldier Wolf thought of his own boyhood, of the unpredictable turns of events which had taken him from the days of hunting and trapping and working on his father's small farm in the valley between the humpbacked folds of the Smokies to the college at Chapel Hill—himself an honor student and ultimately a graduate cast loose into a world in which the opportunities were numerous, but not for him, not for him because he had had the bad grace to be an Indian.

The military, then, but even there he was passed over again and again by men of lesser abilities than his own. But as a regular, he had been able to carve out a niche, his size and strength and quickness of mind gaining him the respect of the other regulars, and his education rendering him valuable to his superiors, some of whom, with their purchased commissions, arrogant though they were, could scarcely read or write.

Thirty years old, he thought, and I've so far accomplished precisely nothing.

He puffed on the cigar, stubbed it out in the snow, smelled the wet, dying odor of charred tobacco.

It's time to head west, he concluded. And now, by God, after eight years of doing other people's work, the federal government is actually giving me my chance. Now that things are coming apart at the seams, they've found something for Jerry Soldier Wolf to do. Send out an Indian to solve Indian problems in the Rocky Mountains. Well, I guess this red-skinned nigger's up to it—whatever it is. There's a new world out there, or at least what's left of a new world. The Cheyennes, the others—still wild, still living a life of wildness, the heritage of all our people. . . .

As he sat there, idly gazing across the Anacostia, Soldier Wolf began to have the distinct feeling that he was being watched—someone close by. He turned slowly, stood up, pretended to look into the gray sky from which the snow had now ceased to fall. But his attention was elsewhere—on the clump of willows just beyond where he stood. A slight movement there? A trickle of steam—someone's breath?

Soldier Wolf moved slowly, casually, toward an opening between trees, just to one side of the willow brush. Under the overcoat, his hand went to his pistol, slipped it out of the holster. Then, with a single quick step sideways, he was behind a maple, gun out, leveled at the willow brush.

"Whoever you are, come on out! And keep your hands in plain sight when you do 'er."

But what emerged:

A little Negro boy in a tattered shirt, torn pants, pads of burlap tied about his feet. The eyes under the tangle of black hair were huge, white.

"For Christ's sake!" Soldier Wolf laughed. "Boy, you damned near got yourself shot. What the hell were you doing?"

"You gonna shoot me, Mister Man?"

Soldier Wolf looked down at his pistol, laughed again, and put the weapon away.

"You got no shoes? Where do you live, son?"

The boy stood poised, wanting to run for his life but uncertain whether the gun might reappear if he did. His mouth was open, but he did not speak.

"Cat got your tongue, little guy?"

"Supposed to find food . . ." the child stammered.

"Where's your mama, boy?"

The boy stared at the ground, glanced sideways, seemed once more on the verge of breaking away.

"Talk to me," Soldier Wolf said, advancing to where the child stood, knelt next to him, patted him softly on the back.

"How come you got that funny hat?" the boy asked.

" 'Cause I'm a heap big Injun. My daddy wears a turban, so I wear one too."

"You a poley?"

"Not me. Are you?"

"How come you got stripes, then?"

"I'm a soldier. The stripes show what my rank is. Don't be scared, now . . . I'm not going to hurt you. Want to help, if I can."

"A sojer? You got any food, Mister Man?"

"I can get some. How long since you've eaten? Where's your mama, child?"

"Dead," the boy said softly. "She's done gone to heaven. My daddy's sick. You gonna turn us in to the poleys?"

"You runaways?"

The boy said nothing, but Soldier Wolf knew. The story was not a new one: field hands . . . head north . . . try to find whatever thing freedom was. Soldier Wolf looked down at the little feet, tied up in wet, filthy sackcloth, the left one matted with what appeared to be bloodstains, the cloth discolored, yellow-black around the toes.

"How long since you've eaten, boy? Answer me, now."

"I don' know, Mister Man."

Soldier Wolf blinked his eyes and shook his head, felt a faint wave of nausea pass over him. He stood up, fixed his gaze across the river, where he could see the buildings of the Army post, half-hidden among the stands of winter-bare trees.

"Take me to your daddy."

"Can't," the boy said. "Pap says don't let nobody know where he's hid. . . ."

"Maybe I can help him. You said he was sick."

"Can't," the boy repeated.

"Okay, okay," Soldier Wolf said, "I understand. You're a good boy. It's best that no one sees your pa. You give this to him, maybe it'll help. I'm going to go buy a box full of groceries. I'll be back as soon as I can get here. I'll leave the stuff right there in the willows, where you were hiding."

He handed the boy a five-dollar gold piece, which the child took, staring at the coin before folding his fingers around it.

"Son, when it's dark, you and your pa go on up the river. Listen good, now. I know some people who'll give you a place to stay and who'll feed you. Up the river, cross the wooden bridge. You'll be in Maryland then, but you still need to keep away from the road. You understand me? Listen good, now. Follow the road, but stay back away from it. The first town is called Hyattsville—there's a sign. Just past the sign's a big white house, back away from the road. Here—you give this paper to your daddy. . . ."

Soldier Wolf sketched a quick map on the back of an old envelope that he took from his pocket. He wrote a note on the other side, signed his name.

"Does your daddy know how to read?" Soldier Wolf asked.

The child looked blank, uncomprehending.

"Doesn't matter. You take the gold piece and the map to your daddy. Then come back right here. Hide over there somewhere and wait for me. I'll bring food, I promise. Go on, now. Go tell your daddy what I said. . . ."

The little dark-skinned face looked up, the eyes searching for some clue. Then the child turned, was running away—not running, limping—was gone.

"Shit almighty!" Jerry Soldier Wolf said to the trees and the gray sky.

Then he turned and strode quickly away in the direction of the

Capital City, his stomach knotted suddenly, a fist of anger and pain.

The winter afternoon had by now nearly run its course, and the darkness had already begun to settle when Jerry kicked the slushy snow from his boots and entered the little grocery store. The bell attached to the door tinkled as he stepped inside, glanced at the man in the white apron behind the counter.

"Just closin'," the man said noncomittally.

"Take me just a couple of minutes. Got to buy a little Christmas present."

"Don't got much in that way," the man said. "Boxes of assorted candies, good leather belts, hand-tooled—not much else. . . ."

"Not what I'm looking for," Soldier Wolf said simply. "You got a big box or gunnysack? That'll do."

He picked out some apples, a couple tins of pickled meat, a couple of loaves of bread, flour, beans, some potatoes, a head of cabbage, and two boxes of wooden matches. He placed these on the counter, returned to the cooler box for a bottle of milk and a slab of cheese.

"Give me a scoop of the chocolate drops," he said to the clerk. "That'll do it. What do I owe the company?"

The man in the apron rang up the purchases. Jerry thanked him, took the cardboard box under one arm, and stepped back out into the twilight, began to walk toward the Anacostia.

The snow had started to fall once more, and by the time he reached the river, the trees had begun to glow a dull white in the darkness. Jerry found the clump of willow bushes and called out, but there was no answer, no sound, no hint of motion. He placed the box on the snowy earth and said to the darkness, "First house after you pass the Hyattsville sign, big house, back away from the road. Try to get there by dawn. Here's the food, and good luck to you. Take care of that little boy, now. He's a good one."

Soldier Wolf walked back toward Constitution Avenue. He whistled as he went—knowing that the father and the son, hiding somewhere close, would thus be able to ascertain his whereabouts and so would know when it was safe to come out from their hiding spot to see what he had left them.

"Well, little god they nailed to a cross, this red devil's done you a Christmas good deed, I guess. You tell me, though, just how it is you let things like that happen. Or is it your brother, Satan, who tends to such matters?"

But the only answer was the continuing snowfall, the heavy, muffled feeling of the night woods, only the squeaking, crunching noise of Soldier Wolf's Army-issue boots on the accumulating snow under the shadowy branches of the great dark trees.

The lights of the city flickered in the white darkness ahead of him, and Jerry Soldier Wolf walked onward. He had a social engagement this night, and there was apparently no way out of it. He'd be missed back at the fort, of course, but the colonel, he supposed, knew well enough where he was.

"Hell," he said to the snowfall, "when the man's enlistment's all but up, I guess he's allowed a little freedom. . . ."

Only then did he realize that he himself had not eaten since breakfast. He was, he supposed, as hungry as a winter-starved bear. Harriman had said something about chow, hadn't he?

Chapter Two

Special dispatch to the Morning News*! Important from Washington! Address of Senator Toombs to the People of Georgia. Propositions for new guarantees rejected! The South treated with derision and contempt! Senator Crittenden's Amendments Unanimously Voted Down! Secession the last and only Resort! Washington, Dec. 23—Senator Toombs telegraphs this morning the following, addressed to the People of Georgia: Fellow Citizens of Georgia.—I came here to secure your constitutional rights, or to demonstrate to you that you can get no guarantees for these rights from the Northern confederates. . . .*

While westward, in the territories, other matters of rights were being discussed: A group of Whitemen, led by Big Phil the Cannibal, visited an Arapaho camp near the town while the men were gone and raped some of the women. And they stole three Indian mules. Chief Left Hand wanted revenge, but Jim Beckwourth talked him out of it, then wrote to The Rocky Mountain News, *denouncing the Denver drunken devils and bummers, warned the Whites that the Indians were as keenly sensible to acts of injustice as they are tenacious of revenge. . . .*

The coal-gas lamps were burning, and the snow was falling once again. A street cleaner was at work, taking up horse droppings, some of the piles already covered with whiteness, others, fresh, still steaming.

Jerry Soldier Wolf was in no great hurry—indeed, the BIA social event did not really appeal to him at all, but he took solace in the fact that two days hence he would have put the Capital City behind him—he would be riding south through the troubled land, south to the upwelled ridges of the Great Smokies and his father's farm, his own people, his own area, Breakneck, Newfound Gap, Clingman's Dome, Cataloochee, Black Gap. . . .

Three prostitutes standing together beneath a gas-lit streetlamp, two White girls and a High Yaller.

Soldier Wolf crossed to the opposite side of the street, waved to the women, continued.

Not tonight, ladies, he thought.

For his thoughts were wandering the misty blue mountains where he could take off for days on end and not be disturbed by the inconsistency of men and their interactions, wandering in a world that had effectively ceased to exist for him that fatal moment when he had decided, yes, he would accept the poor boy's scholarship, he would go to Chapel Hill and see what he could learn about what was in the Whiteman's books, a decision that had led to endless nights of study, constant reading, the mastering of a language that he knew was not really his own at all but a language which held the keys to all those things which he hoped might satisfy his hungry mind and yet which, finally, did no such thing. Each answer brought the inevitable three or four or a hundred further questions, and these unanswerable. Shakespeare, Plato, Dante, Milton, Bacon, Plutarch, Latin grammar, French, German, and the works of the historians, the mudholes of Europe and Asia, the grand White venture to the beautiful land, to the lands of his own peoples, the conquest of those lands, the conquest and slaughter of Red savages, his people, his people. . . .

But now the images of trees standing starkly against the low mist, hovering just above the ground, long trails of vapors, so that the trees themselves appeared to be suspended in the air.

And horses. How he missed the mystical sound they made when calling to each other through the gray curtains of fog. And evenings when the earth seemed to be sheathed in a pink skein as the sun dropped westward beyond the Smokies. The baying of hounds as they treed raccoon or possum during the time of harvest moon. The sounds of water splashing down from the high rocks at night. The good clean smell of the rich earth, the freshly tilled fields on spring mornings, the chatter of crows and the cry of the mourning dove. . . .

A carriage passed him, and he heard giggles coming from behind the drawn curtains, and Soldier Wolf began immediately to condemn the people inside, even as he knew fully well what was going on within. But, after all, what right had he to judge others?

Christmas decorations.

The Whiteman's celebration of the birth of his little hanged god, a god who was served, it seemed to Soldier Wolf, with more of hypocrisy than of faith or reverence. But his thoughts would not remain with this contemplation—and suddenly he could all but smell fresh bread baking, could taste the sweetness of cold winds down off the Smokies. The odor of pine burning in the large hearth.

Soldier Wolf breathed deeply, became aware once more of the smell of coke fumes from the coal fires burning in the homes. And the oddly mixed smell of food odors and the odor of horse manure.

A girl standing in the opening of an alleyway, away from the streetlamp half-dissolved in shadow. Soldier Wolf passed by her, shook his head, walked on.

They learn young, he thought. No more than fourteen, maybe younger. . . .

Jerry arrived at the house he had been directed to, a sprawling three-story affair constructed in the Northern fashion, brick chimneys at either end, a modified formal garden in front. Soldier Wolf walked up to the main door and was about to knock, when the door opened, as if by magic. A Negro in formal dress was working as the doorman, a man wise enough to stand inside, out of the cold, damp evening.

"Your invitation, sir?" the Negro asked.

"Don't have one," Soldier Wolf responded quickly, perhaps too quickly. "Mr. Harriman asked me to come. He's just hired me to work for the agency."

Soldier Wolf was suddenly furious with having to explain his presence, was about to turn around, leave the doorway, when he saw Daniel Harriman hurrying toward him.

"Jerry!" Harriman said. "Don't just stand there—come on along inside. Have some brandy first, and then I'll introduce you around. Come along, my boy. . . ."

The Negro stepped aside, deferential now, unruffled, certain of his position.

Soldier Wolf chucked him in the ribs as he passed, whispered, "Chin up, old fellow. I promise not to kill anyone."

The doorman scowled, looked away.

Then they were inside, at the edge of the great hall in which perhaps fifty people, men in formal dress, women attired in the latest styles, milled about, talking casually, some engaged in animated conversation, some giggling and laughing, some appearing quite serious-faced.

Daniel Harriman poured a snifter of brandy for Soldier Wolf

and asked him if he'd like to remove his turban. Soldier Wolf sipped, shook his head, grinned. He was looking across the younger Harriman's shoulder, staring at a young woman who had caught his attention. Just to look at her produced little sensations of desire in him. Or perhaps it wasn't desire at all, but something else—longing, almost a sensation of loneliness, of loss. Or none of these, but all at once. She was young, not much older actually than the little prostitute he had seen outside on the street in the alleyway, light-skinned, long black hair, eyes that gleamed dark gray. And she was looking at him, studying him. Soldier Wolf felt a tingling sensation along the back of his neck, a weakness in the knees, so that he actually felt it necessary to stand straighter than usual, to thrust his chest forward.

"What are you looking at?" Daniel Harriman wanted to know, squinting up at the big man, then glancing about to see for himself.

"No, nothing," Soldier Wolf said. "That girl, yes, she's staring at me."

"Then you're both staring." Harriman smiled. "Call it fate, I guess. That's Sara Goth, the daughter of the missionaries Frank and Elizabeth Goth. You'll be going out to Colorado Territory with them, Jerry. She's a bit young, perhaps, sixteen I think. Come on, I'll introduce you to them."

Soldier Wolf felt his face flush, and he sipped once more at his brandy.

Jerry Soldier Wolf had already been told about the Goths, but neither Lester nor Daniel Harriman had bothered to mention the girl. Sara, was it? Soldier Wolf emptied the glass and set it down, followed Daniel Harriman across the room. Was it possible that the missionaries would actually take their young daughter out into the wilds? The mere possibility suddenly heightened Soldier Wolf's enthusiasm for the Cramdon mission.

The main room: opulence, light from the cut rose glass of the chandeliers, the confused mixtures of perfumes that permeated the room, the people artificial, the voices a blur of babble.

"Frank," Harriman was saying, "I'd like you to meet Sergeant Jerry Soldier Wolf, as of today our new agent. Jerry, this is Frank Goth and his wife, Elizabeth. And this very attractive young lady is their daughter, Sara. You folks will be seeing quite a bit of each other in the months ahead, so I thought I should introduce you right away."

Jerry shook hands with Frank Goth and then bowed, first to the mother and then to the daughter, who curtsied in turn but looked him straight in the eye.

"You're an Indian," were her first words. "Aren't you, Mr. Soldier Wolf?"

"Sara!" the mother reprimanded. "You must forgive our daughter, sergeant. Somehow we've never quite managed to teach her manners."

Soldier Wolf smiled, nodded.

"Guilty as charged," he said. "North Carolina Cherokee, at your service, ma'am. Mr. Harriman has hired me to protect your ma and pa from the wild Injuns out West."

"Will you scalp them for us?" Sara asked, affecting a very serious expression.

"I guess not," Soldier Wolf answered. "It'd be cannibalism of sorts, wouldn't it? Like I just said, I'm Injun, too."

"The girl runs on," Frank Goth said. "Actually, sergeant, I gather we're all to be peacemakers, if it's possible. I'd wanted Sara to stay in school here in the East, but with all that's happening, Elizabeth and I decided she'd be safer with us, among the Cheyennes."

"You're taking your daughter?" Soldier Wolf asked.

"I'm stronger than I look," Sara said quickly. "And I've been with Mom and Dad before when we lived among the Indians."

"No," Daniel Harriman put in, "I don't think you'll have to worry about this one, Jerry. Now, if you folks will excuse me, I've some business to attend to—have to find my wife. She no doubt has half a dozen young men in tow by now, and all of them enchanted."

Harriman turned and strode away, nodding to various people, and disappeared through a door at the far side of the big room.

Frank Goth clapped Soldier Wolf on the shoulder and motioned to an empty table over against the wall, close by the fireplace. Goth led, and Soldier Wolf followed, the mother and the daughter trailing behind.

Soldier Wolf talked with the Goths for some time, and as he did so, he glanced from time to time at young Sara. Her eyes were so constantly upon him, in fact, that he found himself feeling quite uncomfortable. Frank and Elizabeth, inexplicably, seemed all but oblivious to the silent communication which was occurring between their daughter and the big Cherokee. But Frank spoke with great animation—the problems of the Plains

Indians and of the Cheyennes in particular, the land itself, the high plains, the snow-crested Front Range of the Rockies or Stony Mountains, as they were sometimes called, the frenzied mining activity that had changed the world *out there* so completely since the discovery of gold, the railroad that would, within a few short years, leap across the continent to join the American East and the Far West, the farmlands and mining regions of Oregon and California, the Mormon empire of Deseret, the herds of buffalo, diminishing rapidly and perhaps soon to pass into extinction as the lands were fenced and farmed. The land was huge, Frank Goth said, huge and still wild, a land where the Plains Indians were still essentially wild in most ways, the finest hunters and fighters who had ever lived, cultures based on horse and buffalo, medicine and ritual, honor and immense bravery, nomadic, moving about over vast stretches of land that had belonged to these people forever.

"But it's all going now," Frank Goth said, "going soon. The Whiteman will have what he wants, and when the buffalo are gone, Pawnee, Cheyenne, Arapaho, Crow, Blackfoot, all of them will have no choice but to do as the Whiteman wants."

"Reservations and the government dole, then?" Soldier Wolf nodded.

"That's it, that's it exactly. It's still within our power to change it all, to leave huge areas open for the Redmen, but the grand destiny of the United States will never allow it. As soon as use is found for all that land, it will be used, and the time of the Indian will be gone forever."

Jerry stared at Frank Goth's rugged tanned face—weathered perhaps more than tanned, still bearing the marks of having been snow-burned at one time or another. This was the face, Jerry realized, of a man who had spent a great deal of time out there, in a world of vast horizons, great towering mountains, bitter cold, searing heat, wind and sandstorms.

"Cramdon," Soldier Wolf said. "Why don't they just send the bluecoats after him?"

"My boy, that's what Harriman's doing. You're it. It's an agency problem, though, and the agency feels obliged to handle its own."

Jerry poured himself a glass of white wine, drank it off, shrugged. He was beginning to feel more than just a little annoyed with the Washington social set—the noise, the meaningless chatter that was all about him, the proper ladies with their brightly colored clothing and elaborate hairdos. Frank Goth and his wife seemed genuine enough, and for that he felt relieved. But he was a fish out of water, and he knew it—an outsider, a stranger among these people, outcast by virtue of upbringing, culture, race—even as he was, in some way or another, a minor center of attention. He could feel the eyes upon him, in particular those of an elegant woman with brilliantly blond hair done up in the lastest fashion, her face well-powdered and rouged, one who stood, at the moment, amidst a minor throng of young Army officers, U.S. Cavalry, the very people Soldier Wolf and his regiment trained horses for. And the eyes were green, so green that they didn't even seem real, an air of the artificial, like everything else in the big room.

"Have you ever scalped anyone?" Sara Goth asked.

Soldier Wolf laughed, shrugged.

"Sara!" Elizabeth Goth reprimanded. "What in the world's gotten into you, child?"

"It's all right, ma'am." Jerry grinned. "Us Injuns scalp folks, and the young lady's within her rights to ask."

"Have you?" Sara persisted.

Soldier Wolf stared at the pixielike, delicate face, the long coils of black hair, the full, sensitive lips. Was it possible that this young girl had actually, in some way of which he was unaware, managed to intimidate him? In any case, there was no denying the intense attraction that he felt toward her—but she was, he knew, or so he told himself, simply one more unapproachable, untouchable White woman, and for that matter, not much more than a child. Well, he was going to have her company during the months ahead. He would have to learn to ignore her, to pretend that she was not, in fact, what his insides so poignantly told him she was: an immensely attractive woman, one who had succeeded, without even trying, in shattering his usual defenses.

Soldier Wolf turned from the girl to Frank and Elizabeth Goth, controlled his voice, and said, "Truth is, I've never killed a man except in self-defense or on sheer whim. But once a man's dead, hell, he's got no more use for a topknot. So I scalp 'em and sew 'em into a big blanket and use it to keep my horse comfortable on nights like this."

Frank and Elizabeth glanced at each other, and Soldier Wolf poured another glass of wine.

Injun, you're going to get drunk, he thought.

He glanced across to where the blond woman was standing,

continued to stare at her. To his great surprise, the woman pursed her lips slightly, kissing at the air and then blowing. And Soldier Wolf felt a flush of desire run through his frame—or was it the wine?

He drank and reached once again for the decanter.

"Lester!" Frank Goth almost shouted. "Where did you come from? We thought you'd probably gone south for the winter."

Lester Harriman joined the group, elegantly dressed and looking quite distinguished.

"Talking to the commissioner, Frank. He'll have a few words for us after a while. Have you been filling in our new agent? Sergeant Soldier Wolf, what do you think of the nightlife of the hoity-toity? My boy, it's the price one must pay for being a civilized human creature. You look like you're thinking about running for the woods, and I guess I don't blame you."

" 'Evening, sir," Soldier Wolf said. "Not used to this sort of thing, I guess."

"Well, we'll all be about our proper business soon enough. In the meanwhile, enjoy yourself if you can."

"He was telling us about scalps," Sara Goth said.

Harriman made a wide-eyed expression of mock astonishment, clapped Jerry on the shoulder, and turned to Frank and Elizabeth.

"Can you spare a moment, Frank?" he asked. "Greenwood would like to speak with you. Jerry, can you manage on your own for a few minutes? We'll be right back. What the devil's happened to Daniel, anyway? God save a man from having such a son. . . ."

They moved away, and Jerry stood alone, feeling awkward and somewhat foolish. He poured another glass of wine, emptying the decanter, and drank it off quickly.

The military band had been resting, but now the music began, and the proper Washingtonians paired off in preparation for the dancing. Soldier Wolf leaned against the wall, and his thoughts drifted back to the events of the afternoon, the image of the half-starved Negro boy and the gray waters of the running Anacostia in stark contrast to the perfumed opulence of his present surroundings. Outside in the darkness, around the edges of the city, lay a world of desperation, of poverty, of runaway slaves moving north along the invisible rails of the so-called Underground Railway, human beings trudging through the snowy darkness, burlap sacking tied about their feet, their clothing ragged and inadequate against the cold.

Perhaps the boy and his father had managed to find a spot sufficiently secluded to allow a fire. Perhaps the box of foodstuffs he had left would make a difference, perhaps with immense luck one child, at least, would be able to grow up *free*. But even if fortune smiled and the father and son were able to make it to Hyattsville and on to Pennsylvania or New York, what would the change of location really amount to? More poverty, and maybe worse poverty even than before. Slaves, at least, were relatively well-fed, were provided with adequate clothing.

"A man doesn't abuse his working stock so badly that it can't work," Jerry said aloud, and looked about for another source of wine. His thoughts were already a bit fuzzy, but he wanted to drink. Whiskey would be best, but wine would do. Among all these well-fed, well-dressed people, the idea of getting good and drunk seemed like the most appropriate answer.

Mr. Cramdon, this Injun's come to take you in. If you'll just step this way, sir, we'll go visit the Colorado City jail. . . .

"Will you dance with me, sergeant?"

It was the woman with the golden tresses.

"Hello," Jerry said. "Me heap big Injun. Squaw gottem beautiful scalp. Injun want scalp."

"I know who you are," the woman said. "My husband's told me about you. You speak very poor English for an educated man, Sergeant Soldier Wolf."

Jerry was astounded. "Your husband?" he asked.

"Not important, Sergeant. Shall we dance?"

The music was blaring, slightly off-key, and Soldier Wolf and his admirer moved onto the dance floor. Suddenly everything had taken on an air of the unreal, dreamlike, impossible, something that could not happen but which was happening nonetheless. The woman held him so close that he swore he could feel the pressure of her pelvic area. The bulge that was growing at his loins was downright uncomfortable, and the blond woman seemed to be taking advantage of it. When they drew together, her breasts pressed against his military coat, and he was unable to look away from the cleavage revealed by the low-cut gown.

Look but don't touch. . . .

The dance was a long one, and, Soldier Wolf thought, if the music did not soon stop, surely he would blow up. He imagined himself exploding like a child's balloon. Then, as they turned about, the woman reached subtly down on the pretext of gathering her train and brushed his penis. Not once, but twice.

"Ma'am, I thought perhaps we should sit out the rest of this dance," he managed.

"And why should we do that, Sergeant?"

"If you don't know, I'm not the one to tell you."

"Tell me."

"For one thing, I'm terribly uncomfortable. For another thing, your husband's no doubt watching."

"He's not here. Relax, sergeant. When this girl sees something she wants, she takes it. I picked you out, remember?"

"What do you mean? I don't want to play games with fancy women. . . ."

"You save that for our local women of the evening?"

"I—"

"Do you find me attractive?"

"You are that," he blurted. "You're . . . beautiful."

"Then take me somewhere."

"Ma'am, people are watching us. I think—"

"There's a room upstairs." She smiled. "And I have the key. When the dance is finished, I'll go upstairs. Wait a few moments, Sergeant, and then follow me. I'll meet you at the top of the stairwell. Unless you're afraid. . . ."

"I'm an Indian," he said, staring down at the delicate creature in his arms. He knew he was saying the obvious, but he felt obliged to say it nonetheless.

"I like big strong animals," she said, and then laughed a series of little bell-like syllables.

The music was over at last, and the blond woman was gone. Soldier Wolf blinked at the red-colored light from the chandelier, shook his head. For a moment he toyed with the idea that nothing at all had happened, that he had imagined the entire thing. But the smell of her perfume still lingered about him.

Then he thought about leaving, of bolting outside into the snowstorm, of walking back to the river, of taking an Army horse and riding away into the night, away from Washington, away from the world of dreams and illusions and the governmental buildings of a nation that was itself ready to disintegrate.

Jerry looked around for a familiar face. He saw none. His emotions were mixed, confused. Should he do as the woman had said? When was the last time he'd had a real woman in bed, someone other than the prostitutes of the city? *Too long*. And a woman like this—he'd never even allowed himself to do more than entertain the most fleeting of thoughts.

Soldier Wolf felt a genuine resistance to giving in to this sophisticated female's whim. It was not a matter of loyalty to any other lady, for there was none. A matter of race. Oh, he had seen other Indians who had been drawn to White women, especially in the Southern states. And he knew of some who had been hung for giving in to the fatal attraction, but he was not in the South now. Perhaps in the nation's Capital, all things were possible, and the rich seemed to have no rules except those regarding their own desires.

Sara Goth.

That was it. The vivid image of the black-haired girl with the mischievous eyes came to mind.

Foolish.

Just one more unapproachable White woman, and a child into the bargain. Utterly foolish. At this moment, a beautiful woman whose every movement shouted sensuality was waiting for him at the top of the stairwell—or was not waiting, was acting out some sort of perverse game with him, would take great delight in savoring her exercise of power over him.

The two Harrimans, Frank and Elizabeth Goth, and Sara entered the room, across from him. It was a moment of decision, and Soldier Wolf glanced about the room, avoided eye contact with his new friends. He saw someone's nearly full glass of red wine, unattended, walked over, raised the glass in a toast to nothingness, drank, and moved toward the stairway.

She was waiting for him, just as she had promised. And she led him down the dimly lighted corridor to a doorway into whose lock mechanism she inserted a key, opened the door, and stepped inside. Jerry followed.

The room was lit by two candles, and a fire burned happily in the wall fireplace. Several chairs and a large couch.

The woman closed and locked the door, turned to Soldier Wolf, her head tilted back, her lips parted. He took her in his arms, kissed her, was startled by the quick little tongue that darted into his mouth.

He reached for her breast, but she pulled back, again laughing the bell-like sounds.

"Not to be impatient, sergeant," she said. "We have plenty of time, all night if we wish. Would you like another drink? The cabinet here is well-stocked. Bourbon?"

Soldier Wolf's hands were trembling, and his erection ached.

"Yes, yes, that would be fine." He coughed, was astounded by the strange sound of his own voice.

She poured two glasses, handed one to him. He breathed deeply, drank, set the empty glass down.

"It's true about Indians and alcohol, isn't it?" She laughed. "What does the turban signify? You're Cherokee, aren't you? I've heard that the turban is a sign of high station among your people."

"My father is a leader, yes," he managed.

"Does that mean you're next in line for the kingship? That's what you call it, isn't it? *King*. An amusing word, actually. . . ."

Soldier Wolf attempted to marshal his thoughts. He felt anger now.

"I am the oldest son," he said, his voice strained.

"I've never made love with an Indian before," she said, reaching down to rub her hand across the bulge in his trousers.

He groaned, placed his hands upon her shoulders, held her.

"You're very strong, sergeant. Be careful not to bruise me. White women are fragile creatures. . . ."

"What's your name?" he demanded.

"Amanda," she said, laughing again. "That's all the name I can tell you. Tonight I am yours. After that, no—I doubt that we'll ever see each other again. It's better that way."

Soldier Wolf let go of her, was about to turn, to walk out of the room and back down the stairs.

Door's locked, he thought. I'm trapped. . . .

The woman who said her name was Amanda smiled at him, her teeth glinting in the candlelight, and removed a strap holding up the upper portion of her dress, so that the nearly sheer white cloth slipped down, revealing her camisole and beneath that the boned, half-cupped foundation piece. She turned back to him and said, "Will you unlace me, please? A lady should never make love while she's all trussed up this way."

Soldier Wolf did as he was directed, removed the wrapper, and then turned her about, gazed at her, naked now from the waist up.

"You're . . . lovely," he said and attempted to embrace the woman—but she sailed off into a little frenzy of laughter and pulled away from him.

"Undress, Sergeant Soldier Wolf," she said, her voice distinct with command. "I like my stallions naked. You won't regret it, I promise that. . . ."

Within moments they were lying unclothed on the couch, and Amanda ran her long fingernails, almost painfully, across Soldier Wolf's back. She fondled him, reached down to place her hand upon him, then pulled at his hair. She laughed, the tinkling, bell-like laughter that hardly seemed human at all.

He groaned, bit at her neck, ran his fingertips over her.

"Mustn't muss my hair, mustn't muss," she cautioned.

"I want you, Amanda. . . ."

"Do you love me, Indian King?"

"I want you."

"And I want you. That's exactly what I want, sir."

She guided him, and he thrust into her. The flesh was a band of hot, slippery tightness about him. The woman stifled a cry, turning her head sideways against the bevy of soft pillows upon which she had placed her head. And his body worked, worked in the instinctive, animal rhythm, the ancient pulsing movement that had existed always and forever beyond human consciousness. He thrust rapidly, thrust hard—and she cried for him to stop, to wait, he was causing her pain. But the body was in control, not the mind, and he continued to thrust. The woman cried out, made little whimperings. Then the noises changed, and she was with him, was matching his frantic motions.

Brief fire ran through him, and he convulsed, his body jerking and quivering. He became aware for the first time of the woman's voice: *No, no, no, no. . . .* But whatever the mind was saying, the body was speaking something else, and she continued to arch her hips against his. She clung to him, dug her fingernails into him until he writhed back and forth—and he found it necessary to pin her arms.

Her face was wet. She was crying, she was breathing deep—unwilling for it to be over.

"More . . ." he heard her moan, but he was dropping down through a long, black whirlpool. He dimly wondered if he were dying, but then his mind ceased to function, and he was unconscious.

Awake.

Gray light through the drapes.

At first he closed his eyes, attempted to drift back into sleep, reached over to where the woman would be lying. But she was gone. Soldier Wolf sat up, looked around, at first confused, not sure of where he was. The woman, the blond hair. The people downstairs, the commissioner's speech that he had missed.

He was up quickly, reached for his clothing.

Something written across his chest, something in red—lip rouge, that what it was. Scrawled over his chest and onto his abdomen, the single word "AMANDA."

For a moment Soldier Wolf stared, dumbfounded. Then he could feel the laughter rising, and he roared, shook, tears came to his eyes.

"Good God!" he managed. "What's this half-breed gotten himself into?"

He pressed his fingers to his eyes. Pain shot through his head, or perhaps he had just at that moment become aware of it.

Injun drink too goddamned much.

He had just pulled on his uniform and readjusted his turban when he heard a key turning in the door lock.

The door opened, and Daniel Harriman looked inside.

"Young man," Harriman said, "I don't suppose I have to ask what happened. There's some breakfast ready in the galley downstairs, a bathroom down the hall. Get yourself cleaned up and come on down. Mardi Gras is over, and it's time to go to work."

Soldier Wolf said nothing, but the information concerning the bathroom was welcome intelligence. His bladder was all but ready to burst, and the chamber pot was already full.

Chapter Three

The land was burning, it had been burning for a long while. But as yet the flames were visible in only a few places. Soon the fires would blaze up and sweep back and forth, from North to South, and when the holocaust was over, many things would be changed. Nevertheless, the fires would continue to burn, now hibernating, now erupting outward.

The land consisted of many states and many territories. In some there were slaves, while in others the nature of the slavery was not so obvious. The Whitemen, all of them, believed that God the Father had given the land to them, and yet the land had long been inhabited by other people, dark-skinned people, men and women and children who were called Indians because of an early confusion with regard to geographical location, and so the name stuck.

But the tribes usually referred to themselves simply as the People. The Whitemen were people also, but they were strange creatures, land-hungry, violent, relentless.

The dark-skins lived in tribes, in clans, in villages scattered here and there throughout the beautiful land, and these people had the unfortunate idea that the valleys and mountains and prairies where they had always lived belonged, in some way that they could not state, to them. Because of this belief, they were willing to fight and to die in a futile attempt to preserve the kind of life they had always known.

They fought back, at times, owing to their savage beliefs.

Vouchers were made out, and Soldier Wolf was given BIA authorization for various sorts of miscellaneous expenditure, in keeping with his new job, now that severance from the military was officially completed. Lester Harriman presented him with a new Starr carbine and said, "Jerry, you'll need a good horse, maybe two. Go on down to the militia stables and pick out what pleases you. I'll send Kramer along so there'll be no misunderstanding. Your orders are in this envelope, my boy. You're to meet the

Goths in St. Joseph, at garrison headquarters, the first of February. No railway beyond that, so you'll provision yourselves and head overland to the upper reaches of the North Platte River, by way of Denver. I'd suggest mules for pulling the supply wagons—a hell of a lot more dependable, in the long run, than oxen, no matter what the old-timers say."

"Five weeks." Soldier Wolf nodded. "Guess I'll swing down through North Carolina and take a last look at home. Might be a time before I'm back, I guess."

"Actually," Harriman said, "I'd advise against that. The South may be up in arms by then, if they aren't already, and you'll have God's own time getting out. They'll be wanting to stick another rifle in your hands, and you'll find yourself on the wrong side of things."

"Guess I've got to take that chance. It's been four years since I've seen my father. You understand."

"Have it your way, then. But you've got to be in St. Joseph by the first of February, or Frank will be heading out without you. Jerry, I want to stress just how important this mission is. We must find a way of maintaining peace in the Rockies. The Plains tribes have been fighting among themselves for too long, since the Creator put them there, I suppose. But the world is changing, has already changed. The old ways don't work anymore, not with farmers and ranchers and miners and cities springing up. Better treaties need to be drawn, and if peace cannot be made, I'm afraid we'll see the total destruction of these proud, dignified people. Most of the settlers, I gather, already think that the only good Indian's a dead one. And when we've got a snake in our own midst, a man like Edward Cramdon, preying on both sides and causing the Whites and the Indians to turn on each other, we've got a situation that's simply intolerable. I'm hoping that the chiefs will listen to you, but it won't happen, Jerry, unless you can reach back to your own beginnings and, in effect, become one of them. I'm betting on you. Brownell convinced me you could do the job, and somebody's damned well got to."

"Mr. Harriman, I'll give it my best."

"I know you will, my boy. I'm not often wrong in the matter of judging men's characters, and I figure I've picked the right man. I won't be with the agency much longer, and a man's always remembered for the last things he's done."

Soldier Wolf looked quizzical.

"No, no, it's not the new administration coming in, Jerry. But I've been around here for a long while. Just about time to step aside, let Daniel and the other younger men take over. No one's irreplaceable, you'll come to realize that. As a noncommissioned officer, you were highly thought of, and your unit, it must often have seemed to you, would not be able to function in your absence. But you've left now, and a new sergeant will take your place, and things will go on largely as they always have. Ultimately, we must look at these matters in terms of thousands of years, I suppose. In that sort of scale, no man's life amounts to much. It's all a matter of constant change, change, change. . . . Well, Soldier Wolf, Godspeed."

Lester Harriman held out his hand, and Jerry enfolded it in his own larger paw. The two men shook hands, the old Scot and the young Cherokee. Then Harriman turned quickly and walked back into the interior office, closed the door behind him.

"Shall we go look at the horses?" Kramer asked, forcing himself to be polite to the big man who had so easily thrust him up against the wall the preceding day.

"Sure," Soldier Wolf said, "why not? Let's go inspect some horses."

A fine-looking group of animals was being brought into the stables as Jerry Soldier Wolf and Assistant Clerk Kramer walked in. Soldier Wolf saw a magnificent black with a crescent moon on its forehead, an animal of nearly eighteen hands.

Not a line animal, Soldier Wolf thought. Must belong to the General Staff.

There were no socks on the horse, and its hooves seemed noticeably small. Some regular, Soldier Wolf realized, had spent a great deal of time polishing and waxing the hooves.

In the same group was a mare. It too looked to be an especially fine animal, sixteen hands. The lady was sorrel and had a close gait—would make a fine brood mare. The thought of having the stud and the mare for breeding purposes made Jerry think of home. His father and brothers could, without doubt, use a pair of such animals.

Jerry followed Kramer into the company command post and showed the morose captain his orders. The captain only grunted and muttered something Jerry could not hear—except for one word. *Riddance*. Jerry saluted, since he was still in uniform, and turned quickly on his heels. He was glad to see that the captain was preoccupied with his hatred for Indians, and he rehearsed the details of the man's face. Somewhere, sometime, if fate should allow it, a moment might come when neither of them was garbed in military cloth. Should that time come, Soldier Wolf conjectured, he would without doubt rearrange the man's features somewhat.

Kramer seemed subtly pleased with what had happened.

"I think I can manage from here, Kramer," Soldier Wolf said. "Thanks for your assistance, and my apologies for yesterday. I acted hastily, perhaps."

Kramer nodded, turned, and left the office.

Jerry took note of the stack of requisition forms on the desk. The corporal was looking the other way, intent upon something or other, and Jerry reached down deftly and took half a dozen of the printed pages. Then he walked outside into the corridor, found the lounge area, sat down at a table, and carefully filled out the forms, scrawled in a backhand signature, and sauntered over to the stables.

The sorrel mare was being cared for by the regimental veterinarian.

"Nothing wrong with her, is there, doc?"

"Oh, no. She's the picture of health, sergeant."

"Well, I've got an order here from General Poole. He wants the big black stallion and the sorrel mare delivered to his home. Guess he figures the stud'll fare better out at his farm."

The vet looked up, surprised. "The general wants the horses taken to his plantation?"

"That's it." Jerry nodded.

"In West Virginia? Must be some mistake here, sarge."

"No mistake," Jerry assured him. "Here are the travel vouchers and the orders to move the horses. All signed by General Poole himself."

The veterinarian took the papers, studied them, and said, "Yup, they look like the real McCoy. Whatever the general wants is fine with me. You going to take the animals with you now?"

"That'd be best." Jerry nodded.

Soldier Wolf turned his back and chuckled to himself. He was afraid the man might see his elation and wish to verify the documents.

Within a few minutes, the veterinarian, talking easily and casually, had the two horses fitted out with heavy blankets and fine bridles. Soldier Wolf took the reins, saluted, and led the animals away. Once outside the compound, he mounted the big stallion, and with the mare in trail, rode back across the Anacostia to the fort, where he gathered his belongings together, bade farewell to various friends, checked in his government-issue weapons, filled out a last two or three forms for the commandant's office, and put his military career behind him.

He rode westward, away from the Capital City, the skies above leaden, the air cold, several inches of snow from the previous day's storm, partially melted in places; covering the countryside. Even when the daylight vanished, Soldier Wolf continued his ride, drawing a scarf about his throat and fastening the top button on his military greatcoat. He passed through several small towns and kept going, the houses lighted, Christmas decorations on display in some of the front yards—evidence of a world and a way of life from which he felt himself to be forever an exile.

About midnight he drew the stallion to a halt and fished through his saddlebag for half a loaf of more or less fresh bread. He chewed off a couple of mouthfuls, lit a cigar, and gave thanks to the Creator Spirit for his liberation.

Christmas Eve, he thought, and this Injun's riding alone into the darkness. Now's about the time Christ was supposed to be born, the offspring of a hysterical Jewish girl who got herself in a family way and then convinced her husband that God Himself had done it to her. Well, that's their Messiah. He laughed, slapping the black stallion on the neck. Good name for a horse, though, ain't it? You've been Christened, big guy. *Messiah* it is. And your friend? She needs a name too, that's certain. How about *Virgin?* In honor of the night, and all. . . .

He put his heels to the stallion's sides and moved into the darkness, continued to ride throughout the night, as if wishing to put as much distance as possible between himself and Washington, D.C.

"Truth of the matter," he said aloud, "Jerry Soldier Wolf's turned horse thief. Don't suppose the general's going to be too pleased by that. Cheyennes do it, though, and Harriman told me I had to become one of them. A man's got to have practice. . . ."

When he reached the Rappahannock, the sun was up, and the sky was clear and blue, the trees along the river bearded with snow and hoarfrost, the slow water at the river's edge sheeted with thin ice.

Christmas Day 1860, he thought. Time to build a little fire and cook some grub and get a couple hours of shuteye.

Two weeks, he thought, and horse-thief Jerry will be home again—for a little while, anyhow. Just passing through, Messiah, old beast.

With the land in a turmoil and heating slowly to a boil, Jerry concluded it best to get rid of his military clothing, and at Sperryville he purchased civilian garb, a hand ax and sheath, and a supply of ammunition for the Starr carbine Harriman had given him. Then, riding up into the mountains at Beahm's Gap, he built a fire and ceremonially placed the Army blues upon it, watched the flames devour the cloth, sergeant's stripes and all, until only the brass buttons glowed a dull red in the bed of coals.

"So much for that life," he said. "Guess it wasn't much of a life anyhow."

The new coat felt strange, the unused odor of worked leather—split buffalo hide, frontier style, complete with fringes along the sleeves and across the chest, the raw leather shipped in from the high plains, the work of professional hunters. The great shaggy cattle of the West were being taken in increasing numbers now, and not just for the hides, either, but for the meat as well. As the railways moved westward, whatever animals remained within reasonable distance of the terminus were slaughtered, the meat iced down, shipped eastward to whatever markets were available. When the continent was finally belted with steel, Soldier Wolf knew, it would be just a matter of a few years until the herds, once believed inexhaustible, were cut down to the point where the High Plains Indians would begin to starve and so would become tractable and would, perhaps not gracefully, be forced to move onto federal reserves.

Perhaps at some point in the far, far future, matters would change in a different direction. . . .

But now Soldier Wolf had other things on his mind. He was still perhaps four hundred miles from home, but at least he was once again back in his beloved mountains, with the long line of the Blue Ridge just ahead, the great gray-green swellings now white with recent snow, the folds of the Appalachians rolling, one after another, to the horizon, behind him the lowlands, patchworked with farms and villages, mists gathering in the valleys and hollows between the ridges, the omnipresent blue-gray haze for which the mountains, the Smokies farther south, had been named—mist hanging over everything even after the storm, the dark scars where virgin trees had been cut off or burned as a means of clearing the land, other areas, infinitely larger, where the original growth remained, the aboriginal forests of the Appalachians, sassafras brush, wild tulip, poplar, persimmon, black locust, oaks and hickories, huge, ancient hemlocks, fir up high.

The tracks of gray fox, skunk, raccoon, and bobcat in the snow, chipmunks and squirrels darting about beneath the trees, an old boar woodchuck staring solemnly from behind a pile of boulders. Turkey vultures, crows, ravens, red-tail hawks drifting and darting through the air, ruffed grouse scuttling through the snowy brush, the cry of a mourning dove, the repeated, echoing explosions of the knockings of pileated woodpeckers, the buglings and *ki-week, ki-week* sounds of wild turkeys.

Up high on Hawksbill Mountain's crest, a scattering of balsam fir and red spruce, bent streamers of fog blowing in long bands from the summit.

Good country, Soldier Wolf mused. The long backbone of the mountains. Why in God's name would a man want to head off to Jefferson Territory?

But even as he rode, Messiah and Virgin stepping along the trail through nearly a foot of snow, the whiteness in places untraveled by any others, in places the trail showing signs of considerable traffic, Soldier Wolf's thoughts leaped ahead to other mountains which, as yet, existed only in his imagination, a few paintings and pictures he had seen, of mountains that held their snow throughout the long, hot summers, lands where the temperatures, he knew, sometimes dropped off to forty and fifty below zero and entire rivers froze into long, winding sheets of solid ice. And the Indian Peoples, his own people in some ways that seemed very real, still living in a manner, if somewhat modified by their contacts with the Whites, that the Great Manitou had given them in the beginnings. Soldier Wolf imagined himself astride Messiah, bareback, carbine in hand, staring down from a rim to where a huge herd of buffalo grazed. In his mind's eye, a woman was astride the horse beside him, and she waited to see what he would do. Who was it? He tried to envision her face.

Sara Goth.

"For Christ's sake," he said aloud. "Injun boy, your mind's running wild."

He laughed, urged Messiah onward, and continued his long journey south.

The first week in January, and Soldier Wolf was nearing home. A soft, warm rain had begun to fall, continued unabated, and the thin blanket of snow disappeared even from the highest ridges of the Smokies.

He continued southwestward, generally following the Blue Ridge formation, and shortly after he had passed into what he assumed to be North Carolina, he came upon a pair of black bears happily tearing up an old, rotted hickory stump. Soldier Wolf drew back on Messiah's reins, watched from a distance of a few yards as the bears, intent upon their business of digging after termites, did not notice him at all, might never have become aware of his presence if Virgin hadn't let out a long, mournful whinny. With that, one of the bears stood on its hind legs, waved its arms, and peered about with dim eyes. Soldier Wolf unsheathed the Starr carbine and fired into the air. Grudgingly the bears gave ground and disappeared, stopping to look back over their shoulders, into the persimmon brush upslope.

"Brother and sister," Soldier Wolf said, "this child's back on his own ground, but just passing through. . . ."

Elation filled him. The mountains, his mountains, were still alive and well, no doubt about it. He urged Messiah onward.

He remembered passing through a deep canyon just to the north, but a few years back now—an old man and an old woman, mulatto more likely than not, but free, on their own ground, scratching a living from a small clearing along the tumbling stream, working from *kin see to cain't see*, but making it, taking meat as best they could, deer, wild turkeys, and not at all worried by *b'ars now and again. . . .*

Two days later he came within close view of Grandfather Mountain, the side of the peak eroded into the likeness of an old man's face, the resident spirit of the mountains, a place of very strong medicine for his people. Soldier Wolf passed beneath the Stone Face, crossed over the ridge beyond the mountain itself, shot a deer, the first he had taken since the beginning of his journey, and dined on roasted venison that night, pleased with the good wild taste of the meat. He thanked the Creating Spirit, but only as he ate did he recall the words: *Pass on to the other world, little sister of the woods. I will join you after a time. . . .*

The words were those of his own grandfather, dead now these past seven years, dead, and he, Soldier Wolf, had not been there for the time of the burial.

This night, with a warm, rainy mist blowing in, Soldier Wolf slept beneath the slim protection of the extremely useful government-issue canvas short tarp that he had somehow forgotten to check back in. He listened to the *husha-husha* of the fingertips of the rain, breathed the thin smoke from the still-burning campfire, drifted into heavy sleep, and dreamed: *Fires burning everywhere in the land, carbines and cannons, men on horses, men who all looked alike, shooting each other, cutting each other down with sabers. Back away from the fighting were the Negroes, standing in a great circle about the warriors, not even watching, staring at the earth into which their legs appeared to have sunk. Above, on a ridge crest, were Indians—the peoples of the Western Plains, on horseback, bonneted in eagle feathers, watching, motionless, still as statues. Soldier Wolf attempted to scream out: Stop! Stop! It's no use, it won't do any good! But the voice clotted in his throat, and the only sound that issued was the cry, long and mournful, of a wolf. At this point, the scene vanished, and a man who looked more like a wolf appeared and said: It is all part of the fate that has been dreamed. You cannot stop it, and no man can stop it. It must happen because it has been dreamed, Soldier Wolf. It is not your place to fight, even though ruin should come upon this land you love and consider your own. There are other mountains, far greater mountains, beyond the Father River, beyond the plains that ten men cannot see across, mountains where Father Sun goes to rest each night—that is where you must go, for your fate has also been dreamed and must be fulfilled. But you will not find rest there, either, and will have to continue until you have come to the far ocean. I do not know what will happen after that. But these are my words, Soldier Wolf, and you must remember them. . . .*

Two bears were clawing at a hickory stump. They became aware of his presence, stood up, and spoke to him in unison: It is all right, Soldier Wolf. We are smarter than the White devils. We will live longer than they do. We will always have wild honey and termites and good roots to eat. These mountains are millions of years old, hundreds of millions of years old, they were formed in great upheavals of melted rock, sea floors bent upward, boiling fountains. We were not alive then, and yet we remember. You will remember too, after a time. We will all look back from the Star Path and remember. It will be all right, all right, all right. . . .

Soldier Wolf cried out then, awoke.

First light diffusing through the mistlike rain, crows making a terrible racket down below, then silent once again.

Within moments Jerry Soldier Wolf was up and moving, saddling Messiah, stuffing his gear into the saddlebags, riding onward, with Virgin trailing behind. The early-morning air was filled with birdsong, strange, tremoring cries, and from somewhere close by the scream of a night heron.

The memory of the dream burned through his mind, and he rehearsed it over and over.

"A medicine dream," he said to Messiah. "I have come home to myself, the Grandfather Mountain has accepted me back. But what does it mean? I know what it means—a war is coming between North and South. But we will not be here to see it, Black Boy. We'll be out there, out there somewhere. . . ."

The homeward trail wound onward, and the high point of Mt. Mitchell rose above him, the great mountain of the South, straddling the Blue Ridge. Soldier Wolf skirted the flanks of the peak and came down to the village of Mars Hill, turned due westward, valley and hill country, highland plantations, whitewashed board fences, sleek horses in the fields, little clusters of shacks for the Colored slaves, a group of ragged, black-faced children playing catch with a tied pig's bladder, other shacks where the poor White sharecroppers lived and melted into the red-black loam.

The days passing quickly, the land familiar, almost home.

Up across the lateral range of the New Found Mountains, down to Cove Creek. Snow up high now, the mountains draped with whiteness, just as Mitchell had been, long banks of cumulus pushing up against them. Soldier Wolf rode through an area of sunlight, bright, making him blink after the days of gray sky and dim light, and the high peaks of the Smokies seemed as if they were floating upon the layers of cloud, mountaintop islands in a thick river of gray-white. He rode through thickets of dogwood, redbud, flame azalea, and rhododendron, all but the latter leafless this time of year, and he imagined springtime, when the gray tangles of brush would burst with flower—white, pink, pale orange, soft magenta.

The little city of Asheville lay to the south, part of it under the shadow of cloud, part of it in sunlight, the two areas shifting slowly back and forth, changing, and then the sunlight was gone, had drifted upslope, toward where he rode.

Ten miles, he thought, and I'll be there.

Near sundown, the town of Cherokee was before him.

The great pale orb of the moon climbed higher into the sky, appearing and then disappearing as the clouds moved.

More rain, Jerry thought. Wind's coming up, and it smells like snow.

He looked down into the little valley of Raven's Fork and saw the smoke of the home fire hugging the ground. He drew Messiah to a halt, sat there, savored his contemplation of the place where he had grown up, every rock and path within miles his everyday familiars. He stared down at the lighted yellow squares of window glass in the old log house. He rubbed his face, grinned.

But the contemplation was cut short.

Rifle fire.

Jerry searched the valley below and saw the flashes of two more shots. Someone was at his father's farm, raiders perhaps. He withdrew his Marston revolver, drove his heels to Messiah's sides, and with Virgin galloping along behind, charged down toward the farmhouse.

Rifle fire from the house.

Shadow forms, running, plunging away.

He reached the wagon road, turned toward the house, the big black horse at a full run, with Jerry clinging low to the horse's neck.

He pulled off a shot, then a second—heard a man yelp. He fired once more. Could hear swearing.

A lead ball whizzed past his head as he drew up in front of the house.

"Goddammit!" he yelled in English. "It's Jerry—I'm the wrong target!"

His father's voice, the words in Cherokee: "When it is dark, who can tell a friend from one who is not? Is that you, Jerry?"

"Have you gotten so old you cannot see in the dark anymore?"

"Well enough to pick you off."

The door opened, and Thomas Soldier Wolf came out onto the porch.

"Son, if that's you, get on in here! You make too good a target out there!"

Jerry slid from Messiah's back and ran toward his father, leaped up onto the porch, was about to embrace him when he remembered where he was. The two men stood in the dim light, looking each other over, but for a moment, forgetting about the raiders, they did not speak.

"What happened to the sergeant's stripes?" the father asked. "Son, you look like Daniel Boone with a turban on. You coming in, or not?"

"Who in hell's out there, Pa?"

"Whitemen, nothing else but. Think they've come to liberate some of my stuff, maybe a couple of horses."

A rifle ball thudded into the doorpost beside them.

"White devils!" Thomas Soldier Wolf shouted into the darkness, not really seeming too concerned.

"Let me get my horses out of the line of fire, Father. I'll come in the back way. Don't go shooting me, now."

"Hurry up, then. We got coffee on the stove."

Jerry quickly led Messiah and Virgin to the rear of the house, tethered the animals next to the woodshed, and slipped in through the rear door of the main building. As he entered the house, he was met by Tamara, his mother, who had no qualms about hugging her son. She grabbed him and sobbed as she embraced him.

"Get away from me, White woman!" he said, but his voice was full of affection.

"Jerry, Jerry, is that any way to talk to your own mother?"

He lifted her off her feet, kissed her on the forehead.

A shot rang out from the direction of the barn.

"That'll be Jed." The father grinned. "He and Mike are protecting the animals. . . ."

"My rifle!" Jerry exclaimed. "It's still in the scabbard!"

Without thinking, he was out the back door. Then, rifle in hand, he sprinted for the barn, saw the shadows of two horsemen, the sudden flare of torches lighted.

Another shot, and one of the torches fell to the ground. The other arched through the darkness and landed harmlessly next to the barn wall.

Jerry snapped off a shot with his revolver, missed, and the night rider bore down upon him at a gallop. Soldier Wolf leaped to one side, rolled for several feet, dropped the rifle, spun about, and fired his pistol into the darkness.

The horseman was gone.

The blue spurt of rifle fire from the barn.

"Jed! Mike! Cut out the shooting—it's me, Jerry, your brother, damm it!"

The two hesitated, and Jerry scrambled for his carbine, ran low, entered through the barn door.

"Jesus Kee-rist, fellas, you damned near hit me!"

"That really you, Jerry?"

It was Jed, the older of the two.

Then both of the younger brothers were pounding Jerry on the back.

"Where'd you come from?" Mike asked breathlessly.

"Just riding in when I heard the shots. Jed, what the hell's going on?"

"It's been brewing for a time now. Things were fairly calm around here until last spring. Some folks over near Waynesville decided they needed something we had. They tried to make off with it, and Paw kicked the shit out of them."

"You should have seen him!" Mike chimed in.

"It started when Old Man Carter made a remark about Ma's being White, and Dad thumped him one. That got the Jessups riled," Jed explained. "And things sort of spread from there."

"So who's out there?" Jerry asked.

"Jessups, I imagine," Jed answered.

"But we've been friends with the Jessups for years. I don't figure it. I think I hit one of them with a pistol shot when I rode in—heard someone yell out."

"You think you done killed somebody?" Mike asked. "Jesus!"

"There'll likely be hell to pay if you killed someone," Jed said.

"Maybe we better go look." Jerry shrugged. "A man shouldn't be riding around in the dark shooting at folks and trying to thieve things. If he gets shot, it's his own damned fault."

"The Jessups are White," Mike said, shaking his head.

"Don't make no difference, little brother. But let's go take a look."

The three brothers slipped out of the barn, and Jerry led to the sloping area below the house. The full moon, half-obscured by clouds, still cast sufficient light for them to detect the dark form crumpled in the winter-dead grass.

"Mike," Jerry said, "get that torch they threw at the barn, the damned thing's still burning. And we need some more light. I think this guy's still alive."

Mike ran back, returned with the torch, and held it up over the fallen man. Jerry rolled the body over and saw the stream of oozing blood that matted the man's hair. He felt for a pulse, and the man groaned.

"Scalp wound, nothing more. Knocked him senseless is all. Abner Jessup, isn't it? C'mon, help me get him to the house."

Abner Jessup was placed on the braided rug in front of the fireplace, and the oil lanterns were relit.

"I'll be damned," Thomas Soldier Wolf said. "The Jessup boy—he helped me with woodcutting two years ago. What the hell gets into them? Bad blood gets started, there's no way of stopping it, I guess."

The mother brought a hot, damp cloth and dabbed at the wound, washed the clotting blood out of the hair, then rinsed the cloth, applied it to young Jessup's face.

Within a few minutes Abner had come to his senses, sat up.

"Boy," Thomas Soldier Wolf said, "you damned near got yourself killed. What were you doing out there?"

Jessup shook his head.

"Wanting to play a little trick, was ye? Going to run our horses off?"

"I'm sorry," Jessup said, staring up at the four Soldier Wolf men and then at Tamara. "I don't know what we were doing. I guess it was wrong."

"You're lucky we found you," Jerry said. "You might have bled to death before morning."

"You're Jerry," Abner Jessup said. "I remember you. . . ."

"Who was with you, Abner?" Thomas Soldier Wolf asked.

"My cousin."

"Well, he's halfway to Waynesville by now. Mike, go out and see if you can find Abner's horse. I guess he'll be wanting to head on home. Tamara, fetch the young man a cup of coffee. It'll bring his good sense back, maybe."

When Abner was finally sent on his way, Thomas Soldier Wolf closed the front door and broke into a roar of laughter, pounded his fist against the wall.

"Woman," he said, "is that venison stew about ready? A man could starve to death around here with all the goings-on. And

Daniel Boone here must be just about hungry enough to eat grass. As long as we've got a few minutes between engagements, let's have some chow."

Jerry stared at his father, then at his mother.

"Ma, is this something recent, or has Father been touched in the head all along, and I just never noticed before?"

"Set down, Dan'l," Thomas Soldier Wolf said, "and let's eat. . . ."

The family, reunited for the first time in several years, spent the remainder of the night sitting up and talking about the Jessups and the Carters and Jerry's new job with the Bureau of Indian Affairs. Tamara kept the coffeepot full, and the conversation, one way or another, managed to cover the years since Jerry had last been home. No one wanted to leave the table to get some sleep.

At last a rooster began to crow, and the dark panes of the eastward window began to turn gray.

"Boys," Thomas said, "the sun ball's coming up. Let's have us another cup of coffee and then go out and get the chores started. As my father used to say, the Great Spirit looks after the ones who work, and not the others. . . ."

Chapter Four

"Let the consequences be what they may. Whether the Potomac is crimsoned in human gore, and Pennsylvania Avenue is paved ten fathoms in depth with mangled bodies . . . the South will never submit. . . ."

But in the North, many foolishly persisted in the belief that the South could not actually intend a permanent breakaway. The South, on the other hand, could not conceive that the North would forcibly resist secession. Even President-elect Lincoln saw secession as a bluff designed to win pro-slavery concessions in the territories, concessions he was determined not to make. In the meanwhile, the lame-duck Buchanan "importuned, threatened, warned, begged, pushed, pulled, and shoved in every direction . . . the President at length became distraught and despaired of achieving a solution."

With war in the offing, Buchanan made a final attempt to solve the problem of the Western Indians, and sent Colonel Boone, Dan'l's grandson, with official papers for the Indians to sign, thereby to relinquish most of their lands, in return for federal protection, payments, agricultural implements, and the like. The treaty was consummated at Fort Wise and was signed by Little Raven, Storm, Shave-Head, and Big Mouth for the Arapahos, and for the Cheyennes by Black Kettle, White Antelope, Lean Bear, Little Wolf, Tall Bear, and Left Hand, who signed with the Cheyennes. The papers were dated February 18, 1861.

Jerry had all but decided to forget his mission to the West and simply to stay with his family, to build his own place at the upper end of his father's property, to live out his life in these mountains where he had grown up and which he so dearly loved. Even the thought of starting a family of his own had crossed his mind, for several attractive young women in the nearby town of Cherokee had caught his attention.

South Carolina had voted for sucession, and the likelihood of civil war grew with every day, but in all probability, the violence, whatever it amounted to, would miss the mountain country.

Jerry, Jed, and Mike had been cutting and splitting a big storm-toppled white oak all afternoon, and now, with six mules straining at the loaded drag sled, the three young men were on their way back in.

The house seemed too warm as the boys came in out of the cold. Wind had come up, and clouds were lowering. More snow seemed a distinct possibility.

They found their mother and father sitting at the table. Thomas Soldier Wolf was wearing his turban, and this was a signal to his sons. The elder Soldier Wolf puffed reflectively on his pipe, did not look up. Finally he spoke:

"Eldest Son, a letter has arrived from Washington, D.C. I had hoped that you would stay now and live with us, but I see that you will leave. You have always been restless, and now you will wander off again."

"Letter?" Jerry asked.

Tamara handed her son the envelope. Jerry poured himself a cup of coffee, black, and sat down at the table, opened the missive.

> Agent Soldier Wolf:
>
> First, I want you to know that we are convinced you are the one who took General Poole's stallion and the sorrel mare. Animals were available to you, per our agreement. It was not necessary to engineer an act of horse theft. However, speaking personally, I must admit that I admire your taste in horseflesh. I have managed to take care of the matter, and I trust the black stallion brings you good fortune and that, in some way or another, our project is furthered thereby. Know, however, that no further misappropriations of any sort will be tolerated.
>
> According to our best intelligence, the northern sector of the Rockies may well experience an early spring. If this should be so, then the urgency of our situation is increased. The Cheyenne chief, White Frog, may have already led his people to the south, perhaps because of harassment by the Crows or possibly the Blackfeet.
>
> In any case, Colonel Albert Boone has been appointed chief agent and is to meet with the various Indian leaders at

Fort Wise for the purpose of enforcing a binding treaty, and so putting the worst of our problem out of the way. Boone has received a sufficient supply of goods for the Cheyennes and Arapahos, these being stored at Fort Wise, and he has the full cooperation of William Gilpin, governor-designate of Colorado Territory. The treaty should be signed, sealed, and delivered by the time that you and the Goths arrive in the area.

White Frog's group and the continued unlawful presence of Edward Cramdon, however, put the entire undertaking in jeopardy. It is essential that White Frog be pacified and that Cramdon be brought in to trial. I cannot overstress the importance of all this, Soldier Wolf.

Proceed by the quickest method to railhead at St. Joseph. From there you will travel overland to the upper reaches of the North Platte River, by way of Denver.

South Carolina, as you are no doubt aware, has seceded, and the Union itself seems under sentence of dissolution. You must move with dispatch. Relative peace in the territories is of the utmost importance.

My father has officially resigned from the BIA, so all further directives will come from me.

Amanda sends her good wishes.

With best regards,
Daniel Harriman

Jerry folded the letter, put it into his jacket pocket. Nodded.

"Yes, Father, I must leave now. I must go to St. Joseph and from there into Colorado Territory."

"You do not need to ask your father's permission," Thomas Soldier Wolf said in Cherokee. "In the way of the world we live in, you are a war chief already, my son. It is a bad time to begin such a journey, for it is the time of snow in the air, it is the time of winter furs. The breath is seen even in the dark of the moon. Still, you must go—I see it in your face. My son, I would go with you, but we have trouble here, and that must be cared for. I cannot leave my wife. There is trouble in the land, and only the Creating Spirit knows what will happen. But I would ask one thing."

"What is that, Father?" Jerry said in English.

"Who here speaks like the Whites? Has one of my sons been among the Other People for so long that he has forgotten?"

"What would you know, my father?" Jerry repeated in his native tongue.

"Is this a good thing that you will be doing for the Americans?"

"Yes. It will be a good thing."

Thomas Soldier Wolf puffed at his pipe, then offered it to his son. Jerry took the pipe, tasted the smoke, and returned the carved briar to his father.

"Father, if you hate the yellowlegs, the bluecoats, so much, why did you wish me to join with them years ago?"

"Maybe someday," Thomas Soldier Wolf said, relighting his pipe and blowing smoke in the four directions, "you will know. Our world changed long ago, and we must live with the Whiteman and the Blackmen as well. Perhaps one day there will be a single great tribe to which we will all belong, who can say? Perhaps the Creating Spirit will take pity on all. If we live well, perhaps it will happen. But this thing must be answered by life, and not by some old fool like myself."

Thomas Soldier Wolf placed the pipe on the table and passed his hands over the still-smoking bowl in a gesture.

"Ride well and be careful, Jerry," he said in English. "If it's possible, send us a letter. Tamara, is that roast about cooked? Your sons have worked hard this afternoon, and they're probably ready to start chewing on the furniture. . . ."

The first of February and his rendezvous with the Goths was drawing close now, and Jerry Soldier Wolf crossed the Smokies through Newfound Gap. He rode Messiah, the big animal seemingly glad to be on the move once more, with Virgin trailing behind, snorting, sometimes bolting, excited. The sky was an immense vault of blue, cloudless, and the midwinter sunlight was pleasantly warm, with only a faint hint of chill in the air.

As the big Indian in the turban and the buffalo-skin coat rode northward, down through the ridges and through the little town of Gatlinburg, the carbine in its sheath, the Marston revolver in its holster, a Green River sheath knife next to it, a bowie knife slung loosely from his belt on the opposite side, Soldier Wolf felt distinctly self-conscious. A band of children ran from him, disappeared behind the freshly whitewashed Baptist church, peered around the corner. After years of military garb, the new costume seemed garish, not real, not a part of him, not authentic.

A greenhorn mountain man who's never been west of where he

is right now, he mused, shaking his head. A store-bought buffalo coat and U.S. Army pants and boots. . . .

The nervous laughter of children. As he proceeded down the main street, the children followed, kept their distance. When he reached the edge of town, they began to shout and call out.

He rode on toward Pigeon Forge. After that would come Pine Grove, Sevierville, and finally Knoxville, where he and his pair of refugee horses would board a train. With great good luck, he mused, and if the schedules worked out, he had a bare chance of making it to St. Joseph by the first of the month. But the land was in a turmoil, rumor was in the air, bits and pieces of genuine news mixed with all manner of fabrication and supposition.

If the Goths left without him, he had little doubt that he would be able to overtake whatever wagon train they attached themselves to with no great difficulty. One way or another, it would all work out.

He was heading west. And out there somewhere, beyond the Father River and the great expanse of the plains, were the Rocky Mountains, the backbone of the continent. Cheyennes and Arapahos, Pawnees and Crows—and a man named Edward Cramdon, a man who had never heard of Jerry Soldier Wolf but a man whose fate was somehow to be inextricably bound to his own.

A strange heaviness settled over Jerry's chest as he rode. Was it the leaving of a land he considered his own after so short a visit, the venturing out into a world whose dimensions were clothed with legend and mystery, of strangeness? Or was it the fact that he might well have said good-bye to his father and mother and younger brothers for the final time?

His admiration for his father was so intense that it hurt sometimes. Thomas Soldier Wolf, his father, the man against whom and against whose dimensions and sheer energy and presence he would forever be obliged to measure himself—Thomas, a man in his early fifties and still as strong as any young buck, his black hair just beginning to show grayness, a handsome man. Jerry could see why his mother, Tamara, had been swept away by him, had turned from the traditional ways of her own family to marry him. The image of Thomas' powerful hands wrapped around a coffee cup, looking as if they could crush the cup with the slightest effort.

And Tamara.

The image of Thomas' large hands made Jerry wonder, as he had never wondered before, how such a frail woman could stand up to her husband's power. She was showing age now, more so than his father, and her blond hair was fading to silver, but she still had her girlish figure, despite the hard life, the hard work, the bearing and raising of three sons. It was from her that he and his brothers got their blue eyes, the only apparent feature they had gotten from her.

Jed and Mike, his brothers. They would find their own way. They would, as he himself had, be required to make their own separate treaties with the Whiteman's world, a world that was about to split into halves. The war would come—as a soldier, he had heard talk of little else for the past several months. Lincoln's election was not the cause, only the occasion. Two separate civilizations, bound uneasily together for so long as common interest prevailed, but drawn into conflict on the flood of expansionism, the ambitions of leaders, the requirements of commerce.

Shortly before dark he reached the town of Sevierville, passed through, rode on for a time in the twilight, turned off the main wagon road and into a wooded area through which a small stream meandered. No farmhouses were near, and a barn owl called through the shadowy overhang of elm and oak. A light frost had settled over the world, frost and a thin, stinging fog that seemed to be moving, as though a thing alive, toward the east, against the current of the creek.

Jerry dismounted, watered the horses, found an open area of winter-dead grass, and tethered the animals a few yards apart. He built a small fire, boiled water for coffee, and ate cold fried chicken that his mother had prepared for him and had carefully wrapped in paper and tied into a bundle covered with a flap of old oilcloth.

A fox barked nearby, and again the owl cried. Soldier Wolf could hear a rustle of wings among the brushy undergrowth, pigeons he decided, and then a quiet punctuated only by the soft murmur of slowly moving water.

A new world, as he was well aware, had come into existence. Half a day's ride ahead was the city of Knoxville, Knoxville and the railway that would carry him and his two horses to Chattanooga and on to Nashville and up into Kentucky to Louisville and thence westward across the Mississippi to St. Louis and from there across the Missouri River and westward still to St. Joseph, where the ribbons of steel ended and the West truly began.

Nothing would ever be the same again, for he himself would not be the same.

He tried to think of the wagon train, of his reunion with Frank Goth and his family, of the trip overland to Fort Kearny on the Platte River, of the mountains from which the river flowed, but no images would come.

He thought of Sara Goth. The beautiful young Sara, the girl for whom he had nursed a boyish fixation for more than a month now. Would she in fact be there? Was it possible that her parents would actually elect to take their daughter out into the wild territories, a land filled with all manner of dangers if any of the stories could be believed?

The girl's eyes, like the eyes of a wild creature, perhaps like the eyes of the owl that continued its mournful calling, remained before him even after the rest of the image had faded.

And then he slept.

The horses were making a racket, and Soldier Wolf awoke momentarily. Misty darkness lay heavy over the woods, with winter dawn still an hour or so away. Jerry listened intently but heard no further disturbance. Nonetheless, he turned onto his side, placed his hand on the Marston, then drifted once more toward sleep.

When he awoke a second time, a thin silver light suffused the mist, and half a dozen disreputable-looking individuals were standing in a rough half-circle about him, all of them bearded and wearing worn denim coats and battered felt slouch hats. The older of the men, the father perhaps, was pointing a pistol at Soldier Wolf's head.

"Wal, damn my soul," the man said. "Me an' the boys was out huntin' us some coons, an' we done found us a big 'un—a Churagee coon, judgin' from the turban rag on the branch behind 'im."

"Ain't no Injun got horses like them two unless he stole 'em, Pa," another of the men said.

"Figger you're right, Jimmy me lad. However he come by 'em, he's just lost 'em."

"Let's string the Churagee up an' have us a target practice," another of the young men suggested, grinning.

"What's your name, Injun?" the man with the pistol asked.

Soldier Wolf shifted his position slightly, carefully withdrawing his own weapon from its holster as he did so, the movement shielded beneath the heavy blankets.

"Jerry Soldier Wolf," he answered, "United States government agent. Gentlemen, I'd suggest you be on your way, and we'll forget this whole thing."

"Likely as cowshit," the man with the pistol said. "First place, the goddamn govmint don't hire Injuns, an' second place, they ain't no govmint no more nohow. Luky, fetch your rope. We'll truss this Red nigger up while we decide what to do with 'im."

"Put the dogs on 'im," the one called Jimmy suggested. "If the runnin' bastards ever come back, that is. Probably halfway to Knox County by now."

"They be along," Luky said. "Pa, you never have enough faith in ol' Crooked Spot. He won't let the others run too far. . . ."

"Shit!" Jimmy laughed. "Luke, that big hound of yours is the damn ringleader—the others don't take off at all 'less your dog's with 'em. That's why Pa didn't want you to bring 'im along. . . ."

With one explosive movement, Soldier Wolf twisted out of his blankets, lunging to one side in a crouching position. With his first shot, the old man with the pistol bent backward from the hips, the gun falling from his hand, and a red splotch appeared at his throat. Soldier Wolf fired again, missing, and the five younger men, yelling in rage, dived for cover.

Soldier Wolf scrambled for the brush, followed by a volley of pistol fire, the shots ringing cold and muffled in the foggy half-light.

Then another shot, the sound of a heavy carbine, and one of the boys pitched forward across a downed willow log, his voice a long, diminishing peal of agony. A moment later a second report of the mysterious carbine, and another of the coon hunters spun about, fell, spasmed on the ground, and lay still.

"We're pinned down!" a voice shouted. "They gonna kill all of us. . . ."

Soldier Wolf broke cover, ran to a big maple, and darted behind it as pistol fire sang around him.

Who had the carbine?

He could see Messiah and Virgin now, the two horses straining at their tethers, screaming, rearing, and turning about.

Another shot from the carbine, followed by the sound of someone thrashing about in the low brush by the stream.

Two of the men were running straight toward him, oblivious of his presence, oblivious of everything except the rifle fire from behind. Soldier Wolf considered the wisdom of letting the two men, one of them the man called Luky, owner of the dog called Crooked Spot, pass on by. The thought of a dog with no master flashed through Jerry's mind, while at the same instant he wondered why it was that human brain concerned itself with such details during moments of crisis. Then, without being entirely certain why he was doing it, Soldier Wolf stepped from behind the maple and fired twice, his second shot being drowned by the heavier report of the rifle.

The two brothers, if brothers they were, fell one atop the other, their bodies convulsing, and then lay still, embraced in death.

"Who the hell's out there?" Soldier Wolf shouted into the mist.

But no answer, only the faintly audible sound of flowing water, the distant baying of coon dogs, miles away, running, probably running deer, Jerry thought. He tried to determine distance, direction, and then his mind returned to the more immediate problem of the unknown rifleman.

"Soldier Wolf here! U.S. government agent! Show yourself, dammit!"

When the voice came, it was in back of him.

"Put the popgun away, young feller. This coon don't need no more bullet scars than what he's got awreddy, them's enough."

Soldier Wolf spun about, hit the ground, his eyes scanning the brush behind him. Still nothing visible, not a damned thing. Was it an apparition, a ghost?

"Put the gun away, young fella. If I'd wanted to shoot ye, I'd of done 'er by now. Got ye a mountaineer's coat, but she ain't wore in yet. Got to learn summat, or ye'll get planted, sure. Or ye just playin' pretend?"

"Dammit, where are you? All right, the pistol's in its holster."

"Kin see as it is."

The figure of the old man seemed to materialize out of the mist, no more than a few yards from where Soldier Wolf lay sprawled on the cold earth. The coat the man wore was similar in cut to Jerry's own, but old, brown-black and shiny in places, nearly half of the sleeve and chest tassels gone. He was tall, thin, his face only partially visible beneath its bushy white beard and heavy eyebrows, also white, and his hair, white to silver-gray, hung to either side and behind in three pigtails, a dirty red cloth about his forehead. A butcher knife hung at his side, and an ancient buffalo rifle rested on the crook of his arm, a short-barreled muzzle loader, a Hawken most likely. The man's feet were in moccasins, and his leggings were cross-laced, tight to his calves.

Soldier Wolf nearly burst out laughing—the man looked like an engraving he had once seen of old Jim Bridger.

"What in the living hell?" Jerry managed.

"Name's Farnsworth O'Bragh," the buckskin man said. "Ain't nobody calls me Farnsworth to my face, though, or my scalpin' knife starts singin'. Folks started callin' me Bully back at the turn of the century, an' Bully it's been ever since. Bully O'Bragh. Ye've heard of me, mebbe?"

"Can't say as I have, old fellow. My name's Jerry Soldier Wolf. Guess maybe you saved my life, and I owe you for it."

"Figgered it was ye last night when I come onto your camp, sonny. Wanted to wait for mornin' so's we could get to know each other over a pot of coffee. Got some, don't ye?"

"You were looking for me?"

"Tryin' to catch up. Ride along pretty good on that big black of yourn. Good-lookin' horse, no question, but mebbe not the best for where we're headin'. Me, I ride mules. Ain't so fast, but a damn sight smarter an' more dependable."

"What are you talking about?" Jerry asked, getting to his feet and feeling suddenly both ignorant and awkward. "Following me?"

"Young Harriman sent me," O'Bragh said, fished a pipe out of his leathers, tamped in some tobacco, and lit up, inhaled, shook his head, and blew the smoke out through his nostrils.

"Harriman?"

"Yup. Figgered you an' your preachin' friends might need somebody as knows the land, I guess. Ye got some coffee or not? A man gets past seventy, he needs somethin' to get him started mornings."

Suddenly, the tension gone, Soldier Wolf roared with laughter, held his sides, shook his head.

"Not even sunup," he managed, "and we've killed six men. If you'd had your coffee already, you'd probably have shot my horses too!"

"Naw," Bully O'Bragh said, "horses is worth summat. Only time a man kills a horse is when he's starvin' an' ain't got no choice in the matter. Redneck varmints is different, an' those boys just wasn't bein' friendly."

O'Bragh strode to where the man called Jimmy had fallen, mortally wounded, across the willow log.

"Fix us some coffee, Soldier Wolf," he said over his shoulder, and then sat down on the log, put one knee against the dead man's back, drew his butcher knife, cut a quick circle twice about the scalp, wiped the blade, and put it back in its case. With surprising and, Jerry gathered, practiced dexterity, he grasped the topknot, twisted and pulled in a single gliding movement, and then stood up, the scalp in hand.

"Don't stand gawkin', young feller. Get us a fire goin'. I'll hide these hawgs out in the brush in case anyone comes ridin' through before we're done with that coffee. . . ."

Farnsworth O'Bragh, Jerry learned during the next few days, was indeed a singular man. Raised in the wilds of Kentucky, he had grown up hunting and trapping. His mother was quarter Massasoit, the rest English, a Connecticut woman, and his father, an Irishman whose parents had come over from the old country, was from Boston and had brought a Bostonian's thirst for hard spirits with him to the Kentucky back country.

"Inherited my pa's bad nature and my ma's good looks." Bully laughed as he and Soldier Wolf were loading the two horses and the mule onto the stock car at the railroad landing in Knoxville. "Careful with Porcupine, there—mules is sensitive. Anyhow, when I was fifteen, I sort of acidentally set the woods on fire, an' Pa had in mind to whip me for it, so I took off. Was just the year when Lewis and Clark was settin' off up the Muddy River, but I didn't know it then. Took me a spell to work my way out there, since I had to grow up an' all. You know, one thing sort of led to another. If we get ourselves snowed in up there next winter, I'll tell ye the whole thing. Anyhow, by 1815 or so I was up the river an' livin' with the Rees, trapped a spell with old man La Jeunesse an' Pete Le Blueux, Pierre hisself. Knowed damned near all them coons in my time, Billy Williams, Little Kit, Bloody Arm Beckwourth, Gabe Bridger, Joe Meek, Billy Sublette, Stuffed Shirt Ashley, Davy Jackson, Bible Smith, all of 'em. Now Bridger an' Beckwourth, those coons still be up there, an' could be we'll meet 'em. Meek, he's out in Oregon, from what I hear. An' the chiefs too, this coon's smoked tobaccy with all of 'em. Long Hair, Yeller Belly, Roman Nose, Powder Face, Raven, Big Mouth, Red Cloud, Leg in the Water, White Frog. . . ."

Soldier Wolf squinted at the old man, then slid the door shut on the stock car. Whatever O'Bragh had been, Jerry had decided, the old man loved to lard his stories—but whether the tales were ten percent true or ninety percent, he was not quite prepared to say, though he suspected something closer to the former figure. But the previous morning's shootout in the woods, whatever else Soldier Wolf might have suspected, lent credence, a certain amount of it, to Bully's assertions.

"What about squaws?" he asked O'Bragh as the two men moved the loading ramp back from the tracks. "You got women out among the tribes?"

"No, no. Sonny, I outlived 'em all, an' most of my kids too. Finally I took up with a good-lookin' she-bear, an' we got us a bunch of little ones. You heard about skunk bears? Well, them's our kids. Meanest little sonsabitches alive, 'cause they took after their ma. Tell ye what, though, an' not many know this. Your she-grizzly, once the sun goes down, them ladies turn into the most ungodly beautiful female creatures you can imagine, with breasts like ripe melons and a smell to their snatch that just drives a coon wild. It's the truth, I'm tellin' ye. Get smart, Soldier Wolf me boy, an' ye'll hitch up with a grizzly. . . ."

Within a few minutes they were aboard the train, had found convenient seats, and had sat down. The Negro porter, stiff and proper in his uniform, came by, looked down his nose at the two men, pretended they weren't there, and continued about his rounds. Then the train began to snort and vibrate, the linkages clunking, and, with three blasts of the whistle, the trip down the Tennessee River to Chattanooga was begun.

Soldier Wolf had resolved to attempt to get some straight information from his companion, but almost immediately as the train was in motion, Bully O'Bragh slumped down in his seat and into a noisy, snoring sleep.

The countryside rattled by, a mere five hours to Chattanooga and six more to Corinth, clear across the state of Alabama, and into Mississippi, the daylight passing into darkness, and the train rolling on, clacking, clacking, the occasional blasts of the big whistle, short stops at one small town after another, and a predawn layover in Corinth. Bully awoke, and the two men made their way to the dining car, ate scrambled eggs, and drank coffee. Soldier Wolf bought a newspaper, read, while the older man rattled on about a great battle, twenty years past, between the

Cheyennes and the Crows. The paper was full of material which, taken all together, Soldier Wolf realized, could mean only one thing: *war*. One piece, reprinted from a Georgia paper, insisted that all Yankees were abolitionists, men whose primary and ultimate purposes were the same—to destroy the South as a civilization, to destroy the economic base. *I look upon the whole New England race as a troublesome unquiet set of meddlers*. Following the lead of South Carolina, one Southern state after another had followed suit, and the paper had devoted extensive space to a discussion of the needs for a provisional government to be set up, with a conference to be called to meet in Montgomery, Alabama, the first week in February. Virginia, Tennessee, North Carolina, and Arkansas had thus far held to their places within the Union, the paper declared, and yet it was just a matter of time. Once a new government was established, the remaining slave states would perceive their true loyalties, and a new and powerful nation, the Southern United States, would arise. *From the rattle with which the nurse tickles the ear of the child born in the South to the shroud which covers the cold form of the dead, everything comes from the North. We rise from between sheets made in Northern looms, and pillows of Northern feathers, to wash in basins made in the North. These are not my words, fellow Southerners, and they are not the rhetoric of our present time of crisis. No, indeed—these words are those of a Southern businessman and were written as the result of a commercial convention in 1855. If we would have our freedom, if we would take our place among the nations of the earth, we must break this noxious pattern of dependence upon the North. We must not depend for our very lives upon those who are our enemies. . . .*

Soldier Wolf folded the paper, placed it on the counter, shook his head.

"Newspapers still sayin' the same things they said last week, sonny? That's why I run off from home—did I tell ye that? My ma was determined she was goin' to make me learn to read."

"Thought you said you'd set the woods afire, and your pa was going to give you a whipping." Soldier Wolf shrugged.

"That happened too, that happened too," Bully O'Bragh said. "Between them, they intended to civilize this poor coon, an' I couldn't take 'er."

"Well, it's all falling apart, Bully. By the time we get where we're going, we won't know who we're working for, like as not."

"Don't make no difference, sonny. One govment's just like

another. None of 'em knows which hand to wipe their asses with, an' that's a fact. Besides, Jerry Tsaragi, it ain't like we're goin' out there to do work or nothin' like that. No man goes to the mountains to work, Gawd no. We're just goin' on a little huntin' expedition for a nigger named Cramdon, an' after that we're going to do some talkin' with the Cheyennes, an' explain to 'em how the Long Knives don't mean them nothin' but good. First part'll be easy. Second part they ain't gonna believe, no more'n I do. This child never would of signed on, no matter what Harriman an' his kid said, except I needed a couple of gold pieces to rattle around in my possibles sack. White Frog, he's just gonna laugh at us anyhow. After that, mebbe me an' Porcupine'll mosey on out to California, where the climate's better an' no one's fightin' over nigger slaves. Now that I'm gettin' on in years, the cold winters don't set well. Blanket Chief Bridger, I guess he'll die up in the mountains somewhere, friz to death. Me, I'm gonna lie in the sun an' cook in grand style."

"Bully, I'd almost be willing to believe you've never been further west than we are right now. Probably you've been reading Jim Beckwourth's book and decided to make up one of your own."

"Beckwourth writ a book?"

"I thought you said you knew him. How is it you don't know that?"

"You sure he writ it?"

"Got his name on the cover."

"Don't mean he writ it, sonny."

"Some men know how to read and write. Maybe you should have stayed home and let your ma teach you the magic."

"I kin read an' write too, Soldier Wolf."

"If you ran away, then where'd you learn?"

"Look here, sonny. This child ain't ignorant. I just learned, is all."

Bully O'Bragh lapsed into silence then, and Soldier Wolf wondered if he had pushed the old man too far. Again the shots were ringing through the half-light of the mist, again the figure of the gaunt, tall man was emerging, materializing out of the fog. Besides that, the Harrimans were not fools, whatever else they might be. If they had faith in O'Bragh, then the shootout in the woods was no accident. The man might well be fifty percent noise and grand lies, but the other portion, mysterious, undefined, was more than significant. In any case, there would be time to evaluate

Farnsworth O'Bragh once they were out on the plains and heading for the Rockies. And in addition to everything else, the man was good company. The wild stories, elaborated to great lengths, would provide interesting entertainment on the trip up-country.

Bully tamped his pipe and lit up.

"You sure Beckwourth writ a book?" he asked.

North into Tennessee once more, north still to Louisville, Kentucky, and across the Ohio River, then westward to Indiana and Illinois and over the mile-wide Mississippi River, the great central artery of the land, of the continent, the bridge itself a minor miracle of engineering, parallel humps of riveted and cantilevered steel, a section of it capable of being raised to accommodate the big boats that plied their trade up and down the length of the great river.

St. Louis, the nearly legendary gateway to the vastness of the American West in many of the books that Soldier Wolf had read, but, in truth, looking fairly much like any other city of comparable size, nothing in any way remarkable about it. Back in 1822, when General Ashley had first gone up the Missouri with the song of the beaver in his brain, St. Louis had been no more than a muddy village, the frontier itself. Now a common-enough-looking little city, and no signs of a frontier at all.

They changed trains once again, and the clackety-clack rhythm was resumed and the locomotive, puffing and hissing and belching and whistling, drew its burden westward through another darkness, across the Missouri River, and on toward the end of the line at a settlement called St. Joseph. There, coming once again to the Missouri River, Soldier Wolf and O'Bragh would debark, take to their horses and mule, respectively, join the Goths, and accompany a wagon train westward across the plains, to the Platte River and onward to the Rocky Mountains, where a task of indeterminate dimensions awaited them, undefined danger, uncertain chances of success.

Bully was already asleep—indeed, he had slept for the major portion of the preceding two days and nights. The man snored, Soldier Wolf thought to himself, loudly enough to alert every hostile Indian within a hundred miles of wherever they might find it necessary to encamp. Or perhaps that was his mating call, designed to attract she-grizzlies to his bed.

Soldier Wolf relaxed in his seat, the running lights of the

Pullman dimming and glowing in rhythm, and closed his eyes, tried to drift into sleep.

Images of mountains formed, mountains unlike his own Smokies, mountains of huge proportion, snow-crowned.

Buffalo, a vast herd of the big animals, moving slowly, like cattle. And a woman was riding beside him, riding the mare he intended to breed to the black stallion. Who was it?

The image of young Sara Goth defined itself, came totally clear. She was speaking to him, and yet he could not hear what she was saying.

Soldier Wolf shook his head, drew himself back from the tentacles of sleep, rubbed at his eyes, glanced over at the profile of Bully O'Bragh, the old man slumped forward and appearing quite vulnerable, quite harmless. Was this the man who had helped him to save his own life, who had casually taken the scalp of one of the coon hunters? The man who, even now, had the half-dried scalp of a Whiteman in the buckskin bag he called his possibles sack?

Been needin' some new medicine, sonny, an' the scalp of a Whiteman is powerful stuff. Anyhow, he didn't need it no more. . . .

Soldier Wolf closed his eyes, began to drift once again toward sleep. For a moment, just before the warmth of oblivion, he half-convinced himself that when he awoke, the seat next to him would be empty, that O'Bragh had been no more than a dream, a fantastic illusion.

The illusion continued to snore quite loudly, and the clackety-clack of the steel rims over the steel segments of rail continued. . . .

Chapter Five

February of 1861 brought the formation of a provisional government of the Confederate States of America, thus drawing all the states of the lower South into common bonds. Still Virginia, Tennessee, North Carolina, and Arkansas attempted to remain with the Union, but these warned the federal government that they, too, would secede if force were used against the Confederacy. Restraint was everywhere urged, but few thinking persons believed other than that some manner of conflict was inevitable.

In the face of all this turmoil, the need to resolve the Indian problems in the Rocky Mountain region was perceived as of utmost importance, for ever larger numbers of settlers, drawn by continued and exaggerated news of gold strikes in the Pike's Peak region, were moving westward. Something over a hundred non-Indians had lived near Pike's Peak in late 1858, and in spring of the following year, their numbers greatly increased; they proclaimed the state of Jefferson and sought to authorize a constitution for the new commonwealth.

Congregate a hundred Americans anywhere beyond the settlements, a traveler wrote, and they immediately lay out a city, form a state constitution, and apply for admission into the Union, while twenty-five of them become candidates for the United States Senate.

Emigrants poured westward, drawn by the lure of gold and by tales of lush valleys and land for the taking, and during 1860, as many as five thousand each week found their way to the mines of RussellGulch, Spanish Diggings, Twelve Mile Gulch, Tarryall Creek, Fairplay Creek, and even across the continental divide to Blue Creek, to California Gulch on the upper Arkansas near Leadville, to the San Juan Mountains.

Rock-crushing mills were erected, tunneling was begun. Gold threaded the seams of quartz deep below the surface.

Cheyenne, Arapaho, and Pawnee watched, and some spoke for peace with these new Long Knives, and some spoke of war.

* * *

The plains were frozen but clear of snow, with temperatures dropping below zero at night, the earth iron hard beneath the amazing display of the midnight sky—daytime temperatures, the sky immense and sharply blue, still remaining below the freezing point.

Perhaps a thousand prospective emigrants had huddled in a city of tents and makeshift cabins across the Missouri River from St. Joseph, some eagerly awaiting the spring thaws and yet knowing that these might be as much as a month or more away, others losing heart, beginning to talk either of turning back or of taking up land in eastern Kansas or north in Nebraska. Frank Goth and his family had made arrangements to move west, as soon as Soldier Wolf arrived, with a small group who had decided to take their chances with the winter cold along the Platte River, a train consisting of some ten prairie schooners, the big wagons drawn either by oxen or by Conestoga horses. But then a group of Stampeders, returnees from the frontier villages along the fringe of the Rockies, had come dragging in, their animals half-starved, themselves in very little better condition, and the men mad as hell about their bad luck in the gold-mining areas and telling stories about blizzards and high winds and harassment by hostile Indians.

The leaders of the wagon train, after talking with the refugees from the mountains, held council and decided upon the wisdom of waiting for the weather to turn.

Rumors that Gilpin, governor of the provisional territory of Jefferson, a district which included the newly renamed city of Denver as well as the area of the goldfields, might be asked to step down, rumors that Lincoln, once inaugurated as president, would appoint John Evans as governor, not of Jefferson, but of Colorado Territory.

The frontier territory of Kansas was now a state, its capital at Topeka, a few miles southwest of St. Joseph. The settlements were moving inexorably westward, even as the nation itself was moving inexorably toward civil war.

Frank Goth walked beyond the limits of the tent city, knelt by a frozen creek beneath huge willows, and prayed for guidance. Screech owls called through the brittle night air, and the bare limbs of the willows creaked with the intense cold.

By the time he returned to his wagon and his team of mules, his wife and his daughter, the decision had been made. They would push westward, alone, as soon as Agent Soldier Wolf arrived. If the big Cherokee had not arrived by the first of February, then Goth and his family would undertake the journey alone. Frank knew the trail, had traveled it several times both ways—due west to the Delaware, on to the Little Blue, upstream to that river's headwaters, then to the Platte at Fort Kearny, past the forks of the wide, shallow river, then upstream along the South Platte to Denver. Winter or no, the road was well-traveled, deeply worn, the way littered with cast-off stoves, furniture that peeled and disintegrated, broken-down wagons from which successive waves of emigrants had removed wheels, ironwork, axles. An occasional sod house, some occupied and surrounded by fenced fields and a few cattle, others abandoned. The old Mormon trail to the north of the river, the main emigrant trail to the south.

If Soldier Wolf showed up, well and good. If not, Goth thought, he would leave word, and the young man could overtake them, as he surely would on horseback, somewhere along the trail.

But on the first of February, right on schedule, Soldier Wolf showed up in the company of a tall, gaunt wraith of a mountain man, Bully O'Bragh, one whom Goth had heard tales about, including a story which, on good authority, had insisted that O'Bragh had frozen to death after wandering out into a blizzard while blind drunk, three years earlier.

Soldier Wolf and Frank Goth shook hands, and then O'Bragh extended his bony hand and said, "Howdy, coon. Jerry's told me about ye. Now, I ain't never rid along with a preacher man before, but the boy says you're White enough, so to speak, so I'll give 'er a try. Figger ye'll try and convert me or summat, but it ain't goin' to do no good. Just so's we all understand one another."

"We are all the Lord's children, Mr. O'Bragh," Goth said, shaking hands.

"Naw, we ain't, nuther. First name's Farnsworth, but don't go callin' me that. Call me Bully. Ye ever scalped a man, preacher?"

"Can't say as I have," Goth responded, looking askance at Soldier Wolf.

"Warn't the boy's idee," O'Bragh said, interpreting Goth's expression. "He didn't pick me up nowhere. Naw, the Harrimans got in touch with this child, sent me along to keep Tsaragi here out of trouble. I've lived ten years, off-on, with the Cheyennes. Taught White Frog how to ride his pony, as it turns out, an' rescued Leg in the Water from the Absarokees once. Those coons take me as practically one of their own."

"Aren't you a little old, Mr. O'Bragh, to be undertaking a venture of this sort?" Goth asked, still undecided as to whether he wished to have this disreputable-looking man along.

"Young feller, this nigger's old, but he ain't dead. Me an' Porcupine, we could likely ride backward an' get to Denver afore ye—ain't that what they're callin' 'er now, Denver? A fair town, as I recollect. . . ."

Jerry burst into laughter, clapped both Goth and O'Bragh on the back, and strode over to the wagon to say hello to Elizabeth and to the ebony-haired Sara—Sara, who had occupied his thoughts so constantly for the preceding month and more. She was actually here!

What was he feeling?

Both apprehension and relief that it was so.

The six-hundred-mile trail to Denver went slowly, with temperatures remaining below freezing during the days and dropping rapidly as the sun sank westward and the clear sky glowed orange-red. The little caravan was forced to stop early, start late.

As they neared the Platte, O'Bragh rode off to hunt and returned a few hours later, meeting the Goths and Soldier Wolf on up the emigrant road. He was on foot, leading the redoubtable Porcupine, who was loaded down with fresh meat.

"Ye ever taste fresh buffler, Jerry, me boy? Came on a little group of 'em, an' the old Hawken pulled me down a young bull. Old days, we shot us nothin' but cows, but the herds is gettin' small now. Ye kill a cow, ye kill a half-dozen calves or more. Contrariwise, just one bull can keep a whole herd of cows spittin' out young 'uns. Preacher man, they's a busted-up wagon just beyond the next rise. Good place to camp, an' a ready-made supply of firewood into the bargain. Tomorrow this time, we'll be at Fort Kearny. . . ."

Frank Goth urged his mule team ahead, with Jerry and Sara bringing up the rear, Soldier Wolf astride Messiah, and the girl riding Virgin—at Jerry's insistence.

Once the evening's encampment site had been reached, Jerry set a good-sized fire to blazing, the heat welcome even in the late afternoon, and Bully spit large chunks of buffalo flesh and set them to roasting. Elizabeth and Sara Goth sliced a pot full of potatoes and placed them to boil at the edge of the flames, while Frank prepared a large pot of coffee.

"Them's pizen, ma'am," O'Bragh insisted, gesturing disdainfully at the potatoes. "Once a child gets out past the settlements, he don't eat nothin' but meat if he wants to stay healthy. Mix buffler meat an' potatoes, she'll give ye mountain fever every time. Mark my words, now."

Elizabeth Goth looked up, shook her head, smiled, and returned to what she was doing.

"How long have you lived in the mountains, Bully?" Sara asked, not entirely certain how to take the old man but rapidly deciding that most of what he said was not to be mistaken for truth.

"Shoshones stole me when I was in the cradle," O'Bragh said, "an' I grew up with 'em. When old Lewis and the Red Haired Chief crossed the continental divide, I was standin' there waitin' for 'em."

Soldier Wolf kept a straight face and said, "Didn't know the continental divide was in Kentucky. I'm going to have to study my maps, I guess."

"Sure as hell is," O'Bragh said. "But it ain't map-learnin' ye need, sonny, it's the study of language. Went to college, from what I hear. They teach ye how to speak Cheyenne?"

"French, German, and Latin," Soldier Wolf said, "but no Cheyenne."

"Well, now, I figger it's time for ye to start learnin' Cheyenne. Am I right, preacher man?"

"About the continental divide or the Cheyenne language?" Goth asked.

"Any fool can find the divide if he can tell which way water runs. Don't need no special study for that. But if a coon's goin' to catch the fancy of the warriors, he's goin' to have to speak their tongue, that's all they is to it. Big Mouth, White Antelope, Whirlwind, an' them boys, they know a fair English. But White Frog's bunch an' the People of the Valley, I don't guess they talk much Long Knife. An' sure as hell, the squaws don't, Jerry me boy. If ye want to get friendly with any Injun women, ye've got to know how to talk. Or ye plannin' to be a Catholic priest while ye're out here?"

Soldier Wolf's glance stole to Sara, who was staring into the flames, and then back to O'Bragh's suddenly grinning face.

Both Elizabeth and Frank Goth glanced at their daughter. Sara and Soldier Wolf had spent a good deal of time talking the past few days of the journey, and both the mother and the father had begun to suspect more than simple conversation in operation. The relationship that was developing, they had concluded, was probably not in their daughter's best interests. With sufficient supervision, however, no doubt things would turn out all right. Despite her years, Sara had already spent a good deal of time among the various Indian peoples—but Jerry Soldier Wolf was a different matter, an educated man, charming when he put his mind to it, just the sort who might well turn a young girl's head. The big Cherokee came highly recommended and had been given a position of genuine importance by the agency, but as to the man's moral character, the Goths had as yet scant information upon which to make a judgment. This being the case, cautious restraint seemed the best policy.

"Jerry," Frank Goth said, "O'Bragh's right about that. You're the only one among us who doesn't know Cheyenne. We'll be around as interpreters as you need it, but no doubt it would be a good idea if we used our journey up-country to speak Cheyenne as much as possible."

"An in-service crash course?" Jerry laughed.

"Damn right," O'Bragh agreed.

"I could help too." Sara smiled, smoothing her dark hair back over one ear. "I speak Cheyenne much better than Mother or Father."

Frank and Elizabeth Goth glanced at each other.

"The girl's right," Elizabeth admitted.

O'Bragh slapped his knee, laughed. "Ye got ye a schoolmarm, Tsaragi. Why, hell, we'll all pitch in."

That evening, with the coyotes howling in chorus off across the rolling prairies to the south, Soldier Wolf's lessons in Cheyenne were begun, and the pupil proved more than adept, repeating key words and phrases over and over, impatient sometimes with the pronunciations, but learning with a quickness which astounded Frank Goth. Long after O'Bragh had rolled up in his robes beneath the prairie schooner and had begun snoring loudly, and Frank and Elizabeth as well were preparing for sleep, Jerry and Sara sat next to the fire and the lessons continued.

At length, Elizabeth Goth spoke to her daughter, indicating that it was time to retire. Sara rose, stared down into Soldier

Wolf's firelit face, and spoke the Cheyenne words: "It is time for dreaming now."

Soldier Wolf repeated the phrase, "It is time for dreaming now," and then added, "I wish to give you the sorrel mare, for you ride her well."

Sara had started to turn away, stopped, smiled back at Soldier Wolf, then climbed up into the wagon with her parents.

Soldier Wolf got to his feet, but he was not yet ready to sleep. He placed more wood on the fire, watched the swirl of yellow sparks go up into the darkness and then sat down once more, his carbine across his lap.

Somewhere, a half-mile or so out into the night, the coyotes continued to sing, and Jerry stared up at the stars, fixed his vision on Polaris, glanced over to the pattern of Orion, stared at the glimmering group called the Pleiades.

When daylight came, the temperature had risen. The group ate half-frozen breakfast fortified by hot coffee, and the journey was resumed. In places, now, the ground was no longer frozen, at least at the surface, and as the morning wore into afternoon, the wagon twice threatened to mire in soggy earth.

Soldier Wolf and O'Bragh rode on ahead, came within sight of Fort Phil Kearny and the scattering of houses surrounding it, and then turned back to meet the Goths.

Before nightfall, they were within the barricaded walls, the mules and the horses being cared for in the stable, and quarters, close but comfortable, being made available to Soldier Wolf and the Goth family. O'Bragh, however, declined the hospitality of the fort, and after looking to Porcupine's needs, disappeared in the direction of the cluster of Oto lodges at the western perimeter of the fort.

After a civilized military-style dinner, Frank and Jerry joined Captain Blanchard, the acting commandant, in his quarters, and a long discussion ensued about matters political, economic, and racial in the soon-to-be Colorado Territory. Continued new strikes in the gold areas, Blanchard told them, and the Arapahos and Cheyennes were, to say the least, uneasy—the inevitable impact of some one hundred thousand settlers, more or less, having poured into the area within the preceding two years.

"A good deal less now, I should imagine," Goth said. "When we went down-country last autumn, there was many a good soul both before us and after us along the road, and very few coming the other direction."

"They come and go," Blanchard agreed. "News of a new Leadville or Gregory Gulch or Buckskin Joe, and half of St. Louis is thundering up the river, wives, kids, and all. They get there and find all the claims taken or that the fifty dollars a day they heard about works out to two dollars a day, and back-busting labor at that, and they paint 'Pike's Peak Folly' on their wagons and head back home, if they've still got homes. When you consider all that's happened, the Injuns have actually been damned decent. Last summer, Left Hand's bunch was happily camped just north of Denver. Guess they were coming in at nights to look for dead dogs. Not enough food to go around, and people were killing their dogs so they wouldn't have to feed them. Left Hand's boys would come in, cart the bodies back to their encampment, and dine on roast dog. But they're not ready to move onto reserves yet, not with what the government's offered them so far. Colonel Boone's due through here any day with a new set of offers from Buchanan, all signed and fixed with the presidential seal, from what I hear."

"Will Lincoln abide by whatever offers are made, do you think?" Soldier Wolf asked.

"Afraid our rail-splitter's going to have other matters on his hands—he's not going to be wanting to renegotiate any treaties. The new treaty should stand, once the Cheyennes and Arapahos have agreed to it, until some damned fool discovers gold or silver on whatever lands are given to them."

"Does it seem strange to you," Goth asked, "that we offer them treaties which give them lands that they have owned, in any case, for centuries? After they have allowed us to come into their lands, more or less peacefully, and have even hunted for us and provided us with food when we were on the verge of starvation? It is often not the Lord's work that we do at all."

"You Cherokee?" Blanchard asked, gesturing toward Soldier Wolf's turban.

Jerry nodded.

"Frank, ask your friend here about treaties, then. His people got civilized, for all the good it did them, and they were still herded off to Indian territory a thousand miles west. Not one of the brighter pages in our history, I'm afraid."

"My people will survive," Soldier Wolf said, shifting about in his chair. "Right now we're under directive to see that the same sort of thing doesn't happen to the Cheyennes and Arapahos. Captain, do you have any information to share with us as to the whereabouts of a former BIA agent named Cramdon?"

"Big Ed Cramdon? From what I understand, your friends at the Bureau don't pay very good wages—and Cramdon finally did something about it. He's taken up land out beyond Gregory Gulch somewhere. He's got a ranch and a bunch of bummers working for him—mining gold, trying to get a herd of cattle started, and hauling buffalo and elk meat into Denver. The future belongs to men like Cramdon, men with spunk, if you ask me. If we had more like him, there wouldn't be any Indian problem at all. A man's got to look out for himself, because it's certain no one else is going to."

Soldier Wolf glanced at Frank Goth, then responded: "Turned renegade, according to our sources. A wagon train of supplies was sent out to the Cheyennes last year, and Cramdon resigned from the agency and commandeered the supplies."

"Cramdon's men have attacked several of the mining camps," Frank Goth said. "A couple of Indian villages as well—the People of the Valley, for instance, last summer."

Blanchard lit a cigar and leaned back in his chair.

"The agency ought to take care of its own, I'd say. And Cramdon's no different from a lot of folks out here. If he attacked the Indians, they probably had it coming. We don't always treat the savages right, but most of what they get, they've got coming. Frank, you work for Harriman and his people. But what the hell do they know about how it is out here? I've heard some of those Easterners talk about their noble savages, but they've never been called in to pick up the pieces after the Pawnees have ripped open a caravan. When the Indians get civilized, they're just fine. Soldier Wolf, you've had a college education from what I've been told—you're living proof that the Indian and the Whiteman can live together. But here on the high plains, the Indians are still wild, and I've seen mutilated bodies of men, women, and children. A party of young bucks see a wagon train, and they ride in demanding gifts. The Whites don't understand, and they start shooting. Who'd blame them? A couple of bucks get lead in them, and then the trouble's on. What you have to understand, Soldier Wolf, is that there are still a great many Indians, and they can control the areas away from the settlements whenever they take a notion to do it. Hell, I don't know who's right. But Colorado's on her way to statehood, and so are all the other territories. The Indians are going to have to be pacified and gotten onto reservations. It just won't work any other way."

Soldier Wolf's eyes were gleaming. "Captain," he said, "why not just kill all the Indians? That would solve the problem, wouldn't it?"

"You don't mean that," Blanchard said. "But I'll tell you—there's some that do. Chivington, for instance. He'd put under every Indian in the mountains, if he had his way."

"One of my fellowmen of God," Goth explained. "He runs the Methodist church in Denver."

"The biggest son of a bitch in the mountains," Blanchard said, nodding to Soldier Wolf. "Must be seven foot tall and three hundred pounds on the hoof. If that man ever really gets riled, I figure he could just about handle the Cheyennes all by himself."

"That's not true, not true at all," Goth said. "I know Brother Chivington quite well. He might be six-foot-six, and he is a huge man—as long as we're talking about body size. But I cannot comprehend a man of God with so little compassion for human creatures. I take him for a fraud, a charlatan, and a blowhard, Captain."

"Well," Blanchard continued, "the Indians have got old Jim Beckwourth to look out for their interests, in any case. He got Leg in the Water and his boys calmed down when they were ready to pour in on Denver and kill everybody there. Why is it the Bureau doesn't just make Beckwourth the regular agent? He's old, but the Indians listen to him. The man's half Crow, from what I've been told, and used to be a chief among them."

"He's not a Crow, not by blood," Soldier Wolf said.

"You know him?" Blanchard asked, surprised.

"I've read his book," Soldier Wolf said.

"I heard about that book." Blanchard laughed. "A pack of lies, from what I've been told. He's a good old bastard to have around, though. Him and Bridger both. I remember hearing stories about those two when I was a kid. Strange to see the two of them together, old men, crazy in the eyes and looking like they came out of some fairy tale. Bridger was my guide two years ago, when I took my men on a little tour of Mormon country. The old son of a bitch is half-blind, and he can still see an Indian smoke twenty miles away. He loves to lie—he'll tell stories all night long, if he's got a recruit or two who'll listen to him. But down underneath it all, you get the feeling that the old man's lived a dozen lives or more. Beckwourth's the same way, though I don't really know him all that well. Anyway, they help us to keep a handle on the Indian problem, and I, for one, am damned glad to have them around. Those two and your friend O'Bragh—where'd you pick him up?"

"It's a long story," Soldier Wolf said.

"Heard that he'd gotten shot in a whorehouse down in Taos."

"Apparently not," Goth said, shaking his head. "Right now he's out visiting with the Otos."

"How old is he, Frank?" Blanchard asked. "I remember meeting him the first time back in the early fifties, and he looked to be in his seventies then."

"Meat don't spile in the mountains." Soldier Wolf chuckled. "That's what Bully says, anyway."

Blanchard nodded, rose, and put another chunk of firewood into the cast-iron stove. He relit his cigar and then stood with his back to the stove.

"So," the officer drawled. "You gentlemen are supposed to do something about Big Ed Cramdon, I take it. You at liberty to tell me what?"

"I'm supposed to bring him in for trial," Soldier Wolf answered. "The federal government has issued a warrant for his arrest."

Blanchard shook his head.

"Good luck," he snorted. "But what you're going to find out is that things aren't the way the people in Washington think they are. From what I've heard, Cramdon and his boys shot up the settlement at Gregory Gulch, but no one's too concerned about that anymore. Miners come and miners go. It's the way of the breed. A couple of drunks got shot, but who knows how that happened? And you'd have to have witnesses to do anything about it, in any case. The trainload of supplies is a different matter, but there's no jury in Denver that's going to convict Cramdon. What you don't understand, my boy, is that *civilization* out here is run by gunmen and gold miners. Charlie Harrison, for instance, is one of the most important men in Denver. There's your judge, and he's probably killed twenty men himself. There's no real difference between him and Cramdon, as far as I can see."

"Raping and killing Indian women and children doesn't count for anything, then?" Soldier Wolf asked.

"Not much, my friend. In any case, when Boone gets here with the conditions for the new treaty, the whole matter will be forgotten. The Cheyennes and the Arapahos will get supplies for next winter, and they'll move to wherever the government tells them. Oh, there'll be some bands of young bucks who'll resist, there'll be some skirmishes yet. But the whole business will quiet down once the treaty's in force. Right now, as I understand the matter, the government wants to placate the Red devils—no insult intended, Mr. Soldier Wolf—because we've likely got a war on our hands with our brothers down South. Actually, I've been waiting for orders to move my regiment back down the river. That's probably the message Boone's got for me."

Soldier Wolf stood up, stretched out his arms, and then adjusted his turban.

"Well, Captain," Jerry said, "I was sent out here to bring in Cramdon, and if I have to kill him with my own hands in order to do it, that's how it'll be. If I bring him in alive, and the good citizens of Denver acquit him, then I'll just send O'Bragh hunting."

"For Cramdon, you mean?" Blanchard asked.

"We wouldn't do that," Jerry answered. "Frank's a missionary and doesn't believe in killing. Mr. Goth, you figure it's about time to get some shut-eye?"

When Soldier Wolf and the Goth family arose the following morning, the world was cold with low-streaming bands of ground fog, and off across the river a pair of horned owls were calling dolefully. O'Bragh had the animals ready to go, the mules in their traces, and the old man was whistling to himself. He'd brewed up a pot of what he called "mountain coffee" and suggested that everyone have some.

"Good for what ain't ailed ye yet," he insisted.

Jerry drank some of the thick liquid, closed his eyes, and shook his head.

"What the hell did you put into this stuff, Bully?"

"Secret I larned from the Snakes." The gaunt man laughed. "Special in-gredients. Coffee beans, of course, and then some willer bark and a half a pound of buffler dung. I knew ye'd all like it."

"Buffalo dung?" Jerry gasped.

"Wal, mebbe this child stretched the truth a mite. Mebbe it weren't buffler dung at all. . . ."

O'Bragh poured himself a second tin cup full of the steaming liquid.

"You didn't really do that, did you?" Sara asked.

"Guess not, missy. Young White gals has got delicate insides, so I knew it wouldn't be good for ye. When I'm off by myself, though, sometimes I make 'er out of willer bark and buffler dung by themselves. If I ain't got coffee, that is. Taste 'er, Sara. Keeps off the mountain fever, I tell ye."

"You sure you didn't put in the buffalo dung?" Frank asked.

Elizabeth Goth shook her head emphatically. She wanted no part of anything the old mountain man might concoct.

"Whatever it is," Jerry said, "I admit it takes the morning chill out of a man's bones."

"Damned right." O'Bragh whistled. "Now, let's get this carry-van on the trail. The Otos say that Boone's on his way in this morning, an' I ain't got nuthin' good to say for 'im. Tell ye what he is, Tsaragi, he's a damned slaver, that's what. Has his way, we'll see burrheads picking cotton in Jefferson Territory. That's all a man like Boone can see—his kind makin' other kinds do the work. This old nigger don't want no part of 'im. Cheyennes ain't figgered it out yet, I expect. Give that high-falutin son of a bitch his chance, he'll have Beckwourth hisself fixed up like a clown an' fixin' his breakfast for 'im."

"What are you talking about?" Goth asked.

"Beckwourth's colored, I tell ye. So was Ranne an' Harris an' Rose an' York. Damn fine men, all of 'em. Truth is, I never knowed a Colored I didn't like right off. Time the govment gets done fightin the war that's comin' sure as bear shit, mebbe we'll have Boone an' all that's like him out pickin' cotton. Anyhow, let's get to goin'."

Sara Goth mounted Virgin, pulled the animal about easily, and laughed.

"He's going to spend the whole day telling lies, isn't he?" she said to Jerry.

"Just like all the other days," Jerry agreed.

They moved upriver from Fort Kearny, and then, at O'Bragh's suggestion, turned off, away from the main emigrant trail and toward the Republican River, some fifty miles or so to the south.

"He'll do anything to avoid meeting Boone," Soldier Wolf said.

"Ain't that, ye damned fool. Just better for the mules this time of the year is all. Ye want to see Boone? We'd be in Denver before that coon gets around to leavin' the fort in any case. He'll probably get drunk an' stay that way until the ice is off the rivers."

O'Bragh's cutoff proved easy going, and even Frank Goth had to admit it. Bully snorted, gave close directions for the next twenty miles, and then took off on Porcupine to do some hunting.

Jerry and Sara rode along, side by side, behind the Goths' wagon, and the girl continued her language lessons, obviously pleased with the rapidity with which Soldier Wolf was acquiring the Cheyenne tongue.

By nightfall, O'Bragh still had not returned. Soldier Wolf wondered about going out to look for the old man, but Goth thought the venture would prove fruitless.

"These old mountain men know the land like the backs of their hands, Jerry. He's probably run into some Indians he knows from years back. While we're worrying, they're probably smoking the pipe and lying to each other. He'll be back. You can bet on that."

Goth tended to the animals, and Jerry built a fire. Sara stood close to him but said little. Finally Elizabeth called to her daughter to come help with the preparation of the evening meal.

Elizabeth Goth was scooping heaps of rice out onto the tin plates, and Soldier Wolf was pouring mugs full of coffee when O'Bragh's voice came drifting in on the freezing air: "Halooooo the camp! This here's Presy-dent Lincoln come to set ye free!"

Bully walked in, leading Porcupine. The mule had a dead antelope slung over its back.

"Hyar's dinner, ye damned fools. Didn't I tell ye not to go eatin' them potatoes and fuel for horses? Ye'll die of indigestion."

"We thought the Pawnees had scalped you," Soldier Wolf said. "Sit down and have some real coffee, Bully me boy."

O'Bragh accepted the coffee, pretended not to like its taste, and then, refusing dinner and claiming to have eaten three pounds of raw antelope meat already, he unloaded Porcupine, fed the mule, and within minutes was curled up in his robes beneath the wagon, sound asleep.

Frank Goth nudged Soldier Wolf, gestured out to the edge of the firelight. Four pairs of eyes, gleaming amber, occasionally blinking.

"Brush wolves." Soldier Wolf grinned.

"The song dogs of the mountains." Goth nodded. "They come

in at times to watch—they're not afraid of anything, but they never take chances either. *Little brothers*, the Cheyennes call them. . . ."

"Throw them something to eat, Father," Sara suggested. "Perhaps they've had a bad day for hunting. They're hungry, too."

Soldier Wolf rose from where he was squatting, drew his knife, and cut off one leg of the antelope, at the second joint. He tossed the meat toward the edge of the firelight. The eyes disappeared then, the coyotes making no sounds in their retreat. But after a moment they had returned, and Jerry caught sight of the arc of a bushy tail between intervals of shadow. Then the animals were gone once more.

"A mated pair and two young ones," Sara said in Cheyenne. "They mate permanently, and they let the young ones eat first. The People of the Valley say that coyote families stay near to each other always, just like people."

"Except that people don't," Soldier Wolf said, his thoughts flashing back momentarily to his father's ranch in the Smokies.

"It's strange," Elizabeth Goth said. "The Indian peoples think of themselves as *those who wander the earth*. But it is our people who wander, wander endlessly.

Soldier Wolf asked Elizabeth to repeat the phrase in Cheyenne, and she obliged, saying it over twice, as though suddenly taken with the significance of the words.

At length the Goths retired, but Jerry sat up by the fire, his carbine across his legs. He stared into the flames, added more fuel when the fire began to die back. He listened to the rhythmic snoring of Bully O'Bragh, clearly audible even from beneath the heavy robes. Soldier Wolf grinned into the darkness, breathed woodsmoke and darkness and stars, and felt like singing. Late winter on the high plains, the Shining Mountains ahead. Tomorrow or the next day or the next and he would crest a rise, and there they would be, a long white wall against the west, their grandeur as yet only imagined. This, he concluded, was freedom, this was all of it. Whatever he might have thought earlier, his mind drifting back to the Smokies, a twinge of regret, sharp, now he was filled with the pure excitement, the anticipation of the greater mountains to the west. O'Bragh had known the Shining Mountains all his life—he had known the vastnesses, the seclusion, the solitude—huge canyons, great peaks, lakes, deserts, green-black forests. O'Bragh had seen the Indians in their purely wild state, had seen them at a time when only a few Whitemen had managed to venture into their domains. Now, of course, all that was changed, altered. But what effect could a relative handful of Americans make upon a land of such size, such extent? The wildness was still there, the coyotes still came into the edges of the firelight at night. And mankind was still very small in the face of it all. O'Bragh had known the *shining* times, and he, Jerry Soldier Wolf, would know them too. He could feel the continent, vast, mysterious, stretching westward before him. He could imagine the far Pacific Ocean beating ceaselessly against its boundaries. But what lay between where he was now and that distant and heaving water?

Jerry walked to where Messiah and Virgin were tethered, slipped each horse a pinch of tobacco, and continued on toward the frozen creek, the Stinking Water according to O'Bragh, where great twisted, leafless willows and cottonwoods bent out over the frozen water. He slapped the trunk of a willow, saw the smoke of his own breath in the moonlight, looked back to the gray-orange glow of the fire, the shadow of the wagon where . . . she slept.

"Sara Goth," he said aloud. "Sara. . . . Goddammit, Night, this half-breed Cherokee's fallen in love, sure as hell. She's not much more than a child, and I can't even think about touching her. And I also can't even imagine what it would be like to live in a world without her."

"Touch me," the voice said.

Soldier Wolf sprang to one side, drew his Marston revolver, searched the darkness.

"Jerry, it's me. . . ."

Sara's voice?

Then he saw her, not more than twenty feet from where he stood. But how had she managed to sneak up on him so easily and without his being aware? What was she doing out here? Had she heard him talking to the night? A terrible rush of embarrassment swept over him.

"Sara Goth, what . . . ?"

"I slipped out of the wagon," she said, coming closer. "You weren't by the fire—and then I saw you walking away from the horses, so I followed. You're not angry?"

"Angry? No, Sara, but . . ."

"Mother and Father are asleep. Don't worry about them, Jerry."

"How do you know that? Besides . . ."

Sara turned partly away from him, looked off toward the moon, held her hands to the sides of her face. Then she turned to him once again.

"I heard you talking," she said. "Did you mean all that?"

"I . . ."

"Did you mean what you said?"

"I was talking foolishness, no matter what I meant, Sara. I'm sorry. You're too young. Forgive me for being a damned fool."

She stared up at him, the moonlight turning her dark hair to silver—like spiderwebs, he thought, spiderwebs that he wished to touch, to run his fingers through.

Sara moved closer to him, and suddenly he half-wished to flee, to be away from her, this woman-child, this female presence that, without even trying to, exercised such immense power over him. But another part of his mind remained completely calm, almost detached, almost away from him—and that part of his mind told him to press her face between his hands, to put his mouth down onto hers.

"Will you kiss me, Jerry?" Sara asked, and the tone in her voice told him that she was afraid, indeed, that he might not wish to do it.

He started to say: *I must not, I cannot, Sara, your parents would hate me if I ever did that.* But the words would not form, and, as from a distance, he watched himself touch the girl's face, lean over to kiss her, as from a distance he could feel the heat of her flesh, the pale odor of autumn leaves in her breath, and he realized that she was clinging to him, that she was pressing her mouth hard against his own, that she didn't really know how to kiss at all, that there was moisture on her cheeks, that she was sobbing convulsively and between kisses he could hear her choked words: *I love you, I love you, I want you to take me Jerry I want to be with you always*, and he heard other words, his own voice, his own words, words uttered without his willing them: *I love you Sara I want you to be with me we'll go to California we'll go wherever you want how did this happen Sara I knew it had happened the first time I saw you I knew it had happened before I ever even spoke to you or knew your name. . . .*

And Soldier Wolf realized that something was in his hand, something awkward as he held Sara in his arms.

He had forgotten to reholster his pistol.

Chapter Six

In 1859 Horace Greeley had visited the Pike's Peak region, arriving in Denver on June 16, from which city he wrote of his observations of the Indian peoples and in particular of the perpetual warfare between the Arapahos and the Utes:

". . . the Indians are children. Their arts, wars, treaties, alliances, habitations, crafts, properties, commerce, comforts, all belong to the very lowest and rudest ages of human existence. Any band of schoolboys from ten to fifteen years of age are quite as capable of ruling their appetites, devising and upholding a public policy, constituting and conducting a state or community, as the average Indian tribe.

"I have learned to appreciate better than hitherto, and to make more allowance for the dislike, aversion, and contempt wherewith Indians are usually regarded by their White neighbors, and have been since the days of the Puritans. It needs but little familiarity with the actual, palpable aborigines, to convince anyone that the poetical Indian—the Indian of Cooper and Longfellow—is only visible to the poet's eye."

Such, in one form or another, was the assessment—and again and again actions were taken against the Indians based on such an assessment. Drunken devils and bummers raided the lodges when the warriors were away and raped and otherwise sexually humiliated Indian women and young girls, even gray-haired grandmothers. These same men stole horses, mules, and anything else that might serve them.

The April 18, 1860, edition of The Rocky Mountain News *contained a letter of protest and called for "Justice to the Indians":*

"The Indians are as keenly sensible to acts of injustice as they are tenacious of revenge, and it is more humiliating to them to be the recipients of such treatment upon their own lands, which they have been deprived of, their game driven off and they made to suffer by hunger, and when they pay a visit, abused more than dogs. . . .

All our Indian troubles are produced by the imprudent acts of unprincipled Whitemen. . . ."

The letter was written by James P. Beckwourth.

By sundown of the following day, the Goths, Soldier Wolf, and O'Bragh had reached the Republican River, just below its forks with the Arikaree. Crossing the latter stream provided little difficulty, for the thin sheet of water was completely frozen. Frank Goth guided the wagon on upstream for perhaps another mile to a grove of box elders and there made camp.

Goth and Soldier Wolf went out together to cut firewood, and Jerry knew that some way or another he had to bring up the matter of his feelings toward Sara. How would Frank respond? The two men were rapidly becoming close friends, but the goodwill might easily be shattered if the subject of Sara were broached.

The conversation, however, drifted in quite another direction.

"How long have you been a missionary to the Indians?" Jerry asked.

"God, man, don't call me that. I'm a BIA agent, just like you. The Cheyennes are like family to me. Ten years with them all in all."

"BIA man with a Bible?" Jerry suggested.

"I believe in carrying on God's work wherever I am, that's true. But there's a difference. Some don't even see me as a true Christian. Ask Chivington when you meet him."

"You don't intend to convert them, Frank? Guess I misunderstood somewhere along the line. . . ."

"I see it this way, Jerry. True religion, a genuine religious sense, works nothing but good upon the human spirit. I studied for the ministry, and my training has formed and improved my life. I've taken the Lord for my personal Savior, and I'm content in that. But Christianity derives from a European and Near Eastern tradition, and in many ways it simply will not translate directly for the Indian peoples. For this reason, what I take to the Indian peoples is not a strictly Christian doctrine. No—I try to gentle their natures, but I do it by utilizing the basic elements of their own religious awareness."

Soldier Wolf carried a great armload of wood and dumped it into the cart they had brought for the purpose. He slapped his hands against his legs in the cold, breathed out briskly into the moonlit darkness. Goth adjusted their flare, and the two men started back toward the wagon.

"The religion of the Cheyennes, for instance," Frank continued. "It's far more practical than anyone in the White world seems to believe. Unlike the European who prays to an Unknown for actions desired or feared, the Indian prays to a Trickster who governs by whim. Old Man Coyote—he has to be amused or pled with or reminded that the people are hungry. He exemplifies the world as the Cheyennes perceive it. The European goes down on his knees to pray for release from hunger, but the Indian knows that if he goes down, he may never get up again. The best time for prayer is after an elk, for instance, has been taken. The Cheyenne prays for the spirit of the animal, for in that way, other elk will be less unwilling to be shot. And the soul of the elk goes to the Spirit World, and so do the souls of the people. No heaven as the Whitemen know it, and no hell either. The good will prosper in the Spirit World for the same reasons that they prosper in this world. And the evil will continue to create their own misfortunes."

"Does Sara believe as you do?" Jerry asked.

"Ah, that girl! Her mind's her own. She loves the Indian people—they've been like a great family to her for the past several years, and she's half Indian herself, despite appearances. Yes, yes—I think she'd like to carry on our work, Elizabeth's and mine. Next year, God willing, we'll send her to Christian College down in Missouri, or perhaps Cazenovia or Bradford, back East. She's a bright one, and Elizabeth and I have tended to her education as well as we're able. But she needs to be with people her own age, she needs formal training. Then she'll be equipped to make her own decisions."

They approached the firelight, and Jerry could smell the sizzling meat. O'Bragh himself was sitting with his back to a wagon wheel, and he seemed to be asleep. The man was able to fall asleep in a matter of moments, and it was his practice to catch catnaps whenever the opportunity allowed.

Elizabeth and Sara were attending to the preparation of food.

"Your daughter's beautiful," Soldier Wolf blurted out, instantly aware that he should not have let the words slip. He glanced at Frank's face, but the Bible man merely nodded and dumped the contents of the wood-gathering cart onto the frozen ground a few feet from the campfire.

One of O'Bragh's eyes opened, and his hand was instantly upon his Hawken.

After the evening meal, Soldier Wolf's language lessons were continued, and Sara, for the first time, showed signs of impatience with her student.

O'Bragh cackled and lit his pipe, shook his head.

"Tsaragi, ye've got a strict teacher there. Maybeso ye should take off that there turban. Likely it's constrictin' the flow of blood to your brain. Bareheaded, an ye'll learn faster. This child guarantees 'er."

Soldier Wolf raised one eyebrow and shook his fist at O'Bragh.

"You must pay attention, now," Sara insisted.

"The student hears his teacher," Soldier Wolf said in Cheyenne. "The student will listen to the birds of the air and the voices of the earth so that he will learn more quickly."

"It will be good," Sara responded.

"It is a good day to die," Soldier Wolf said, keeping his face straight.

"It is a good night to learn," the girl said, shaking her head.

"The wolf who fights with all must pay close attention." O'Bragh laughed.

"I said she had a mind of her own," Frank Goth said in English, then switched to Cheyenne: "The young teacher's medicine bundle is full of small green snakes because her student has stepped in fresh buffalo droppings."

"Frank!" Elizabeth said softly. "You're not helping at all."

At this point Porcupine let out a long melancholy braying sound, and immediately O'Bragh was up, rifle in hand.

"Someone's ridin' in," he said. "Women folks into the wagon. Tsaragi, get ye over into the shadows an' keep us covered."

Jerry snatched his carbine and moved away into the night, took position a few yards off, prone, his rifle resting in the fork of a sagebrush.

"Hellooo the camp!" came the voice, and a young soldier rode in, dismounted, and strode to the fire.

O'Bragh grunted, called to Jerry, and put his rifle away. Frank Goth shook hands with the soldier and offered him some coffee, which the young man gratefully accepted.

"Private Johnson," he said, "Colonel Boone's brigade."

"Dispatch rider?" Goth asked as Soldier Wolf came in from the shadows.

"Yes, sir. The colonel sent me on ahead, and I followed the tracks of your wagon."

"Won't be no tracks to foller from here on," O'Bragh said. "Jest foller the Republican to 'er headwaters an' drift up the prairie, northwest, to Aurora. Denver town's just beyond. Can't miss 'er, as my pappy used to say."

Soldier Wolf also shook hands with the soldier, squinted, asked what the big news was.

"The whole South has followed suit," he said. "A provisional government's been set up in Montgomery, Alabama, and war's inevitable. The colonel wanted me to get the word through. Even facts like these are better than rumors, I guess. Mr. Goth? Is it agreeable with you if I spend the night in your camp?"

"Of course, of course," Goth said.

Sara brought a portion of cold meat and the remains of the fried potatoes, and the private, coffee cup in hand, stood by the fire and ate silently.

"Boone's a pro-slaver," Soldier Wolf said to Goth in a low voice. "What do you suppose he's going to do?"

"He'll be loyal to the Union, no matter what," Goth answered. "You're from Carolina, Jerry. What about you?"

"I'm Cherokee, not a slaver. Guess I've been loyal to the government too long now to think about changing."

"The damnedest thing," Goth mused. "The South—the Democrats, that is to say—still have control of Congress, and they've got the Supreme Court as well. If the North actually attempted to destroy slavery, then secession would be a logical tactic. But there's no threat yet—Lincoln won't even take over until the first week of March. For ten years the South has been after its share of federal territories, and maybe that's what it's really all about. Slavery itself couldn't last much longer in any case."

"A quagmire," Soldier Wolf growled. "A damn political quagmire. I'll tell you, Frank, I'm grateful to your god or mine or both of them together that I'm out here and not back there. I'm a coward, maybe, but choosing which side to fight on is not a choice I want to make. My younger brothers, though—they may not have a choice. But maybe the good Southerners won't want Indians fighting in their army. It's a bad world. . . ."

The language lessons were over for the night, and O'Bragh had disappeared, apparently not wishing to spend the night in close company with the young soldier. The Goths retired to their wagon, and the soldier spread out his roll next to the fire. Jerry wrapped himself in his robes and sat with his back to a wagon wheel, dozed. But sleep did not come, and he rose, built up the fire, and reheated the remains of the coffee, drank the bitter liquid, stared down at the sleeping soldier.

At length he walked over to the horses, ran his fingers above Messiah's eyes and down the length of his neck, slapped him softly across the withers, and then walked off a few yards and stood, staring back at the wagon. He was nearly ready to return to his robes when he saw Sara slip out of the rear of the wagon, and he whistled to her.

She ran toward him, stopped to allow her vision to adjust to the darkness, and then continued.

Soldier Wolf took a few steps toward her, then caught her as she threw herself into his arms.

"I was hoping you'd come," he whispered.

"Didn't you know I'd join you?"

"I hoped you would."

"Kiss me, Jerry. I want you to kiss me."

Their mouths found each other.

"You were short-tempered with me tonight," Jerry whispered. "I thought perhaps you were angry."

"You were trying to ignore me," she said, standing on tiptoe and demanding to be kissed once more.

"I could never ignore you, little dummy."

"Did you say anything to my father, Jerry?"

"I wanted to."

"Perhaps it's best not to—for a while, anyway. Are we going to be happy?"

Her question rang in his ears, but his mind could not make sense of it. What was she asking? Surely she could not be thinking about marriage? His own thoughts had not yet proceeded that far—he had not yet adjusted even to what he considered his immense good fortune. *Sara wanted to be with him.* The way ahead was dark, inchoate, undefined. Was it possible? *Impossible, impossible*, the detached portion of his mind told him.

"We will be happy, little one," he said in Cheyenne.

"Yes," she said, "yes, we will be happy."

His hands were trembling, whether from the cold or from

anticipation and fear, but he held her to him and kissed her hair, slid his hand down over the small of her back, the thin, wiry body, the body that smelled somehow different, a delicate, wild odor, the odor of Sara Goth, the odor of the woman he wanted so desperately, the child-woman he was mad to hold, to possess, and yet, as he knew, he could not now even allow himself the terrible luxury of imagining what it would be like to possess her. He let his hand drop, cupped her buttock, felt her body go tense, her breath catch. And then she relaxed, molded herself even more tightly against him.

To his amazement, she pressed her hand against his groin, she felt for the bulge of his swelling penis.

He groaned and held her more tightly.

"I'm not ever going to let you go, Jerry. And I'm not ever going to share you with anybody." She paused then and said softly, in Cheyenne, "You are the one I wish to lie with."

The words had not even fully registered upon Soldier Wolf when the girl had spun away from him and was running back toward the wagon. He stood there with a bulge in his pants and watched her slip carefully into the wagon where her parents slept.

"Son of a bitch!" he said aloud. "What's this Injun boy gotten himself into?"

"Figger she's chosen her buck is all."

The voice was O'Bragh's. Suddenly Bully was standing beside him, and the tall, gaunt mountain man was slapping him on the back.

"Where the hell did you come from, O'Bragh?"

"Always had a weakness for peep-Tomming, this child has. For a while there, Tsaragi my friend, I figgered ye an' Sara was goin' to do a bit of humpin' right before this old man's eyes. Tell ye, it's not all that bad on froze ground, no sir. I've seed Pawnees do 'er on Platte River ice. Sary's willin', for sure, but I'm wonderin' how ye be goin' to make it right with the preacher man an' his missus. Ye've got complications to work out, Jerry me boy."

The young soldier was gone before the first light, and breakfast conversation was somewhat subdued, with Sara seeming to make a point of not looking in Jerry's direction.

Had her parents caught her in the act of slipping back into the wagon? Soldier Wolf glanced at Frank, who was intent upon his coffee and warmed-over potatoes.

"Crows splash water all over themselves even mornin's as cold as this one—do if they can find any unfriz water, that is. Injuns do some damn fool things, this child's thinkin'," O'Bragh said, trying to fill up the silence.

"And the Irish eat potatoes for breakfast, just like we're doing." Soldier Wolf grinned.

"Not this Irish nigger," O'Bragh snorted, rubbing at his bearded mouth.

The Goths said nothing, didn't even glance up.

They know—dammit, they know, I should have said something yesterday, what would I have said?

"Give you a hand with getting the mules into harness, Frank?" Jerry asked.

Goth looked up then, nodded, and drank off the last of his coffee.

They wrestled the animals, balky this cold morning, into their traces and fastened the buckles, gave each mule a portion of oats. Goth checked the cordage, tested the cinches, and slapped his hands together, whistled.

"She's a cold one," Jerry said.

"Ever been married?"

He knows, sure as hell.

"No. Never was in one place long enough to think about marriage. Someday, though. A man's got to settle down eventually. . . ."

Goth nodded, stared at Soldier Wolf, nodded again.

"Agent Soldier Wolf, I think we're about ready to get this show on the road. Two hundred and fifty miles or so to Denver, seven, eight days if the Lord is willing. As soon as the weather turns the corner, we'll head north to Laramie and then across to North Park—it'll be like coming home for the Goth family. The People of the Valley, Jerry—I guess they really are our family, at that. Then all we have to worry about is friend Cramdon. After that, your work will be done—you'll be moving on?"

"One thing at a time, Frank. I haven't even seen the Shining Mountains yet, and already you're trying to get rid of me. Right now, let's get the wheels turning. Where's O'Bragh?"

The old mountain man had disappeared, but within a couple of minutes he was back.

"Had more than one visitor last night, coons," he said. "Found sign out there, other side of them boulders. A dozen Cheyennes, from the looks of 'er. Checkin' us out, it appears. Bully O'Bragh must be gettin' old or summat. No way they should of been able to sneak in here without my catchin' wind of 'em. Porcupine, he was frettin', but I guessed we must of had a cougar prowlin' about, lookin' things over. Instead it was Cheyennes. No harm done, though. If they was wantin' trouble, they'd of had us dead to rights. Probably headin' north to Pawnee Buttes, figgerin' to take some meat. Ain't no good, this gettin' old. If ye got a choice when the times comes, Tsaragi, don't do 'er, Stay young. Next time, by damn, that's what I'm goin' to do."

"Nothing to worry about with the Cheyenne people," Goth said. "Elizabeth and Sara! Everything packed away and ready to go?"

Two days later, with the weather growing more temperate and good trail ahead of the wagon, Soldier Wolf accompanied O'Bragh on a hunting foray. With Jerry astride Messiah and Bully on Porcupine, the two men moved westward from the South Fork of the Republican toward the drainage of Arikaree Creek, Bully being of the opinion that prong-horned antelope might be found in good numbers close to the extensive sandy areas near what the old mountain man called Idaho Springs. A pack mule trailed behind them as they rode, occasionally setting its hooves and pulling back against its lead rope, at other times frisking along and giving evidence that it wished, most devoutly, for O'Bragh to turn it loose so that it might run to its heart's content.

The day passed without sign of game, and Soldier Wolf had come to question O'Bragh's wisdom in continuing in their present direction. A warm wind had begun to blow, and the sky was an immense gray above them, the cloud bars roiled and charged with electricity. The dead-grass waves of prairie surrounded them, a vast open country that seemed to ripple on forever. There were no birds in the air at all, and Soldier Wolf had the feeling that a downpour might begin at any moment.

"You sure you know where we're heading?" Jerry called out to his companion between gusts of wind.

"Headin' to the little-horn pastures, that's where," Bully assured him. "Ever seed one of them before, Tsaragi? Hell no, ye ain't. Goddamn green'un is what ye be. Look over there."

O'Bragh pointed to a low rise in the waste of broken grass and sagebrush, and Soldier Wolf saw a peculiar rock formation—or was it rock? As they rode closer, the rocks took on the form of some sort of prehistoric animal before what it actually was became evident: several boulders piled together, and on top was a huge buffalo skull which, in turn, had a flat rock placed on top, as if to hold it in place.

"Big medicine, Soldier Wolf, me lad. The Injuns think the Buffalo Skulls are alive, move around all over the place. Hate to be disturbed, they do. So the Red devils weight 'em down, make 'em happy, keep 'em in one spot. Likely we'll find us half a dozen more of 'em close about. Little valley on the other side, I figger. Magic place for buffler huntin' years back—years when they *was* enough bufflers to hunt right. The Injuns put 'em in a *surround*, better yet if they could find some bluffs to back 'em up against. Then they'd ride in or even come up on foot an' shoot the varmints, sometimes take a hundred or more at a time. I've hunted buffler with 'em, Jerry. There's no sport like it, I'll tell ye. Bad years now, and the buffler stay away from the Buffler Skulls. Me, I think it's just they ain't many buffler. Bufflers is near all gone, just like me an' my kind. Damned near all my old companyeros is dead, Soldier Wolf—what do ye think of that?"

"Think we're going to get wet," Jerry said, brushing at a couple of raindrops that had spattered against his face.

"Maybeso ye be right. Limestone ridge a mile or so up ahead—ye see 'er? Chances are we can find us a hole in the wall an' get out of Isakawuate's way."

"Isaka-what?"

"Old Man Coyote, green'un. That's what the Absarokees call 'im, Isakawuate. Like the sound of the name myself. Let's keep movin' here."

They reached the low rim just as the sky broke open, the rain falling so heavily it actually produced a low humming sound as it struck the earth. Within minutes the shallow ravine below where they had taken shelter was running a brown torrent, and the rain continued to pound down, punctuated now and again by thin flashes of lightning and deafening waves of thunder.

"Might be we can figger on spendin' the night here, coon.

Think we can get some of that deadwood up here an' get 'er to burn?"

"You want me to go down, get soaking wet, and drag wood back up here so you can have a fire, is that it?"

"Right," O'Bragh said without smiling. "Old man like me, he couldn't probably make it down there an' back. Jerry, she's up to ye."

"All right, all right, you crazy old possum. I'll do it for love of you. Guess I owe you some sort of debt for saving my life back in the Smokies. This pay us off?"

"Shore, shore. For a little while anyway, Tsaragi. You go fetch us some wood now, and we'll cook up some of the elk meat I got in my saddlebag. Might be it's a bit ripe, but once she's cooked, she'll taste like Saint Looey beefsteak, I promise ye."

The rain cooperated, diminishing to a drizzle for a few minutes, just long enough for Soldier Wolf to gather in a good supply of firewood, wet as it was. O'Bragh utilized his bowie knife to shave the wood into thin strips and then used some black powder and his fire-striker to kindle a small blaze. The two men tended their little fire, adding wood shavings until a respectable cone of flames was licking upward. O'Bragh spit the sections of meat, the surface of it dark and crusted, and soon it was dripping fat and sizzling nicely. Bully ate greedily and wiped the grease from his beard, winked at Soldier Wolf, and reached down into the saddlebag, produced a bottle of whiskey.

"Been savin' 'er," he said. "Seems like now might be a good time to take a couple of pulls, what do ye figger?"

"By heavens, Bully," Soldier Wolf said, "I do believe you're right."

"I've got a powerful dry mesself," O'Bragh said as he withdrew the cork and passed the bottle to Jerry, first taking a long pull himself.

Jerry drank, snorted, shook his head.

"Don't tell me," he said. "You tried to milk a buffalo cow and got hold of a bull by mistake."

"Somethin' of the sort." O'Bragh nodded. "So what ye goin' to do about the Sary? Ye ain't said nothin' to Frank, I take it."

"I haven't said anything—guess maybe I should have. But he knows, Bully, my friend. He's thinking the thing over, and probably hoping nothing will come of it before he can get Sara sent off to some Bible college."

"Ye ready to take a wife, Tsaragi?"

"Never thought about marrying, to tell the truth. But damn me, I'm in love with that black-haired little shit. Right now I'm feeling about as lonely as a man can get."

"Need ye a Cheyenne squaw. Once ye've been to bed with an Injun gal, ain't no White gal'll ever please ye again. Probably ye've had a Cherokee gal or two, but she ain't the same. You Tsaragis is *civilized*. I'm tellin' ye, wild Injun women is different."

"That's what I like about you, O'Bragh—you're so utterly, so perfectly crude. Goddammit, man, what have you got against *civilization*, anyhow?"

"One or two things, one or two things. Ye live as long as this child, ye'll be feelin' the same way, mark my words."

"Give me another snort," Jerry said, gesturing to the bottle.

"Don't expect ye'll be a temperance man." O'Bragh coughed. "No damned resistance to temptation at all. . . ."

Soldier Wolf took a mouthful, swallowed hard, closed his eyes and concentrated on the burning sensation that passed down his throat and into his stomach.

"I'm going to marry her. And we're going to go to California and homestead and have us a farm."

"In a badger's ass." O'Bragh chuckled. "Tell ye what's goin' to happen. Yes sir. Old Cramdon's goin' to fill ye with rifle balls, an' this child's goin' to cart ye up into the mountains and pile rocks on top of ye!"

"Cramdon's a dead man already. I'm going to bust his back over my knee, and then I'm going to marry Sara and head for California."

"Met Cramdon once, four, five years back—when he was still being Injun agent. Big son of a bitch, I'll tell ye."

"You figure I can't do it?" Jerry asked, taking another drink of the whiskey.

O'Bragh reached over, put his hand on Soldier Wolf's arm, gave his bicep a scrutinizing squeeze, nodded.

"Ye got arms on ye like oak trees, Tsaragi, but might be it'll take more than just *strong*. Being a soldier, they taught ye all the wrong things. I keep watch, though, an' ye're learnin' fast. Ye got the makin's of a man to ye. Keep watchin' O'Bragh, me boy, ye got a heap to learn yet. Me, I'd been dead three, four years when Harriman got hold of me and says, Bully, I hate to wake ye up this way, but there's a young feller ye got to teach summat. Ye been restless down in that grave-hole anyhow. . . ."

"The Prince of Lies, that's what you are."

"My tongue is straight," O'Bragh said in Cheyenne. "I speak only of those things that are true."

"At least you can cook pretty good," Jerry said, staring out into the rain and the gaining darkness.

"Cook? I'll tell ye about *cook*. A man's got to learn. You, for instance. You try boilin' water for coffee, and ye end up burnin' every damned drop of it. Some figger cookin's a squaw's work, but it ain't so. Give me two toothpicks, an' I can build fire enough to cook supper for twenty men. Take that time over to the Big Horn, for instance," O'Bragh continued, lighting his pipe and sipping some more whiskey. "I had just two regular matches, an' we was in the middle of a blizzard, God's own blizzard it were, too. So I lit the matches an' crossed 'em and was able to cook for nigh on two weeks, an' that blizzard was so bad it froze the eyeballs out of two big buffler bulls."

"That when you were with Lewis and Clark on the way across the mountains?"

"By God, it were. Probably ye read about 'er in a history book or some such. An' it's the plumb truth, too, and I kin prove 'er. Just ask old Fiddlehead Clanihan—he was there at the time."

"Who's Clanihan?"

"Fiddlehead? Ye never heard of 'im? Irishman, he were. Come to the High Shinin' back in twenty-six."

"You sure it wasn't oh-six? You said you were with Lewis and Clark."

"Nope, I didn't. Ye said that. It were twenty-six, just after the Rendezvous."

"Thought they were in the summer."

"True enough, Tsaragi. Just checkin' on ye. That was the year we had one hellacious blizzard in the middle of the summer. Well, Clanihan had a kinda funny head. Said he got hit on both sides of the skull at the same time by a couple of Cheyenne war clubs. Squashed in the middle, ye know. Said they'd of kilt him good, only he'd been drinkin' Ashley's Special, so the war clubs didn't do nothin' but change the shape of his head."

"I wish Sara were here," Soldier Wolf said, humming to himself.

"Pay attention, now. Forget about the little squaw. Now,

Fiddlehead, he had a squaw wife, in fact he had eight of 'em. But that's a different story, an' mebbe I'll tell 'er to ye sometime. Anyhow, old Fiddlehead learnt a lesson after he got hit from both sides—an' that is, don't never get drunk with no wild Injuns."

"Tell me what happened to Fiddlehead. The top of his head finally come off, or what?"

"Hopin' ye'd ask. It was sad, damned sad. Got his pecker caught in a virgin gal that happened to be a Piegan warrior woman, and she got to hoppin' up an' down, tryin' to get loose ye see, an' by God she fucked 'im to death. He just kinda shriveled up until they was nothin' left but his scalp, an' the Blackfoot gal kept it next to her bed for ten years after."

O'Bragh took another pull at the bottle, then grinned.

"Now, ain't that a *sad* story, Tsaragi?"

"It is that. Let me have another snort, Bully."

"Be glad to oblige, except for one thing."

"What's that?"

"Jerry me boy, it do appear we've drunk 'er dry."

Dawn came in a rush of crimson across the east, and the high, rolling prairies of dead grass and rocks and occasional sage were endless, utterly beyond the human capacity to comprehend it all. A soft wind was blowing from the south, and the turf itself smelled different. A dozen vultures had taken shelter in a giant, deformed cottonwood some two or three hundred yards up the arroyo, and now the big birds fanned their wings slowly for several minutes and then took to the air, vaulting themselves upward one or two at a time and drifting in ascending spirals, moving off in separate directions, dispersing.

Soldier Wolf and O'Bragh continued their ride toward the northwest, and finally, by midmorning, overlooked the drainage of Arikaree Creek.

"Look at 'er, Jerry. The very beasties we been lookin' for. . . ."

A small herd of buffalo, perhaps no more than two hundred animals, grazed desultorily at the thin grass near the awakening creek, beyond which rose a low sandstone bluff.

"Big brown cows," Soldier Wolf said, nodding.

"I hate to kill even a one of 'em anymore," O'Bragh said. "Time was when a man could sit an' watch a herd go by for hours, they was so many. Millions, this child figgers. An' time was when they weren't but mebbe a thousand goddamn Americans in all the land—just bufflers an' bears an' Injuns. Damn my eyes, we've done a poor job of 'er. Still big herds around, but harder an' harder to find 'em. Time was when the Cheyennes an' the rest of 'em didn't need no supplies from the govment. All they needed was the land Old Man Coyote had given 'em—that an' to be left alone. But it just ain't the goddamn American nature to leave things alone. I ask ye—ye be educated, Tsaragi—what the hell good is it to dig up the mountains after gold? Ain't a coon I ever saw could eat the stuff."

"Like anything else, my old friend," Soldier Wolf replied. "If there's not much of a thing, or if it's hard to come by, then it's worth more than something that's plentiful."

"Then answer me this. Why ain't *freedom* worth more? Looks to me like most niggers don't never give it a thought one way or another. Or else they do everything they can to get rid of 'er. They all crowd together an' set up a goddamn bunch of rules an' laws, an' then they build a jail to put coons in what don't follow the rules. That make any sense to ye?"

"Guess it doesn't."

"Damned right it doesn't. But I'll tell ye, Tsaragi, years back a man could find freedom out here—cause they wasn't no one to tell him which way to ride or which way to think. Only rules he needed was his Hawken and his good wits. If either one failed him, then he ended up dead, an' that was an end to 'er. I done lived too long, I reckon. Whatever we all come out here for, we sure as hell ain't found it. Or we found it an' didn't know. Well, a man shouldn't think too much. We'll leave our varmints here—walk down, real slow, an' shoot us a buffler, a young bull like I told ye before. . . ."

The two men moved downslope, did not speak again until they had approached the buffalo, the big animals hardly noticing them. At fifty yards O'Bragh stopped, pointed to a particular animal, and motioned for Soldier Wolf to assume a prone position.

A few of the buffalo now seemed to sense their presence, ceased to graze, moved their heads from side to side, staring myopically toward them and yet apparently still not seeing them clearly.

"Bufflers don't see too good," O'Bragh whispered. "Now look. We both fire at once, take steady aim for the heart, just a hand's width down from the brisket. Damnedest thing about bufflers. Ye knock one down without it bellerin', an' the others'll just stand there, they don't figger out what's happened. But if the varmint bellers an' the lead cow figgers it out, they'll run until hell freezes over. A good hunter can make a stand an' just fire off one round after another sometimes, bring down a hundred or so. An' that's the truth. When the Injuns hunt 'em, they make a *surround.* Be a good place for it here, with the sandstone rim behind 'em. Or they'll herd 'em up into a box canyon, get 'em confused. Use to be they'd even drive 'em over a cliff if they could, an' take a load of meat in a short time. Ye ready?"

Soldier Wolf nodded, drew aim.

"Okay, then, let fly. . . ."

The two rifles made nearly a single report, and the young bull dropped in its tracks. The other buffalo ceased to graze but did not run. The heads moved back and forth, back and forth. Then O'Bragh stood up, waved his arms, and let out a loud and repeated *Heeeyah, heeyoo!* And the stampede was on, the big cattle moving away in an explosive fluid motion downstream along the Arikaree.

Soldier Wolf shook his head, watched until the animals had disappeared from sight.

"How far will they run, Bully?"

"Nobody knows. Heard a story once about some bufflers that started to runnin' down in Texas an' kept goin' until they was in the Dakotas. Might be they're still runnin'. . . ."

They walked up to the fallen animal, and Soldier Wolf watched as O'Bragh expertly opened the young bull's paunch with his skinning knife, took out the liver, sprinkled a few drops of gall upon the steaming meat, and took a bite—then offered it to Jerry.

"Keeps the mountain fever off," he said.

"You sure of that now?" Soldier Wolf asked, one eye squinted.

"Sure as I am of anything."

Jerry sampled the delicacy, admitted that it wasn't bad.

They turned the animal over onto its back and began the process of skinning it out, and Soldier Wolf was forced to admire the extreme dexterity of the old man's hands as he worked.

"We'll save the hump rib until we've got caught up with our friends," O'Bragh said. "Them Goths get a taste of 'er, an' they'll forget all about their damned potatoes an' such. A coon gets addicted to buffler meat. It's habit-formin', just like rotgut. Only difference is, it's good for ye. Main reason I ever started gettin' old is I started eatin' other things. Man goes back to the settlements an' starts eatin' flour an' rice an' such—that's when he starts dyin'."

Soldier Wolf looked up from the butchering, glanced back toward where they had left Messiah, Porcupine, and the pack mule—and for a moment he was unable to breathe.

Along the crest, Indians on horseback—perhaps three hundred of them.

"O'Bragh!" he managed.

Bully looked up, glanced along the line, shrugged.

"Ye come out here to find Injuns," he said, his voice utterly calm. "Well, ye just done found 'em. Don't do nothin' foolish, now. Them's Cheyennes an' some of their Arapaho friends. Big fella in the center, the one on the spotted horse—looks like White Frog. Next to him's Roman Nose, the Arapaho medicine man. An' next to him's Whirlwind, a Cheyenne war chief. Just stay calm, Tsaragi. If they'd wanted to kill us, they'd of done 'er before now. . . ."

Chapter Seven

Legend says that the Pawnees stole horses from the Spanish, strange people with hard shells and hair on their faces. In any case, in the year 1640 the Pueblos rebelled against their Spanish overlords, killed many of the Europeans, and freed thousands of horses over the Plains. There were other revolts, and each time more horses were liberated, and wild herds formed, the mesternos or mustangs. For the Plains Nations, these animals were God Dogs or Magic Dogs or Medicine Dogs, and the effect was devastating and immediate upon the preexisting cultures. Whole tribes vanished and reemerged, and the Kiowas and Apaches, the Crees and the Blackfeet came into being. The Cheyenne people moved north into Minnesota and then out onto the Plains. The Sioux split, merged again, split once more, and Mandans, Crows, and Dakotas emerged. A marginal group from the eastern Rockies became the warlike Comanches.

Almost overnight the Medicine Dogs transformed what had long existed, and new tribal personalities were born. Indeed, Old Man Coyote had told the people: "Yes, you may have the Medicine Dogs if you wish, but then, afterward, everything will change, and nothing will be the same again."

Then, with greater mobility, the Nations were thrown into conflict with one another, thirty languages mingled among the warrior tribes, and a universal sign language arose.

The fur traders came, both British and American, and the trappers themselves became Indian, a new kind of tribe, dispersed throughout the High Plains and the Shining Mountains and the lands to the west. Emigrant trails to Oregon and California were opened, and news of gold brought the White tide westward.

Then gold was discovered in the Shining Mountains, and the stage was set for the final confrontations between the Long Knives and the People.

White Frog, Whirlwind, and twenty or so of the warriors rode slowly down to where Soldier Wolf and O'Bragh stood next to the buffalo they had slain. Soldier Wolf started to draw his revolver, but O'Bragh placed his hand upon Jerry's arm and said, "Let this nigger handle it. Stand tall but don't make no moves. . . ."

The Indians drew up ten yards distant.

"It is the old man with long bones," White Frog said in English, "but who is this other with the strange headdress?"

"Damn right it's me, ye Red devils!" O'Bragh called out. "Ye know me well enough. Whar's Chief Big Mouth—or don't ye take 'im out ridin' anymore?"

"His tongue is as bad as always," Whirlwind said.

"Who is this one?" White Frog asked, gesturing toward Soldier Wolf.

"Ye've heard of the Tsaragis? Well, this one's a big chief among 'em—cain't ye tell by the turban?"

"What is your name, Tsaragi?"

"Soldier Wolf—Jerry Soldier Wolf. The White Father has sent me to find the man named Cramdon, who has stolen supplies intended for the Cheyenne and Arapaho peoples. I will capture him and take him in to stand before the White man's justice."

"The White man has no justice, and we do not have a White Father," Whirlwind said, his face betraying no expression of emotion.

"I have come to capture Cramdon," Soldier Wolf said in the Cheyenne language.

White Frog and Whirlwind glanced at each other, and an apparent murmur of approval went up from the warriors.

"You speak the tongue of the Morning Star People?" White Frog asked.

"O'Bragh and my friends the Goths have taught me. Do you know the Goths?"

"The Long Knife with the black book," Whirlwind said, nodding. "He is better than the other Americans."

"Damn right, ye heathen savages." O'Bragh snorted. "An' me an' Soldier Wolf here has been sent by the govment to help ye."

"The Irish Vulture has grown old because no one wished to take his scalp," White Frog said to Soldier Wolf, and Jerry detected what he supposed to be the hint of a smile on the priestly chief's face.

"Ain't it at all," O'Bragh insisted. "Just that this child's tougher than the lot of 'em, an' they know it well."

"He is the one who rides the jackrabbit that was born of a mare," Whirlwind said, also nodding.

"Fifty years I've been tryin' to teach these savages about mules," O'Bragh muttered.

"The big black horse is yours, Soldier Wolf?" White Frog asked.

"The Medicine Dog is mine," Jerry answered.

"I will buy him from you, then."

"I'm keeping him. He is my war horse, and I stole him from a powerful chief among the bluecoats. He is part of my medicine."

The eyes of the two Cheyenne chiefs were glinting with laughter, but still they held their faces straight.

"Aren't you a blue coat with no uniform?" Whirlwind wanted to know.

"Indian agent—agent to the Cheyennes and the Arapahos. I have told you my purpose—I have been sent to take revenge upon the man named Cramdon, for he has betrayed the White Chief."

"He is not your father either, then?" Whirlwind queried.

"No. I am not a Whiteman. I am Cherokee, Tsaragi, just as Irish Vulture has told you."

"Does O'Bragh work for you?" White Frog asked. "Will he do what you tell him?"

Soldier Wolf glanced at Bully O'Bragh before answering.

"He works with me. We both work for the White Chief. But he will only do what he wishes to do."

The two Indian leaders actually smiled, and Soldier Wolf felt a tremendous sense of relief. He had said the right things, and the immediate danger was past.

"It is good," Whirlwind said. "You may keep your black horse, for probably no one else could ride him anyway. Stallions are very bad-natured sometimes. And Irish Vulture has always done just what he wanted to do. He listens to no one, and yet he has never been scalped. It is very strange."

The Indians were in pursuit of the buffalo herd that O'Bragh and Soldier Wolf had come upon an hour earlier, and the two BIA agents rode along quietly, not as prisoners, but as guests. The big animals had not run an excessive distance after all and were discovered some five or six miles on down the Arikaree, once again peacefully grazing.

"Now, pay attention, Tsaragi," O'Bragh said, his eyes twinkling. "Ye're goin' to see somethin' that not many eddycated coons ever see, White nor Injun nuther."

After conferring briefly, the Indians fanned out, keeping a good distance between themselves and the herd, the smaller band of Arapahos taking position downstream from the buffalo, the Cheyennes moving upstream and across to the far side of the little river. With the herd completely surrounded, they began to close the circle, some of the warriors slipping ahead on foot, others mounted. The buffalo seemed, inexplicably, not to notice until the big circle had been drawn close—and only then did a few of the animals cease to graze, looked up, the heads moving back and forth just as they had when O'Bragh and Soldier Wolf had approached them.

At this point Roman Nose and Whirlwind both gestured, and Soldier Wolf was half-expecting to hear the famed war cries. But the hunt was commenced without fanfare, the warriors moving forward quickly now, dropping to prone positions, beginning to fire. A number of the Cheyennes were armed only with bow and arrow, and these men, coming in from the upstream quarter, at the distance of just a few yards, stood erect and began to fire their arrows—a method, as Soldier Wolf perceived, fully as effective as that utilized by those armed with rifles. A few of the braves, knives in hand, actually ran in amongst the now milling and confused, roaring and snorting buffalo, striking by hand. The big brown cattle fell on every side, the animals trampling one another in their panic. Then a cow broke free of all the main body of the herd, and the remainder of the animals followed her, the stampede now in full progress and careening almost directly toward where Soldier Wolf and O'Bragh, astraddle their respective mounts, waited.

The Indians parted to allow the passage of the stampeding buffalo, and O'Bragh clapped his heels to Porcupine's sides and shouted, "Move 'er out, Tsaragi!" Jerry pulled Messiah about and on sheer impulse urged the black stallion in a direction nearly parallel with the movement of the herd. He acted without actually knowing why he did it, but once in motion he knew what he would do. Messiah didn't at all like what was happening, but Jerry controlled the stallion and edged closer and closer to the flank of the charging herd. When he had drawn to within a few yards of a wild-eyed bull, he drew his Marston and fired, was surprised that his first shot seemed to have no effect at all. He fired again, then again, and then a fourth time. The bull, as though growing tired, suddenly disinterested in the mad flight, began to slow. Then, instantly, it collapsed in mid-stride, flipped end over end, and lay still, its head canted, the neck apparently broken by its fall, the hind legs pitifully spasming for a moment or two.

Then O'Bragh and several of the warriors were next to him. White Frog rode up, glanced down at the dead bull, and said, "The man with the funny hat rides well. Perhaps we will not kill you after all. . . ."

Soldier Wolf and O'Bragh were taken to an encampment of some two hundred lodges perhaps ten miles back upstream along the Arikaree. A small band had been left behind to work at the task of skinning and butchering the slain buffalo, and a larger group, many of them women and young men, were dispatched back to the kill site upon the arrival of the hunters at the village. Numerous pack animals were taken along, and the people were in high spirits, for food supplies had grown desperately low during the previous weeks of bitter weather. A number of the women were singing and chanting as they left the village.

Soldier Wolf and O'Bragh were summoned to the lodge of Whirlwind, where the chief, White Frog, and Roman Nose, the Arapaho medicine man, awaited them. One of Whirlwind's wives had, at her husband's direction, killed a fat dog and had set it to cooking.

When Soldier Wolf realized what was to constitute the dinner fare, he immediately lost all appetite.

"Eat and praise the taste, coon," O'Bragh cautioned. "Dog's a great delicacy with 'em. Ye're bein' honored, Tsaragi. Guess ye've managed to impress 'em."

"Irish Vulture," Roman Nose said, "your friend rides well. Is he as strong as he appears to be?"

"Stronger'n that." O'Bragh nodded, his expression serious.

"He is also very tall, almost as tall as you are." Roman Nose then turned to Soldier Wolf and said, "You speak for the Long Knives? Does this mean your words cannot be trusted?"

"I speak for the Long Knives, Roman Nose, but I am no Whiteman. You can trust me."

"He belongs to the Funny Hat People, perhaps," White Frog said.

The three chiefs nodded and waited for some further explanation.

"My people are the Cherokees. We have lived among the Whites for a long time."

"Cheragis? Were your people not driven from their lodges many winters ago?"

"That is true," Soldier Wolf said. "Many were forced into the lands where the Kiowas live, but others remained in the Eastern mountains, beyond the Father River. That is where I have lived."

"I do not understand," White Frog said. "If the Long Knives, the Americans, have done this thing to your people, then why would you wish to speak for them?"

"Many things change," Soldier Wolf answered. "The Whitemen sent me to their school, and I learned to read their books. I learned much of their ways, and they were good to me. After that I served in their army, I was a bluecoat for seven winters. Then they asked me to come to the lands of the Cheyenne and the Arapaho so that I might help your people."

"The Whitemen have never helped us before," Roman Nose said. "They dig holes in the mountains in order to get the yellow metal, and they build their villages everywhere in our lands. They do not wish us to send war parties against our enemies, the Utes, and they tell us about how good a thing peace is. Then they attack our villages and murder our women and children. They promise us food for the long winters, and then they take it away. They kill the buffalo so that we cannot feed ourselves, and they tell us we must stay in one place or another and not hunt anymore, even though these lands have always been our own and were given to us by Saynday, Old Man Coyote."

"Our great warrior, Leg in the Water, has grown old now," Whirlwind said, "and yet he counsels us to drive the Long Knives from our lands. For after that, he says, the buffalo will return, and all will be as it was before. What do you think of this counsel, Soldier Wolf?"

"There are many Whitemen," Soldier Wolf said slowly, "many more than you can even imagine. I have lived among them, and I know. But it is possible to live with them in peace. When the world changes, the people must change also."

"Do you bring us the new treaty we have asked for?" White Frog wanted to know.

"I do not bring a treaty, White Frog. But the new treaty will be brought to you. I have not seen it, but I am told that it contains those things you asked for. Colonel Boone is at Fort Kearny right now, and he will bring the treaty."

The three chiefs looked at one another, and their eyes narrowed.

"We do not trust this Boone," Roman Nose said. "He will try to use his soldiers to force us to accept a treaty that will not work. Then we will starve to death."

"No," Whirlwind said, "we will not starve. We will do as Leg in the Water urges us. We are the ones who control the plains and the mountains, and the Whitemen who live in the big villages do not know how to fight. They are all cowards. And Boone does not know how to fight either. We will kill all of his soldiers and darken our lodges with their scalps. That is what we will do."

"Boone must do as he is told," Soldier Wolf said. "There is a new chief among the Whitemen, for that is their way. They choose a new chief during the fourth winter, and this new chief of the Whitemen wishes to have a treaty with the Cheyennes and the Arapahos and all the other Indian peoples. He wishes to have peace. Boone can do only what he has been told to do."

"And you, Soldier Wolf," White Frog asked, "is that also true of you? You must do as you have been told?"

"It is true."

"What has the new chief of the Whitemen told you to do? You do not bring a treaty, so it must be something else."

"Soldier Wolf and O'Bragh have been sent to capture Cramdon, the one who stole your supplies and murdered some of your people."

"What good will that do?" Roman Nose asked. "We have seen what happens when a Whiteman kills a Cheyenne or an Arapaho. If the man is caught, then he is turned loose again so that he may murder more of our people."

"Yes," Whirlwind agreed, "we have seen how the Whiteman's law works. There is no justice in this law. If you capture Cramdon, the men in Denver will only turn him loose again."

"Beggin' your pardon," O'Bragh sputtered in English, "but this old hound ain't come all the way back out here to turn that feller loose once we gets our hand on 'im."

White Frog laughed at the mountain man's outburst, then glanced at Roman Nose and Whirlwind.

"Irish Vulture is old. He speaks what is in his heart, but perhaps his medicine has all dried up. Cramdon has many men with rifles and pistols, and there are only two of you. We could kill this Cramdon if we thought it wise, but then Boone or some other bluecoat would bring his soldiers against us, and many would die."

"The mountains and plains are very large," Whirlwind said. "So we stay away from Cramdon's ranch, for that way he does not bother us. But one day soon a party of young warriors will not listen to the words of their chiefs, and then they will go to the valley where Cramdon and his people are and kill them all. When the bluecoats come to us, we will say that the Pawnees or the Crows have done this thing. If we say it was the Pawnees, then Medicine Calf will agree with us, and the bluecoats will believe him."

"Jim Beckwourth?" Soldier Wolf asked.

"Yes," White Frog said, "he is the man. Medicine Calf is our friend, even though he was our enemy years ago, many winters ago, when he lived among the Absarokas and was their chief."

"It won't be necessary," Soldier Wolf said. "O'Bragh has told you the truth. We were sent here to get rid of Cramdon, for he disobeyed the wishes of the White Chief. Perhaps I will kill him myself."

"Then there will be one less bad Whiteman." Roman Nose laughed. "Will that make the buffalo come back?"

"No," Soldier Wolf agreed, "but at least your people will know that the word of the White Chief may be trusted. If one of his agents does not do the right thing, then he will be punished. And you will see that the treaty which Colonel Boone brings is generous and fair."

"You believe that this new White Chief speaks the truth, then? Do you know the man yourself, Soldier Wolf?"

"I have seen him, but I do not know him. But I do know the men who gave me my orders, and I trust those men."

"The new White Chief's name is Lincoln," Roman Nose said. "We have our ways of learning things also. And we knew also that you were being sent here, Soldier Wolf, and Irish Vulture with you. Also Frank Goth and his wife and his daughter, who has become a beautiful woman. We know the Goths, and we trust them, even though they are crazy because they are always reading out of their black book. And we also know that Harriman's son has sent you. The father came to visit us more than ten winters ago."

This sudden flood of information astounded Soldier Wolf, and yet, somehow, he was not truly surprised. He nodded slowly and glanced at O'Bragh, who was grinning from ear to ear, the broken yellow teeth glinting firelight.

"It is good," White Frog said. "This man does not lie. We will smoke now, and afterward we will eat. . . ."

The pipe was blessed to the four sacred directions, filled with tobacco, lit, and passed around, and Soldier Wolf was pleased that this first step had been taken—not at all when he supposed it would be, but taken nonetheless.

And the dog stew, he admitted to himself, was actually quite tasty.

White Frog offered Soldier Wolf the youngest of his wives for so long as Jerry should choose to remain in the encampment. O'Bragh had told Jerry that such an offer might be made and had encouraged him to accept, for to do otherwise might be interpreted as a rejection of hospitality. Jerry considered the prospect, for, as he reminded himself, he had not had a woman since that drunken night in Washington, D.C. But the truth of the matter was that only one woman was in his thoughts, and that was Sara Goth—his impossible and totally irrational love for the dark-haired girl who, almost certainly, could never be his. And yet who could say what the whims of Old Man Coyote might be? The longer he thought upon the matter, the more impossible everything that had happened to him in the previous four months seemed. Who could have predicted that Frank Goth would have such a daughter, or that he would decide to take her with him to the Shining Mountains, or that the girl would actually be attracted to a thirty-year-old half-breed? Was there a plan to all of this, some fate predetermined by whatever force it was that decided such things? *Call it Old Man Coyote. Hear it in the chorused cries of the brush wolves at night. Hope that his own intense yearning, spontaneously and inexplicably triggered the moment he had laid eyes upon the girl, might somehow find fulfillment.* Indeed, there was reason to hope. And right now, he reflected, the beautiful Sara Goth might well suppose him dead. Soldier Wolf pictured the girl, wrapped warmly in the rear of her parents' Conestoga, crying herself to sleep, mourning the death of the man she had, for no good reason at all, decided to love.

"I am White Frog's guest," Soldier Wolf said carefully in Cheyenne, "and I am grateful for his offer, but among my own people a man who has decided upon one woman must not sleep with another."

"We were not told that you have a woman, Soldier Wolf. Have you left her in St. Louis perhaps?"

"I am not married, but I have decided upon the woman I wish to marry."

White Frog raised one eyebrow. "This woman must be very special to you, Soldier Wolf."

"She is."

"Is it Goth's daughter that you wish to marry?"

Soldier Wolf was stunned. *How in hell does the son of a bitch know that?*

White Frog realized what Soldier Wolf was thinking and said simply, "Some of my warriors came close to your wagon. They saw the girl leave her parents and come to where you were. Why do you not offer Frank Goth a marriage price, for that way the girl will not have to sneak off to meet you?"

Soldier Wolf grinned, shook his head. "Is there anything about us that you don't know, White Frog?"

"Yes," White Frog answered. "We don't know why your people dig for the yellow metal."

"Not my people. I am Cherokee."

"This is what you have told us, and your skin looks like ours. But you are a warrior for their tribe, and that makes you one of them."

The days flowed by now. The spring thaws had certainly come, and the remaining ice disappeared from the water. Grass had appeared as if by magic from the apparently dead earth, and a warm, moist wind was blowing, breathing across the land. The village was moved, the women and boys disassembling with amazing quickness the lodges of buffalo and elk hide stretched over poles. It took but half a day for everything to be loaded onto travois rigs, these drawn by packhorses. Even the camp dogs, whose population had been severely diminished during the hard winter, the seemingly endless rains and snowstorms and ice storms of this long year, had small travois fastened to their shoulders and so dragged along their own loads.

The combined village of Cheyennes and Arapahos moved northwestward from the Arikaree toward the Fort Morgan outpost, and on the third day, with Soldier Wolf and O'Bragh riding near the front of the trailing caravan, riding along with Whirlwind, Roman Nose, and White Frog, they came in sight of the Rocky Mountains, the peaks still some seventy or eighty miles away and yet vivid in the clear air, a long, jagged white wall that seemed to boundary the world.

"It do shine," O'Bragh said. "Every time this child comes back and catches his first sight of 'em, he swears to God he ain't never goin' East again. They get to ye, Jerry. Ye'll see. The mountains get inside your head, I say, an' after that a coon ain't never the same again."

Soldier Wolf was stunned. Even at so great a distance, these Shining Mountains were huge, a long, seemingly endless white wall of immense proportions.

"Amazing!" he said. "They don't even look real."

"Real enough," O'Bragh said. "An', Tsaragi, they go on damned near forever, higher in some places, lower in others, clear across to the Great Salt Lake an' Seedskeedee country, where we all gets together every summer and gets blind drunk an' shoots each other an' sells our plew. Used to, that is. Damn, it was good. All gone, an' old Brigham the Mormon's got him a city built out there now, an' his people is raisin' corn an cows an' God knows what-all. Ye should of been with us, Soldier Wolf. Only the mountains is left, but they is somethin', ain't they?"

"Guess I was expecting the Smokies, only bigger. I've never seen anything like this, Bully. . . ."

"Ain't seen nothin' yet. Mark this nigger's words."

"Beyond those mountains," White Frog said, "is where your friend lives."

"Who'd ye have in mind, ye Red devil?" O'Bragh snorted.

"The man you intend to kill. That is where he lives."

They crossed the Platte and moved on to the Cache La Poudre, then north along Box Elder Creek, where, in a grassy swale, the village was reassembled. Above them rose the Shining Mountains, and the stream, picking up melt water now, was running high and milky green.

Soldier Wolf continued as a guest in White Frog's lodge and continued as well to decline White Frog's repeated offer of a bed companion. Bully O'Bragh, after a relatively few days among these people, was completely at home—and indeed, he had moved into a lodge with a squaw whose husband had died the previous year of the Whiteman's lung disease, as it was called. When Soldier Wolf inquired about the nature of this arrangement, O'Bragh winked and said, "Jerry me boy, I knowed this gal from years ago. Ain't the first time I've lived with the Cheyennes, ye know. Well, me an' Marsh Flower was close years back, after she lost her first husband to the Absarokas. When she got done with her mournin' an' wasn't gettin' asked to marry again, me an' her did a bit of pokin' an' rubbin' out in the willers, as it's called. Then I went away, an' when I come back again, she was married. So it's like we're old sweethearts."

Soldier Wolf clapped O'Bragh across the shoulders and laughed.

Since his departure from military service, time itself had grown less and less meaningful for Soldier Wolf. It had taken a bit of getting used to, this unstructured passage from day to day—no reveille, no meals at appointed hours, no universally agreed-upon moment for lights-out and sleeping. But there had been, at least, a single, significant date—a place he had to be, St. Joseph, on the first day of February. Then had come the icy trail up-country, and the days flowed and merged. Even so, the routine had been essentially without variation—up early, quick breakfast, the animals into their harness, the journey taken up once more, midday to rest the animals and to eat, move forward again, the evening campsite, the cooking fire, the day's big meal, conversation, Sara teaching him the language of the Cheyenne people, sleep.

But now, among the Cheyenne people, the routine of the trail was gone, and all that remained was the early rising, and not even that was enforced. The business of the village, Soldier Wolf observed, managed to get done without specific direction, the world of the women on the one side, almost a separate society, a separate culture which from time to time overlapped with the different culture of the males. And yet it all worked, and worked admirably.

Time took on less rigid but greater dimensions, defined only by the immediate weather and village site and by the inevitable progression of the season. Once more the village was moved, the large herd of horses having exhausted the new pastures, and the people trekked northward, avoiding the White settlement at Laramie, and then westward and southward along the Laramie River and back into the mountainous fastness to broad meadows between ridges and peaks that rose precipitously to either side.

And weeks drifted by. Soldier Wolf could feel, as a thing almost tangible, this new kind of life taking hold of him. During the days he and Bully sometimes rode up-country through dark forests of spruce and pine to highlands where the snow remained in deep drifts—they wandered and hunted, it seemed to Jerry when he thought about it, like two small boys, like grown children with nothing else to do.

But nights were a different matter. O'Bragh had entered into a *de facto* marriage with Marsh Flower, and for a time Soldier Wolf remained in the lodge with White Frog and his wives, the women attentive to all his needs but one, and that as a result of his own choosing. He and White Frog talked of many things, and Soldier Wolf felt that he was coming to understand, truly understand, the needs and whims of these people who had either captured him or taken him in. He and White Frog were becoming close friends, and the priestly chief—a war chief as well, as Jerry realized—was deeply interested in Jerry's reflections with regard to the existence of a Creator and a Spirit World as well as his somewhat skeptical responses to the "true religion" that Frank Goth and other such men professed and attempted to teach the Indian peoples. Again and again White Frog called upon Soldier Wolf to speak of the Whiteman's school, this strange place where the young people read books and wrote things and did nothing else.

"How is it possible to *learn* in such a place?" White Frog demanded.

But the Indian leader was not impatient, and Soldier Wolf had the distinct impression that White Frog was learning of the White world more certainly, more systematically than he, Soldier Wolf, was learning of the world of the Cheyennes, even though he was living among them.

When the lodge fire had died down and White Frog and his wives were asleep, then Soldier Wolf became aware of the smoky, human odor of the lodge—of that and of the quiet, punctuated only by the occasional yipping of a camp dog or the more distant wails of coyote or wolf. And he thought of Sara Goth, wondered if she indeed supposed him dead, knew that he would have to return to her, find her, soon.

She inhabited his dreams as well. *One night they were together in a lodge of their own, but there was no village and no one else in the world about them—only animals that came and went, deer, antelope, buffalo, hawks and eagles, and a great grizzly like the ones the*

Cheyennes had come across on the journey up the Laramie River and had given wide berth to, for as O'Bragh had said, "White bears is touchy when they first come out of their holes, don't ye know?" But now the animals wandered about outside the lodge that he and Sara shared, and two bears built a campfire and sat beside it, speaking in a language which Soldier Wolf could only partially understand. Other dreams as well, and in one O'Bragh came to him and announced that he would ride off into the mountains to die. Jerry protested, but the gaunt man turned and strode away. Soldier Wolf followed, began to shout at him, but O'Bragh vanished. In his place lay the body of an Indian girl, facedown. Soldier Wolf looked about, not knowing what to do—but when he spoke to the Indian people, they did not seem to hear him and continued with whatever they were doing. He leaned down, turned the girl over, discovered it was Sara, a knife thrust into her stomach, the face clenched in an expression of horror and fear and pain.

He awoke sweating, shaking, hardly able to breathe, and was unable to sleep for the remainder of the night.

The days drifted on. Roman Nose and the Arapahos had left, had gone north to find the buffalo herds, and in the evenings the Cheyenne warriors spoke of undertaking a war party against the Crows, to steal horses. O'Bragh was excited by the prospect and convinced Soldier Wolf to accompany the expedition. Jerry shrugged and agreed.

"Trouble is, coon, ye ain't got no medicine bundle. Half Injun ye may be, but ye ain't this *kind* of Injun until ye've acquired some medicine."

Then a scout came in with news of an Arikara encampment some forty miles away, in the mountains to the north. And immediately a horse-thieving party was formed.

The Ree encampment was quiet, and the big fire at the center of the village had died away to a dull orange glow. The herd, half a mile distant from the lodges, milled slowly in the late-March half-moon, some of the animals continuing to nibble at clumps of grass in the darkness, some asleep on their feet, a few lying on their sides and revealed as little more than shadowy humps in the thin silver night.

Whirlwind's horse thieves had been patiently waiting for several hours, and now the chief passed the signal, and the warriors, on foot, began to glide down the brush-and-pine-covered slope toward the horses.

"They ain't expectin' nothin' a-tall," O'Bragh whispered. "The Rees is got a couple of guards posted, for sure, but their fires is gone out, an' this child guesses they be sleepin'. Cain't never tell, though. Look, Tsaragi. If somethin' goes amiss an' we have to take to our heels, don't ye go waitin' for me. Cain't run like I once could, or I wouldn't be sayin' nothin'. But a nigger takes his chances, an' I know better'n to be doin' this sort of thing, even if I cain't resist temptation. No point in both of us losin' our topknots."

"Forget about the doomsday stuff," Soldier Wolf said. "You got me into this, O'Bragh, and I fully expect you to get me out of it."

"Hold on to your ha'r, then, Jerry me boy."

Like shadows the Cheyenne warriors moved in amongst the horses, dropping their lead loops over the animals' necks, beginning to move the creatures away from the main group.

A coyote sent a series of sharp, ululating yips into the night air, and the horses, growing nervous, began to flutter their nostrils and stamp about on the marshy ground.

Soldier Wolf, following the examples of the Cheyennes, moved among the horses, selected out a light-colored mare, and was about to slip his loop around the animal's neck when a shout went up a few yards from where he stood. Soldier Wolf spun about, his knife in his hand, and studied the dimness.

A hand pulled at his coat, spun him to one side. An arm was about his neck, and he struggled against it, was pulled down to one knee.

A good day to die, a voice far back in his skull repeated over and over, as though some intelligence within him and yet detached, at a distance, and watching with grim humor, had spoken.

Soldier Wolf kicked with both feet, felt contact, was aware of the grunted expulsion of breath.

A long gash down his left shoulder. Knife wound—he knew what had happened, had not been aware of its happening, did not feel it.

He leaped upon the shadow form, brought his own knife down, missed his antagonist's throat, felt the blade slide through flesh along the cheekbone. The Ree twisted aside, groped for his own knife. But Jerry was on him, had brought his blade up into the

Indian's stomach, withdrew the knife, and slid the steel upward into the throat.

The Ree collapsed without making any further sound, and Soldier Wolf rose to his feet, hardly aware of what had happened, only dimly realizing that he had actually slain a man.

The horses were running, and further shouts went up.

O'Bragh was next to him.

"Ye done kilt 'im, now take his scalp, ye damned fool!"

Soldier Wolf's mind was blank.

O'Bragh leaned over the fallen Ree, drew his knife in an arc about the top of the head, and said, "Pull 'er off, Jerry me boy. Yank hard, an' let's get out of here. Goin' to get crowded real soon. . . ."

Soldier Wolf grasped his victim's hair, pulled, pulled harder, heard the muted, sucking sound of torn flesh.

Like skinning a fox or a raccoon. . . .

Then they were running, running toward the low rim where their horses were waiting. Shouts behind them.

Soldier Wolf slipped the bloody scalp inside his coat as he ran, slowed to wait for Bully, and then realized the old mountain man was no longer with him. He stopped, turned about, searched the nearly total darkness now that he had entered in under the cover of a spruce grove—but no O'Bragh. His impulse was to go back, but go where?

Then he remembered Bully's words, realized there was nothing he could do, only the gesture, a gesture that would probably cost him his own life.

"Where'd that skinny son of a bitch get to?" he groaned.

"Soldier Wolf! This way!"

It was Whirlwind, and he moved toward the sound of the voice. Then the chief was there, standing beside him in the faint moonlight, and he followed numbly, blurted out, "Bully's back there. . . ."

Whirlwind did not answer.

They reached their horses, the little clearing quite crowded now with more than a hundred additional animals, those driven off from the Arikara herd.

"Damn ye, boy, ye give this child a start. Thought we'd lost ye there. . . ."

"I'll be a son of a bitch!" Soldier Wolf exploded. "O'Bragh! What?"

"Ye zigged when ye should of zagged. Git mounted an' let's move!"

Within moments the scene of commotion was resolved into one of organization, and the Cheyennes rode out, driving their newly acquired horses before them. They rode through the remainder of the night, stopped shortly after dawn to rest and water the animals, ate scraps of cold meat from their saddlebags, and continued their forced march.

By late afternoon one of the scouts had overtaken the main group and announced that the Rees had turned back.

"So, you have taken coup and have an Arikara scalp to show for it, Soldier Wolf. Now I begin to believe that you are Indian and not White. Is your arm cut badly?" Whirlwind asked.

The bleeding had stopped hours since, and the pain was merely that of a dull ache, the wound crusted over with dried gore.

"I am not hurt, Whirlwind. These things happen."

The Cheyenne chief nodded, urged his mount forward, and reassumed his position at the head of the troop.

"No need to worry 'er," Bully said. "Like I've told ye, meat don't spile in the mountains. Wrap 'er up with a mite of blackroot poultice, and ye'll be good as new, mebbe gooder'n that."

Chapter Eight

Just as in California and Nevada, the early mining communities in the Shining Mountains seemed to take shape almost overnight following a rich strike in the gold fields, for there was always a sufficient supply of merchants of one sort or another who were eager to relieve the miners of their nuggets and dust. Gambling houses thrived, and staple foods and clothing sold at outrageous prices. There were relatively few women in the camps, and a majority of these were ladies of the evening (or morning or afternoon) who had been brought up from St. Louis and the river trade. The supply was never great enough, however, and in many cases Indian women were lured away from their villages, or, in some cases, actually kidnapped and forced to enter into the "oldest profession."

The miners, for their part, received cash for their back-breaking labors, and since the earth was pregnant with riches, they were not inclined to save what they had earned. Irreligious and footloose, the typical miner very seldom arrived in the mountains in company with his family. When he had money to spend, he did. And after days of working in knee-deep freezing water and endless muck, he was mad for the clamor and easy company that only the towns could provide.

Miners lived in tents or in makeshift log cabins, many of these consisting of no more than a single room sufficient to accommodate bunked beds and a cast-iron stove. The shacks and tents commonly dotted the areas around the diggings, apart from the towns—for claims were guarded jealously and at gunpoint.

"The people were camped all around . . . in wagons, tents, and temporary brush houses or wickiups. The principal business houses were saloons, gambling houses, and dance halls, two or three so-called stores with very small stocks of general merchandise and little provisions. . . ."

In addition to the prostitutes, the saloonkeepers, and store clerks, other professionals also arrived early: the speculators, the freighters, the salesmen, and the lawyers.

How long would the gravels hold out? Double the damned prices, boys, and double them again. . . .

The victory dance had just begun, the village in a festive mood indeed. A supply of whiskey appeared from some indeterminate source, and many of the braves were drinking heavily, joined in this indulgence by a gleeful Bully O'Bragh.

Soldier Wolf, who had taken one of the two Arikara scalps, was pushed forward and required to recite the details of his struggle, which, with some confusion, he did. When he came to the part in which Irish Vulture had to show him how to remove the scalplock, the warriors began to laugh good-naturedly, and when he was finished, they whooped their approval and forced him into the dance.

Roast venison, antelope, elk, and buffalo—including two large black pots filled with simmering buffalo tongues—were the fare of the evening. Soldier Wolf extricated himself from the dancing, ate, eluded the advances of one zealously amorous Cheyenne woman, and began to walk toward White Frog's lodge when the camp dogs began running about and barking wildly.

Immediately the dancing ceased, and the warriors raced for their weapons.

At this point two riders appeared at the edges of the firelight, having somehow passed through the sentries undetected.

"Hellooo the camp!" the larger of the two riders shouted. "This is Medicine Calf and Gray Blanket! Leg in the Water has told us where to find you—we wish to speak with Whirlwind and White Frog!"

O'Bragh was instantly next to Soldier Wolf, the old man grinning from ear to ear.

"By damn, Jerry me boy, it's them, sure as hell. Jimmy Beckwourth—ain't seen 'im for twenty years or more, but this child'd recognize 'im anywhere. An' Hawk-Face John Smith, a White coon that married into the Cheyennes with Big Mouth's bunch an' is a subchief on the council. Him an' me trapped together one winter—had to show 'im how to set a trap, an' that's a fact!"

O'Bragh stood for a moment as if not certain what to do next, and then he bellowed out a long "Hoo-ki-hi!" and followed that with, "How's the stick floatin', coons?"

Beckwourth turned on his pony and held his hand to his

forehead, stared out into the shadows in the direction of Soldier Wolf and O'Bragh.

"Who gives the Crow war cry?" Beckwourth shouted back.

Bully stepped forward.

"It's the Vulture, damn ye, Farnsworth O'Bragh!"

Beckwourth and Smith swung down from their horses as the Cheyennes came up to cluster about them, and O'Bragh and the other two old mountain men embraced, pounded one another on the backs and shoulders.

"Wagh!" Smith snorted. "Me an' Jimmy come looking for yuh. This here the Cherokee? John Smith's my handle, an' I'm pleased to meet yuh, too."

"Soldier Wolf," Jerry said, shaking hands first with Smith and then with Beckwourth, astounded somehow that the latter, though a large man, was not at least a foot taller. *Legends are supposed to be bigger than ordinary men. But this is one old man I sure as hell wouldn't want to get into a scrap with. . . .*

Whirlwind and White Frog appeared and also embraced the two mountain men, seemed genuinely pleased to see them.

"Why do our brothers search for us?" White Frog asked. "Has something happened to Big Mouth or Leg in the Water?"

"Got sent out to find these here two Injun agents," Smith said. "Folks was gettin' worried about 'em."

"Have you treated these men well, Whirlwind?" Beckwourth asked—but his eyes were glinting with good humor.

"The one with the turban has taken coup and now owns an Arikara scalp," Whirlwind said. "We were celebrating when you rode in. How did you get past our wolves, Medicine Calf?"

"Gentlemen," Beckwourth said, "if I didn't have any trouble sneaking in on the Cheyennes thirty years ago, why do you think I'd have trouble now?"

"Medicine Calf has always been a very good sneak, Soldier Wolf. It is good that he is our friend now and not our enemy. Gray Blanket Smith, your brother is pleased to see you again. Have the two riders eaten since morning?"

"The Medicine Calf smells roast venison," Beckwourth said, rubbing his hands together. "For that I am always hungry."

The festivities were renewed in honor of the two new guests, and after Beckwourth and Smith had conferred with the chiefs, they spoke with Soldier Wolf and O'Bragh.

"Your Bible friends are up on the headwaters of the North Platte by now, Agent Soldier Wolf, and I gather they'd like your company. There's a pretty little gal in particular who'd like to see you again—you know who I'm talking about?"

"I think so," Jerry said.

"Ye didn't ride all the way up here to tell us that, did ye?" O'Bragh asked.

"Talk was goin' round the Injuns had scalped yuh," Hawk-Face Smith said. "People in Denver an' Aurora is just lookin' for reasons to put the bluecoats onto the Cheyennes an' Arapahos."

"Be Chivington an' those boys ye talkin' about?"

"Chivington," Beckwourth said, "yes. But Boone's back in Denver now, and he wants to keep a lid on matters. Soldier Wolf, there are a couple of things you don't know about—not unless White Frog has told you."

"For instance?"

"First off, the new treaty's been signed—mid-February, down at Fort Wise. You boys and the Goths just missed Boone, or I guess he would have told you. Little Raven, Storm, Shave-Head, Big Mouth, Black Kettle, White Antelope, Tall Bear, and the others have all fixed their marks to it. What it comes down to is this: the Indians have relinquished claims to all lands except a chunk of southeastern Colorado Territory. . . ."

"A place that's dry an' without game," Smith added.

"That's right. In return the U.S. government is supposed to protect the Indians and to pay them thirty thousand dollars a year for fifteen years, half to each tribe. The money's to purchase stock and farming equipment, outbuildings, fencing, plowing and so forth. The government's supposed to set up a sawmill, houses, and mechanic shops. Going to send people to work on the farm machinery for them. And each Indian gets forty acres of land, with timber and water if possible."

"Only there ain't no timber, an' precious little water," Smith added.

Soldier Wolf was incredulous, glanced at O'Bragh.

"And the Indians signed it?"

"They went through the motions," Beckwourth said. "Apparently didn't take the matter too seriously, though, or Whirlwind's bunch wouldn't be up here. Big Mouth is off wandering around right now, and so is Roman Nose, and so is Black Kettle."

"I don't understand," Soldier Wolf protested.

"Neither do them coons back in Washington, or they'd never of wrote up such a treaty," Smith said. "Just want the Cheyennes an' Arapahos to join civilization right now, is all."

"The tribes are getting ready for the summer buffalo hunts," Beckwourth said, shrugging his big shoulders in a gesture of futility. "Commissioner Greenwood was out here last summer—he should have known better. If he did, Congress sure as hell didn't, but in any case, by the time the summer buffalo hunt's here, this territory could well be Confederate instead of Union. Strong Southern sentiment in Denver and Colorado City."

"Has war actually begun, then?" Soldier Wolf asked, his voice subdued.

Beckwourth shook his head, and Smith said, "Not as we've heard yet, but word is it's just a matter of weeks or days."

"They be bad times, bad times, this child's thinkin'," O'Bragh said. "Now, this boy here, he don't remember—but we remember, don't we, lads? All of us together out to Bear Lake, summer Rendezvous? An' beavers so thick they choked up the criks, an' so many bufflers they'd run on for hours an' ye still couldn't see an end of 'em."

Beckwourth and Smith nodded, and Soldier Wolf could see the distance, the time in their eyes—three old men now, but men who had seen it all, had known it all in a way that he, Soldier Wolf, never would. The talk drifted on, the Big Hole, Jackson's Hole, Seedskeedee, bullboats on the Roche Jaune, South Pass, Colter's Hell, white bufflers, grizzlies swarming over the land, the sky filled with birds, the tribes wild and fierce and in constant warfare, Here Before Christ, American Fur, Smith, Jackson, and Sublette, Rocky Mountain Fur. . . . The three old mountain men, Beckwourth and Smith in their sixties, O'Bragh in his seventies, were hardly even aware of Soldier Wolf's presence. Jerry rose, walked out of the lodge, stood by the diminishing flames in the central fire pit.

White Frog came to stand beside him.

"The old ones are lost in their memories, my friend?"

"Yes," Soldier Wolf said, "that's what's going on."

"I understand. I have listened to Leg in the Water and the other old warriors talk about how things once were—before the Whitemen came, so many of them."

"White Frog, why didn't you tell me about the treaty?"

"What treaty is that, my friend?"

"What was signed at Fort Wise."

"Was it important to know? This government of yours says many things, and none of them makes sense. They wish us to stay near Sand Creek, and they say they will bring us food for the winter. We listen, but we do not believe them—we have heard the words before. So we will go to find the buffalo herds, we will hope that they are somewhere. If we find them, we will have food, the squaws will make much pemmican. There are still deer and elk. The Whitemen have promised us much, but they will not give us these things until we go to Sand Creek and live there. Agent Boone will hold our annuities until fall, when the cold weather comes. He thinks that we will be destitute by then and so will be willing to do as he wishes. But it may not happen that way."

"I'm beginning to realize that I'm on the wrong side."

White Frog reached up, put his hands on the taller man's shoulders.

"You are part Indian and part Whiteman, Soldier Wolf. Your blood is Indian, though your people are different than mine. But you have lived your life among these Whitemen and have gone to their school. Medicine Calf was the same. He has had to live in both worlds—he is one of us, but he is one of them also. It is the same with Gray Blanket and Irish Vulture. When the time to fight comes, you will have to choose."

White Frog's words echoed and reechoed through Soldier Wolf's brain: . . . *part Indian and part Whiteman.* Not even White Frog realized what utter truth he had spoken. *Don't know for sure just what the hell I am. Cherokee father, White mother. Should never have come out here, didn't know about freedom until I saw the mountains, the long white wall of the mountains, until I heard the coyotes and wolves howling, until I took that scalp. . . .*

With morning, Beckwourth and Smith left to return to Denver, able now to grant assurance to those who might otherwise heed the words of Chivington and set out to take revenge upon the Indians for having done away with the special BIA agent.

White Frog drew about himself some seventy young warriors and announced that he would accompany Soldier Wolf and Irish Vulture to the village of the People of the Valley, and before noon the little caravan rode toward the northwest, where they would cross through the low pass, around the upper end of the Medicine Bow Range, and down to the North Fork of the Platte.

O'Bragh was ebullient, since Marsh Flower had decided to accompany her new friend—for indeed, the people had already granted the relationship the status of a marriage.

"Maybe I'll get me a couple more younguns. Got children scattered all over the Shining Mountains, Jerry me boy. Cain't even keep track of 'em all—Shoshones, Crows, Utes, Kaws, Otos. Ain't never got me no Cheyennes, though, not until now. A man shouldn't give up on livin' too soon, I tell ye."

Soldier Wolf smiled, reached over and swatted Porcupine on the rump, causing the animal to step forward indignantly.

"Don't go doin' that, now. Ye'll be hurtin' 'er feelin's. Tell ye what. Ye're looking like either a melancholy bull or a lovesick calf, that's what I figger. Thinkin' on little Sary, are ye?"

"Where are we going, Bully?"

"Goin'? Why, that's a damn fool question. To the People of the Valley, of course."

"And where are they going? Where's our world going?"

"Turnin' poet on me, are ye? Well, all right then. I'll tell ye. It's time to start over, that's what. Tell ye. Medicine Calf an' Gray Blanket be talkin' about makin' one more trappin' party out to the Seedskeedee, just us old guys. We'll do'er, too, next year or the one after. Don't make no difference when. An' it don't make no difference that plew ain't worth nothin' much anymore. We'll be goin' back to find the young bucks we used to be. We'll come ridin' in, an' there they'll be, young Jimmy Beckwourth an' Johnny Smith, an' Graybeard Le Blueux, he'll be there too, an' Davy Jackson an' Jed Smith, little Prayin' 'Diah, an' Black Harris, an a whole string of other coons that has gone under. We're goin' to pray to the Great Coyote, an' off we'll head. How's that sound to ye, youngun?"

Soldier Wolf stared at the tall, gaunt man on the mule and whistled, laughed.

"Sounds good," he said. "You old guys interested in taking a half-breed Tsaragi along?"

"Don't guess the boys'd mind. This nigger sure wouldn't, no sir. Somehow or another, Jerry, I guess ye be one of us. Just had the bad judgment to get born too late is all. Wagh! I can hear the wind singin' up through the Tetons right now. . . ."

* * *

The Medicine Bow peaks rose lonely and brilliantly white above the dark cloaks of their fir and spruce forests, and the April weather was warm, with even the nights pleasant.

The party encountered snowdrifts across the back of the low pass, but the difficulties were minimal, and soon they were on their way down the western slope.

In the interior now, Soldier Wolf thought. Part of the Shining Mountains now, now they're real. . . .

They reached the eastern branch of the North Fork, the stream O'Bragh called the Canadian, and they moved upstream through canyons and broad meadows. One day's ride above the confluence of the Canadian and the Illinois—and a wolf came in with news that the encampment of the People of the Valley was only a couple of hours' ride ahead.

"But there is trouble," the scout told White Frog. "Some of the lodges have been burned, and the people are in mourning."

White Frog nodded gravely, turned to look at Soldier Wolf and O'Bragh.

"We must ride on through immediately, even though the darkness is nearly upon us. These people are our brothers, even though they do not hunt the buffalo, and they may need our help."

"In mourning?" Soldier Wolf asked the scout. "Some have been killed, then?"

"I did not enter the village, Soldier Wolf. I saw what had happened, and I turned my horse and rode back to meet you."

White Frog ordered a forced march, and the remaining distance to the encampment was covered despite the darkness.

The Cheyenne warriors came to a halt outside the village. A great fire was burning in the central circle—and indeed, what the scout had told them appeared to be true. The half-burned remains of several lodges stood out in the firelight, and the people clustered about, subdued.

The warriors, at White Frog's command, discharged their weapons into the night air, thus signifying peaceful intentions, and then rode slowly into the midst of the village.

Frank Goth and an old Indian with an extremely wrinkled face stood together before the big fire to welcome the visitors.

"It is Morning Star Fox," White Frog said. "He is their shaman and also their leader. They have no war chief because they do not go on the warpath. These people separated from my people many winters ago, but they are still Cheyennes."

With this explanation, he called out to the old chief: "I am White Frog! My warriors come in peace, and we bring the friends of Frank Goth with us!"

"Enter in peace," Morning Star Fox said quietly, his deep voice carrying easily, though he spoke in normal tones.

Frank and Elizabeth Goth and Sara were overjoyed to find Soldier Wolf and Bully O'Bragh still alive and well, for the disappearance, naturally enough, had caused them to entertain the gravest fears. Frank and Elizabeth embraced both Soldier Wolf and O'Bragh, and Sara, standing back a few steps in a state of either shock or forced restraint, nodded simply and said hello.

Soldier Wolf realized there were tears in the girl's eyes.

Morning Star Fox welcomed the new arrivals and apologized for a lack of immediate hospitality due to the calamity that had befallen the village just two days earlier.

Several tree-hung graves were faintly visible in the shadowed firelight just beyond the village, and a number of women as well as men wore bandages of one sort or another. Frank Goth's right arm was in a sling bandage, for he had taken a rifle ball in the shoulder.

"Our friend Cramdon and his men," Frank explained. "No reason for it at all, surely no possible reason for attacking these peaceful souls, no threat to anyone. Cramdon was just passing through, apparently, and decided to wipe out the village. It was Edward Cramdon, no doubt about it. Jerry, he just sat on his horse and watched and laughed while his henchmen came roaring through the village, shooting and tossing torches into the lodges. He took us totally by surprise, and his people killed three of the young men and also a woman with her infant on her back. They trampled her down and killed the child as well."

"You were shot?" Soldier Wolf asked, stunned by the brief account.

"Frank was hit when they came through the village on the first pass," Elizabeth said, "just as though he was the one they wanted to kill."

"The speaker of Whiteman's religion decided to fight then," Morning Star Fox said. "He found his rifle and helped to defend us against the raiders, even though he was wounded."

"I killed one of the sons of bitches," Frank said, his voice flat and emotionless, "and I think I wounded two others. When it was all over, I knew I should pray for the souls of Cramdon and his people, as well as for my own forgiveness. I have never slain a man before, and I—"

"Be a strange God who couldn't forgive ye," O'Bragh said.

"God save me, Soldier Wolf, I couldn't bring myself to do it until the next day."

"And yet these men were attempting to kill you and your family and these people you live with. . . ."

"That is true. But, Jerry, in accepting the service of the Lord, I disavowed violence as a solution to the problems of humankind. Cramdon's attack has caused the dark, primitive force within me to emerge. And it is not the first time, God save me. Do you remember when I told you I was probably not a true Christian at all? Lord forgive me, the point is this: I actually enjoyed it—I was no different than Cramdon's wild animals. I became someone else, not Frank Goth at all."

"This coon's thinkin' ye started bein' Frank Goth." O'Bragh shrugged. "Ye got to keep things in per-spective. Them boys was tryin' to kill ye, preacher."

Goth shook his head, turned back to Soldier Wolf as if for understanding, as if for vindication.

"Perhaps one day the world will be as you want it to be, Frank, I don't know. In fact, as Farnsworth himself might say, this child is just starting to realize how damned much he doesn't know. It's even occurred to me that the fate of mankind might lie in precisely the opposite direction from what you envision—and God only knows what that means. Except that maybe violence is not, ultimately, a bad thing at all. *Keep your dukes up*, my Pa used to say. *That way a man doesn't have to fight, at least not most of the time.*"

"Friends don't call me Farnsworth." O'Bragh snorted.

"You know what the Cheyennes call this man, Frank? Irish Vulture. Now there's a name that fits."

Goth, still obviously troubled, nonetheless managed a weak smile. "I don't know, I don't know," he said. "But what am I thinking of? Morning Star Fox, we must feed these people—they have ridden a long way."

Throughout the conversation, the shaman of the People of the Valley and the priestly chief of the Cheyennes had stood to one side, listening. Now the old chief called to his woman and told her to bring food as quickly as possible.

And White Frog turned to Soldier Wolf and asked, "What will you do now? Shall we ride against this man who has attacked the people? You are the chief now, my friend, and you must tell me what it is that you wish to do."

When Jerry and the others had finished eating, Sara said to him, her voice hesitant, subdued, "Do you see the big crooked pine up on the hill? I have gone there many times since you disappeared. It's a good place to be alone, to think about a friend who is probably dead. Sometimes I even go there at night, after Mother and Father are asleep. . . ."

"Will you go there tonight?" Soldier Wolf asked.

"I might."

She turned away then, walked across the lodge, her lithe body maddeningly attractive in the white deerskin dress, her long black hair braided in Indian fashion now that she was living among these people once again. Jerry watched Sara walk away from him, then caught Elizabeth Goth's eyes upon his face, and turned his gaze upward toward the smoke hole in the top of the lodge, feeling awkward and embarrassed as he did so.

Was the girl glad to see him or not? Why the restraint, why the distance? And the whispered words about the crooked pine, what did that mean? Perhaps she wished for him to go there and wait, wait as she had waited during these long weeks of his absence. Perhaps she was angry with him because he had not gotten word of his safety back to her somehow.

But now a host of other matters was running through Soldier Wolf's mind as well, not the least of these being the apparent duplicity of the treaty Jim Beckwourth had described, sanctioned by Congress and with the approval of both Commissioner Greenwood and President Buchanan. Honest Abe the rail-splitter was president now, a man whose public reputation, at least, bespoke both fairness and a concern for human rights. Some hope in this, and Soldier Wolf began mentally to compose a letter concerning what seemed to be the desperate plight of the Cheyenne and Arapaho peoples, a letter sent directly to Lincoln himself? And Byers, the newspaperman in Denver—here was a possible ally, a man at least modestly sympathetic toward the Indians, a man, according to Beckwourth, who had in the past published items in behalf of the Cheyennes in the attempt to gain a modicum of public support for their claims and needs. But with even the local churchmen, like this fellow Chivington, in apparent favor of either eliminating the Indian problem by eliminating the Indians themselves or of driving them onto a meager reservation consisting of lands that were of no foreseeable value to the Whites, the situation locally seemed almost hopeless. Here were two churchmen, Goth and Chivington, whose views represented the difference between night and day. The one had no church and doubted the validity of his own position as a Christian, while the other dominated the most influential church in the area and at the same time self-righteously called for the extermination of the Indians, as though they were nothing more than wild animals whose very existence posed a deep and immediate threat to the settlements.

And Harriman? With the father retired as chief clerk of Indian affairs, had Daniel, the son, taken over his father's position? Was the man still an ally, or had the entire venture been no more than lip service to a problem—something set into motion merely as a cover, the Harrimans knowing all along exactly what the nature of the new treaty would be? Or had someone else been put into Lester's position, over Daniel's head? In any case, a copy of the letter would have to go to Harriman, who remained, after all, the one relatively certain source of sympathetic support. O'Bragh trusted the elder Harriman, and that had to mean something. And perhaps there was still time to effect adjustments in the treaty, some way of preventing yet another Trail of Tears. Or was that, ultimately, the Great Plan? All the Indian peoples driven into a single Indian territory, the prison of the Oklahoma Territory, and that safe only until such time as the pressure of White expansion dictated genocide?

And Cramdon? Why the unprovoked attack on the People of the Valley? If the man were construed as *pure evil*, Soldier Wolf supposed, then such an attack might be understood. Men shot wolves and hawks and buffalo at times for no other reasons than those of whim, of malice—and so perhaps no further explanation was necessary. And if Cramdon and his men had made a venture to the south, to one of the mining camps maybe, then it was conceivable that no further motive existed. But what if there were gold here at the headwaters of the Canadian? That might explain it. The grasslands were rich, to be sure, but of little use to one whose ranch lay across the mountains, on the Cache La Poudre.

Or, indeed, was the motive no more than that of simple hatred?

Soldier Wolf said nothing. He rose, stepped through the lodge opening, and walked out toward the central firepit, where O'Bragh, White Frog, and Morning Star Fox were standing.

"Do you wish to ride on a warpath against these men?" White Frog asked again. "My warriors are ready."

"Wagh!" O'Bragh snorted. "That's what we come for, ain't it, Tsaragi?"

But the old chief shook his head, his expression one, Jerry thought, of nearly timeless resignation.

"If these men who have attacked my village are slain, the White Chief will send his soldiers against us. It will make no difference to the White Chief that my people have been murdered. Our medicine tells us to remain on the path of peace—that is the way we have lived for many winters, and that is how we must continue."

"It was different in the old days, Morning Star Fox," White Frog said. "You are a wise man, and your ways have helped your people. Even so, the Utes have sometimes forced you to pay them a tribute, even though these lands belong to your village. And I remember that once the Utes killed many of your people, and Leg in the Water learned of this and made a revenge-taking against the Utes. Afterward all of our people rejoiced, and the Utes did not enter back into the mountains for a long time."

"That is true," Morning Star Fox said. "I have grown old, White Frog, and my mind is no longer clear. I will die soon and go to the Spirit World, and then one of the younger men must take my place. My medicine has been that of vision and prophecy and peace, but now I can no longer see the future days. Perhaps it must be now as you suggest. Yet I fear that the bluecoats will come, and many more of my people will die."

"If we capture Cramdon, then I will turn him over to the authorities in Denver," Soldier Wolf said. "The Whiteman's justice will take care of him."

"I do not trust your Whiteman's justice," White Frog said. "I have not seen any justice. If the Whiteman kills the Cheyenne, he is not punished. Only when the Cheyenne kills a Whiteman is there any justice, for then the miners attack one of our villages."

"She-it, Tsaragi!" O'Bragh said. "This child didn't come all the way back out here to *arrest* that son of a bitch! What ye thinkin' of?"

Soldier Wolf stared at Bully's firelit face and toyed with the idea that O'Bragh had told the truth when he'd claimed that Harriman had forced him to get up out of his grave. Perhaps

O'Bragh himself was only an illusion, a figment of his own imagination. . . .

"White Frog," Soldier Wolf said, "we will ride in the morning."

The Cheyenne chief grasped Jerry's hand with both his own and said, "It is good. There is no other way to end the time of mourning for the People of the Valley."

When the fires had died down, and the people were sleeping, Soldier Wolf left his robes and walked out under the waxing April moon, the moon of the new grass, that hung low above the westward range and suffused the meadows and the spruce thickets with a soft glow. He passed around the small herd of horses, the animals unguarded this night, and entered the darkness of the forest, climbing to the big crooked pine that Sara had pointed out.

He reached the tree, which grew from an open shelf, grass-covered, perhaps two hundred feet above the level of the encampment, but the place was empty—the jet-haired white girl in Cheyenne clothing was not there. Soldier Wolf, truthfully, had not expected that she would be. He walked about the area, noted that the grass indeed showed signs of human presence, matted in places but regenerating.

Four days, he thought, perhaps five since she's been here. Before the attack on the village. . . .

He sat down on the mound of bark fragments that surrounded the bole of the big tree and stared off into the night, the countless stars strewn across the blackness of sky, the yellow-red half-moon suspended above the dark, recumbent forms of the mountainous sprawl to the west, the white crowns of the Park Range glinting white and clearly visible above the lower ridges.

He did not hear but could feel the close passage of wings—a great horned owl—it held in the air for just a moment, revealed in the moonlight, ghostlike, and then was gone. And far away, perhaps two or three ridges removed, a wolf, the true dog of the mountains, quavered the stillness with its protracted, lonely-sounding wail.

He waited for some time, perhaps an hour, until the moon had touched the rim of the far mountains, and was about to return to the encampment, when he heard a faint sound in the brush below, the sound of chokecherry, perhaps, rubbing against deerskin clothing.

Soldier Wolf rose, stepped quickly behind the pine, and waited.

In a moment the girl stepped out into the clearing, was illumined in the diminishing moonlight, the Cheyenne quillwork clearly visible on her dress, her dark hair glinting almost silver.

Sara approached the tree slowly now, and Jerry stepped out from behind it.

Startled at first, she let out a surprised burst of laughter that sounded, to Soldier Wolf's ears, like a fusillade of small bells in the night.

"Sara!" he said.

And then she was in his arms, the small, lithe body, and he placed his hands beneath her arms and lifted her above his head.

"What are you doing?" she protested. "Put me down!"

Soldier Wolf laughed, a laughter that came from deep inside him, and he set her back on her feet.

Then their mouths were nailed together hungrily, the girl almost in a frenzy now, their tongues interpenetrating, her hands clinging to the fringed shoulders of his coat.

She pulled away and laughed again. They were both laughing, all the tension of their earlier meeting in the village now gone.

"Damn you!" she said. "I thought you'd left me. I thought you were dead! I'm not sure what I thought. . . ."

"Bully and I got kidnapped . . ." Jerry managed, unable to think of anything else. "God how I've missed you, Sara—it's all so crazy. Have you said anything to your mother and father yet?"

"Yes, yes, but . . . he wants to send me back to St. Louis, he says I'd never be happy with you, he says I'd be better off, that you'll drift away, leave me . . . and then I was afraid something had happened to you, Jerry! Do you truly love me? I want to lie down with you, I want you to take me to the willows, I want to be your woman. . . ."

"I love you, little Sara, my Sara. . . ."

And they locked in another kiss, as his hands, with a will of their own, sought for her body, touched at her breasts.

"We'll be happy together, won't we?" Sara pleaded. "I'll do anything you want, I know what to do even if I've never done it, the Indian women have told me. They laugh at me because I'm seventeen and have never had a man, but I'll have you. . . ."

They pressed their pelvic areas tight together, held on to each other desperately.

"Sara, Sara," Jerry whispered, "what if your mother and father are right? I have no future, what could I give you?"

"I want to be with you, no matter what. We could go anywhere. We could stay here—you have a job with the agency, just like my father."

Her voice was urgent, pleading.

"Nothing is permanent, Sara. My commission lasts until the end of the year, that's all. They might renew, they might not. And there may not be a government to worry about by then—Colorado could end up as Southern territory. Civil war may be under way right now, for all we know."

"It doesn't make any difference, damn you, Jerry! Can't you see that? I'm not a child, I don't need to be taken care of—I'm a grown woman. We can work together. We could mine gold or live with the Indians or go to Oregon and homestead. I'm not afraid of anything!"

Soldier Wolf held her small face between his hands and grinned at Sara's outburst.

"Guess you're not, at that. Maybe it's just me."

"And you don't want me because you're Indian and I'm not," Sara said, pulling suddenly away from him.

"No!" he said, "no! I just want you to be happy, I want—"

"Well, I want you," she said, and turned and ran away from him, down the hill, into the dark spruce woods.

The half-moon had disappeared behind the mountains to the west.

Chapter Nine

Lincoln's inaugural speech had been conciliatory but also firm:

"A husband and wife may be divorced, but the different parts of our country cannot. . . . Intercourse, either amicable or hostile, must continue between them. . . . I am loath to close. We are not enemies, but friends. We must not be enemies. Though passion may have strained, it must not break, our bonds of affection. The mystic chords of memory, stretching from every battlefield and patriot grave to every living heart . . . will yet swell the chorus of the Union when again touched, as surely they will be, by the better angels of our nature."

But the Confederates seized most United States property in the Deep South, and Lincoln did not attempt to reclaim this property. Only Fort Sumter, located on an island in Charleston harbor, and Fort Pickins, in Florida, remained in federal hands. Lincoln sent a naval expedition to supply the Sumter garrison, and the Confederates opened fire on the fort early the morning of April 12, before the ships had arrived. A day and a half later Major Anderson and his men surrendered, and the Civil War had begun.

The war. Highly important news from Washington. Offensive war measures of the administration. The President's exposition of his policy toward the Confederate States. A war proclamation. Seventy-five thousand men ordered out. Thirteen thousand required from New York. Call for an extra session of Congress. Preparations for the defense of the national capital. The great free states arming for the conflict. Thirty thousand troops to be tendered from New York. Strong Union demonstrations in Baltimore. The battle at Charleston. Evacuation of Fort Sumter. Major Anderson to sail for New York. Important news from Montgomery. . . .

The news would spread, would eventually reach every corner of the continent-spanning nation. But for Jerry Soldier Wolf, the news—if it had reached him—would have made little difference, for one thing only was on his mind. And the long journey from Harriman's office to Cramdon's ranch was resumed.

White Frog, O'Bragh, Soldier Wolf, and the band of Cheyenne warriors crossed directly through the Medicine Bow Mountains, the pass still deep with snow but Cramdon's trail clear before them. With the way already broken, they progressed across the range, the mountain weather, always unpredictable, holding good.

They found two dead horses and one hastily excavated grave along the way, and O'Bragh said, "Guess the preacher-man done killed him two men after all, Jerry me boy."

On the third day the warriors reached the Cache La Poudre and entered into the broad meadows. With Cramdon's ranch no more than a few miles ahead, White Frog sent out his wolves, while the main band worked its way up a thickly forested side canyon and made camp. The men ate a cold evening meal and pitched into their robes without benefit of campfires, even by cover of darkness.

"Smoke drifts," O'Bragh remarked, "an' sometimes ye can smell trouble ten, fifteen miles off. Cold drops down off the mountains an' runs through the valleys just like a river of air."

"Figger ye're talkin' to a green'un, do ye?" Soldier Wolf mocked. "Hell fire, man, this half-breed Injun was born knowin' that."

"Just talkin' is all," O'Bragh said, raising one eyebrow and squinting. "Ye goin' to get ye another scalp tomorrow, Tsaragi?"

"What color's Cramdon's hair?"

"Ain't never met the man. Figgers it'd be yeller, though, don't it?"

"It is red," White Frog said. "That is what Raven calls him—Red Face with Red Hair."

"Wal, now, we'll just take 'is red ha'r an' give 'im a little red hat instead." O'Bragh chuckled. "Tell ye what. I'll kill 'im. Nothin' they can do with me, old as I am. Wagh! I been dead three years already. No way ye can hang a dead man, is they?"

White Frog slipped away, drifted through the encampment, spoke with his warriors, and then disappeared into the firs and pines.

"Goin' to consult 'is medicine," O'Bragh said. "Might not be a bad thing to do, when ye take all into account. Unless we take 'em by complete surprise, they goin' to have buildings to shoot out of, an' we're goin' to be in the open."

"Surprise sounds like the best method to me. Cramdon's got no idea we're following behind him, and there'd be no reason to fear Morning Star Fox, and he knows it well enough. Any guards he's got posted are no doubt downriver, watching the trail to civilization."

"Ye be likin' some medicine of a different sort, Tsaragi?" O'Bragh asked, producing a half-full bottle of whiskey.

"Where'd you get that, Farnsworth?"

"Name's Bully. Just say I got 'er, that's all. Old niggers like me got to keep a few secrets. Never can tell when a child's likely to need a glug of Rocky Mountain Tonic."

He tilted back the bottle, snorted, rubbed at his bearded mouth.

Soldier Wolf took the bottle, took a mouthful, and swallowed hard.

"By God, Bully, that's good stuff, it's actually good!"

"Damn right it is. Don't think I'd be drinkin' any of that cheap swill, do ye?"

"I suppose not. So where'd you get it, O'Bragh?"

"Guess it wouldn't hurt none for me to tell ye."

"Hell no, wouldn't hurt a thing."

"This'n is all I got, ye understand?"

"Where'd you get it, Bully?"

"God damn me, I found 'er alongside the trail—up by the pass it were."

"The truth, the truth."

"Beckwith give it to me. That's where she come from."

"Beckwourth?"

"Straight from Vasquez' store, as I gather. Jimmy Beckwith's workin' for 'im, Vasquez' kid's place in Denver. Now Looey, the old man, I trapped with 'im four, five years. Later on I spent a winter with 'im up to Bridger's Fort on the other side of South Pass. Good days, I tell ye."

"Beckwourth's being a store clerk? Come on, Bully, don't pull this greenhorn's leg."

"It's the truth, Jerry me boy. Old Medicine Calf told me so hisself. The years keep movin' on, an' each of us ends up playin' different parts in the big play. Like me, for instance. Tsaragi, to tell the truth, I was happy asleep in my grave when that damned Harriman come scratchin' an' yellin'."

"O'Bragh, you're so full of buffalo shit you could fertilize the entire state of North Carolina."

"Naw," O'Bragh said, "North Carolina don't need no fertilizin'. Ain't that where ye be from?"

Jerry shook his head, and Bully rolled over in his robes and began to snore immediately.

Soldier Wolf turned about, and White Frog was standing there.

"One of the scouts has returned, my friend. The ranch of Red Face with Red Hair is beyond the third bend of the river. There are four buildings—a house, a long house for the men, a stock barn, and a shed. The other men live in lodges of elkskin, like those of my people. And there are no guards. Do we attack with the first light?"

"How many men does the scout think he has?"

"Maybe twenty, maybe thirty. We have more."

"Will the warriors do as I tell them, White Frog? I would like to accomplish this purpose without anyone getting hurt."

"Is that possible in war, my friend?"

"I've got an idea. Can you keep the braves under control for as long as necessary?"

"I think so, Soldier Wolf."

White Frog drew the warriors into a group and then dispersed them along the rim above the Cramdon ranch. From here they watched as the sun rose, deep red through low trailings of cloud to the east. Smoke began to filter upward from the main building and the bunkhouse, and a few of the men, yawning, walked out to the horse trough to splash water on their faces.

At this point Soldier Wolf, astride Messiah, rode slowly down and brought his horse to a stand a few yards from the bunkhouse. The men at the watering trough looked up, glanced at each other.

"What you looking for, stranger?" one called out. "The boss ain't taking on no new men just now. Come back next month if you're still looking for work. . . ."

"I'm looking for Ed Cramdon!" Soldier Wolf shouted. "I'm a government agent, and I've got to talk to Cramdon—alone!"

"That a fact?" the man said, toweling off his face and hands and nodding to his companion, who walked away briskly toward the main house. "You Union or Confederate, mister?"

A number of men had now issued from the bunkhouse and the

several tipis, and, as Soldier Wolf noted, two or three were wearing pistols, one was carrying a carbine.

A large heavyset red-haired man appeared at the doorway of the main house. He was rolling up the sleeves of his faded blue shirt.

"What's goin' on over there?" he yelled. "We got a visitor? Bring 'im on in—see what's on his mind."

Soldier Wolf urged Messiah a few more paces forward, drew the animal to a stand once again.

"Edward Cramdon?" he called out.

"That's my name. What's yours, fella?"

"Jerry Soldier Wolf—I'm a government agent. We've got business, Cramdon."

"Not if I don't think so, we ain't. What's on your mind?"

"You're wanted in Denver—to testify in a matter before the BIA inquiry board."

"I'm wanted for what? Get the hell out of here before I have my men fill you with holes. You crazy or somethin'? Get your ass out of here. You come back, and you're a dead man. You tell your friends in Denver that Cramdon says *fuck all of you!*"

"Cramdon, I'm not leaving unless you come with me. Get your coat on and fetch your horse—we've got a long ride ahead of us."

"Well, you dumb son of a bitch! You keep your brains in that funny hat, or did a white bear whop you on the head?"

"I'm waiting, Cramdon! Have one of your men get your horse. I'm not a patient man—get your ass moving!"

Cramdon stared at Soldier Wolf as if not believing, shook his head, and then burst into a fit of laughter. He held his sides, roared.

"That thing on 'is head's to hold in his shit for brains. Jackson! Get around behind him, keep him covered. A crazy man might do anything. Let's find out if he's a government agent. . . ."

Flames had begun to shoot up from the cedar shakes on the roof of the main house, but only Soldier Wolf was aware of what was happening. The bonfire was burning quite nicely, taking the side of the house and the roof like tinder.

"Your house is on fire, you dumb bastard!" Soldier Wolf shouted. "You going to watch it burn, or you going to do something about it?"

The men turned, saw the flames.

"Water!" Cramdon shouted.

"Get the buckets!" someone else yelled.

"Jesus Christ, she's going to burn to the ground!"

Cramdon, forgetting momentarily about the man on the black horse, stood as if spellbound. At this point Soldier Wolf clapped his heels to Messiah's sides, and the big stallion bolted forward, directly at Cramdon—who turned quickly when he heard the horse's hooves, went for his pistol.

But the horse was on top of him, swerved, and Soldier Wolf sent a well-aimed kick to the man's chest, sent him sprawling backward. Soldier Wolf drew Messiah about sharply and leaped onto the fallen Cramdon, who was gasping for breath. A forearm to the side of the face stunned the former agent even more, and within a moment Soldier Wolf had his arm around Cramdon's neck from behind and his Marston revolver to the side of the man's head.

"Like I said, Mr. Cramdon, you're coming in with me. . . ."

Now the fire was forgotten. The water buckets were dropped, bounced on the ground, and the men, a number now with gun in hand, circled their boss and his captor.

"Tell them to back off or I'll blow your brains out!" Soldier Wolf hissed.

"Back up, boys," Cramdon managed. "Give the crazy son of a bitch space. I'll go with him—you follow. No way he's goin' to make it to Denver."

"Gentlemen!" Soldier Wolf called out. "Look up on the rim—look over there!"

A few heads turned.

"I've got a hundred Cheyenne warriors up there, all with carbines. Anyone follows me, he's a dead man. Cramdon's going in for trial—he's under arrest for theft from the United States government. Anyone interferes, he's an accessory to the crime!"

But as Soldier Wolf attempted to wrestle Ed Cramdon about, gunfire erupted from the rear window of the bunkhouse, and immediately the Cheyenne warriors on the rim above also opened fire. Everywhere men were diving for cover, and pistols began to go off.

Cramdon, despite the gun at his temple, lunged sideways, broke loose from Soldier Wolf's grip, and scrambled for the horse trough. Jerry stumbled to one knee, saw his plan dissolve, and leaped onto Messiah, clapped his heels to the stallion's sides, clung low to the horse's back, and raced toward cover.

The impact of the bullet nearly threw him from his mount, but he clung, held on, waited for the pain to come, thanked God when it did.

Gunfire and battle whoops from the rim above.

Upstream along the stock trail, through a group of straggling longhorns, their eyes wide at the sudden disturbance, then up through the brush, the powerful movements of the big black horse, the great muscles straining beneath him, Messiah lunging, lunging.

And then he was on the rim.

He was bleeding.

He drew the horse to a halt, breathed deeply, tore open his leathers, stared down at the ragged wound in his side.

O'Bragh came running.

"Ye goin' to make 'er, coon? Let the old man take a look at 'er. . . ."

Soldier Wolf took a deep breath, held the wound tight with his fingers.

"Let me look at 'er, damn ye!" O'Bragh commanded.

Jerry removed his hand—his hand dripping blood.

"She hurt, son?"

"She hurts, goddammit."

"Flesh wound, nothin' more. Just grooved ye a bit. Ain't nothin' serious a-tall, just messy."

O'Bragh reached down, scraped through the duff, and brought up a handful of coarse dirt—held it tight to the wound.

"Bully, dammit, you trying to kill me?"

"Stops the bleedin', coon. Ain't nothin' to worry about. . . ."

"I know, I know. *Meat don't spile in the mountains.* Who the hell started the shooting?"

"Cramdon's niggers it was. Now the firefight's on. Grab your carbine, me lad. Looks like we got some target practice ahead of us."

The battle went on for several hours, with bursts of rifle and pistol fire alternating with periods of silence. Cramdon's main building had now burned to the ground, was no more than a smoldering gray heap of charred logs.

White Frog cleansed Soldier Wolf's wound, applied a poultice of sage and alum root mixed with tobacco, then cinched Jerry about the middle with a wide band of deerhide.

"My friend's plan nearly worked," he said, "but we should

know that not all things happen in the right way. What will we do now? They cannot get away, and yet we cannot get them without losing too many warriors."

"They's always a way of smokin' out rats," O'Bragh said and turned and walked away, down along the rim. Then he was over the edge and out of sight.

"What in hell's the old fool up to?" Soldier Wolf groaned.

"We do not need to worry about the Irish Vulture," White Frog said. "I think he is going to light another fire, just like the first one."

Within a few minutes O'Bragh was back, having climbed up through a fracture in the stone shelf. And smoke was rising from the rear of the bunkhouse.

The Cheyenne warriors cheered, took aim, waited for the inevitable exodus from the flaming building. When it came, the rifles crackled as Cramdon's men came out, coughing, gasping for air, firing wildly in the direction of their hidden antagonists.

The warriors poured down over the rim, and gunfire rang through the air, powder smoke drifting up everywhere—much greater smoke, black smoke, spiraling up from the cone of flames that was rapidly devouring the bunkhouse.

A group of Whitemen made it to the horses, escaped down the canyon amidst a hail of rifle fire.

Hand-to-hand fighting.

And then it was over. Nearly twenty Whitemen lay dead, the bodies scattered at seeming random about the fiery remains of the bunkhouse. Four Cheyennes were also dead, and the warriors, in solemn rage, proceeded to scalp their dead enemies. Then they took up the bodies of their own dead and quietly awaited direction from White Frog.

Cramdon was not among the corpses.

"Wal, the fat's in the fire now, me boy. Don't know what's likely to come of what we done," O'Bragh said, "but likely it ain't goin' to be good."

"We have made our revenge," White Frog said softly, "but now we must take our dead back to our village. Red Face with Red Hair has escaped. What will you do now, my friend?"

"Well, the game's not over yet, but we've evened the odds a bit."

"I do not understand your meaning."

"What Soldier Wolf's sayin' is, Cramdon's not goin' to the law in Denver, not if he thinks they're after 'im. But he ain't likely to be givin' up, either. He'll try to hire on some more men, an' then he's goin' to come lookin' for the big fella with the turban."

They fought their way through a late snowstorm mixed with freezing rain across the back of the Medicine Bow Range, Soldier Wolf, O'Bragh, and the dozen young men from Morning Star Fox's band, and made it to the drainage of the Canadian, rode on to the high meadows where the People of the Valley made their home. Soldier Wolf's wound was healing—Bully O'Bragh had sewn the wound together with fine-gauge wire from the spool that he carried with him for the "stitchin' of man nor beastie." Riding was particularly painful at times, but Soldier Wolf gritted his teeth, locked his jaw. O'Bragh laughed and spoke of the inevitable "nicks an' scrapes that come of livin' in the High Shinin'."

The last few miles they rode through heavy snowfall, but at midday, just before they reached the village, the clouds split open, and the world was bathed in rich sunlight. The overcast drifted away quickly, and by the time the warriors entered the village, the sky was blue, and trees, meadows, lodges, everything glittered white in the warm sunlight.

"She's a good omen!" O'Bragh laughed. "We've whupped our enemies, an' Old Man Coyote's give us a spring snowfall an' then sunlight. These mountains is the damnedest place in the world, I'm thinkin'. I've heard coons say the snow don't never melt up here, it just wears out from blowin' around. An' they's only three months—July, August, an' Winter. But this child wouldn't trade 'er for anywhere else on earth."

The people came out to meet them, mothers and fathers relieved to find their sons still alive after the warpath.

And Sara.

She bolted past her parents and old Morning Star Fox, ran excitedly through the few inches of fresh-fallen snow that shone in the sunlight, shouted, "Jerry! Jerry!" and then tripped and pitched face forward into the whiteness. She arose, didn't even bother to brush the snow off her clothing or out of her hair, and continued running.

"Think she's glad to see someone," O'Bragh said.

Soldier Wolf grinned, pulled Messiah to a halt, and slipped carefully to the snow-covered ground.

Sara threw herself into his arms, and he grunted, said, "Easy, girl. Old Cherokee managed to get shot, not serious, easy. . . ."

"Shot?" Sara asked, her gray eyes widening in immediate concern. "Jerry, are you all right? What happened?"

"He ain't permanent damaged." O'Bragh laughed. "Ye just got to be gentle with 'im for a time, Sary. Don't want to give Tsaragi no re-lapses."

"What happened?" she demanded.

"Pistol wound in the side. Bully sewed me up with fish wire, and that was worse than the gunshot."

"Do you still love me?" she asked.

During the interval that Soldier Wolf and O'Bragh had been gone, Marsh Flower had been busy, and now a large new lodge had been constructed near the perimeter of the circle of tipis.

"There is room for both my husband and his friend, as well as for anyone else who might choose to live with us," the old woman said, her worn teeth showing in a self-satisfied grin and her deep brown eyes gleaming with mischief. "Does Irish Vulture like his new home?"

"Flower," O'Bragh said, "it's the finest lodge the Big Vulture has ever lived in. Woman, ye're a wonder. But how . . . ?"

"The other women have helped me, and Morning Star Fox has given us the skins for me to sew together."

"Looks like a good place to plant us some seeds," O'Bragh said, one eyebrow raised.

Marsh Flower laughed, a girlish giggle, it seemed to Soldier Wolf.

"Perhaps I have not lived too many winters yet," she said. "I must still go to the menstrual lodge each month, so it may be that my earth will still allow my husband's seeds to grow within my body."

O'Bragh embraced her, and the two of them entered the new lodge, the husband to give it his official approval.

"Got to hurry, gal"—Soldier Wolf heard O'Bragh's voice from within—"if we ever want to have us some grandchildren. . . ."

Then Marsh Flower's laughter. Then whispered sounds. And then silence.

Soldier Wolf shook his head, whistled, and turned away.

The year drifted toward summer, and the last of the snow vanished from the ridges near the encampment of the People of the

Valley. Soldier Wolf took his place in the new lodge, and the days went swiftly, his time spent at hunting—often with Sara as his companion.

The issue of their future life together, the possibility of it, remained to be solved. Frank and Elizabeth Goth were cautious and spent a good deal of time in attempting to convince Sara of the folly of making such a choice—and, at every opportunity, Frank would accompany Soldier Wolf and Sara on their ventures or see to it that one or two of the young warriors went with them. For their own part, Jerry and Sara had agreed between themselves not to enter into lovemaking for a time and thereby to respect her parents' wishes so far as they were able.

Finally, on an evening when Jerry was eating dinner in the Goth lodge, Frank said, "Soldier Wolf, it is time that we talked, all of us. Sara has told us that she loves you and that she wishes to be your wife."

The girl lowered her head and did not look up.

"Is this what you wish also, Jerry?" Elizabeth asked.

Soldier Wolf glanced at Sara, and then said, attempting to keep his voice quite calm, "Yes, yes, that is what I wish also. That is what I wish, if Sara will have me."

"Sara?" the mother asked.

"You know what I wish," Sara answered.

"All right, then," Goth said. "Elizabeth and I have discussed the matter at great length. Jerry, you know how highly I think of you, but you must understand that we have to consider Sara's future. And you know that it has been our deep hope that we would be able to send Sara to a college, a divinity college for young women. That will require two years, at least. Are you willing to wait for her?"

"I will wait as long as necessary," Soldier Wolf said, speaking carefully, choosing his words.

"Sara?"

The dark-haired girl looked up, searched Soldier Wolf's face, then turned to her parents and whispered, "Yes." But there was disappointment written evidently upon her features.

"There's yet another matter to be resolved," Goth said. "You know what kind of a man I am, Jerry. And you know that my faith is not that of a normal Christian—I've lived among these people for too long to be spouting the usual dogmatic platitudes. Still, I am a Christian, just as Elizabeth is—and Sara as well.

We know that the Great Spirit, the Manitou, and God the Father are one and the same, and we see in the belief in Saynday the rudiments of a belief in the Christ, primitive and based on intuition, but nonetheless real. The People of the Valley recognize this as well, and when I speak to them of Jesus as the Son of the Divine, they understand my meaning."

"You have seen how interested they are when Frank speaks to them about the great fire," Elizabeth said.

Soldier Wolf nodded.

"But what of you, Jerry?" Goth continued. "You know my thoughts, and yet we do not truly know yours. Would you call yourself a religious man? You are capable of great violence, we have seen that—and yet I, too, have slain my fellowman. Perhaps it is living with these people, in their world, that makes us what we are. We were attacked ruthlessly, and we had little choice but to fight back—our survival depended upon it. Such were the ways of the people in the days of the Old Testament, before the coming of the Savior. And these children, the Cheyennes, are much like Old Testament people, I believe. Do you believe in the Almighty, Jerry?"

"Yes, Frank, I do indeed."

"Good, good. But what of the Christ? You were raised within a different tradition, and yet your people are civilized, not like the Cheyennes. Did you have a Christian upbringing?"

"I went to the church. We all did."

"And yet I do not believe you to be a Christian, not even of the abnormal variety, as we are. Are you willing to become a Christian in order to have our daughter's hand in marriage?"

Jerry and Sara, startled, stared at each other. Soldier Wolf could see doubt in the girl's eyes and wondered if that same doubt were evident in his own.

"Yes," he said finally.

Frank Goth nodded. "Then it's settled," he said. "Elizabeth and I are prepared to grant our permission."

Two years! Soldier Wolf's mind was spinning when he left the Goth lodge—his thoughts incoherent, confused. It was not just a matter of the time he had agreed to wait, an interval specified, he realized, not only to see to it that Sara was sent to an institution of proper indoctrination and so to be given time to come to her senses, but time also to see if he, Jerry Soldier Wolf, would be able to readjust to the "civilized" life of the settlements, to find a steady job, to settle down.

He thought: This Injun's just starting·to find out who he is, and now they want him to forget about all that and turn into a storekeeper—like Jim Beckwourth. Jesus Christ in heaven, if there ever was anyone named Jesus Christ, and I've got my doubts about that, too.

The vision of Beckwourth drifted through his mind. The living legend who had turned storekeeper! The demigod he had read about a year before he'd ever walked into Harriman's outer office and strong-armed the goddamned clerk, what was his name? And now Beckwourth was an old man, trusted by the Cheyennes and listened to, apparently, by the Whites! Still, there was wildness in the old man's eyes, just as there was in Smith's and in O'Bragh's. Soldier Wolf recalled his first image of Medicine Calf, the big slope-shouldered man astride his pony, slipping through the Cheyenne guards and calling down to the encampment, mysterious at the edges of the firelight.

Don't know why he's working in a store, he thought. But he hasn't been tamed, he hasn't been civilized. No, dammit, and I'm not going to be, either. I was a child of civilization's *institutions* long enough, precocious child to college student to sergeant in the U.S. Army. I've had enough of that! California's out there, and Oregon, yet that's civilization too, maybe. But endless mountains and deserts between here and there, and no Civil War or Constitution of the United States is ever going to change that, not completely. Even the Smokies are still wild, even after two centuries and more of the Whitemen living there. The mountains—*only the mountains live forever*. Sara, I love you—but the cost's too high. A man can't stop being a man, not when he's just learned how, not even for the woman he loves. I learned to love you, and I can forget it the same way. There's one of my own kind out there somewhere, a woman who won't try to change me, won't try to put me behind any damned store counter!

But it wasn't Sara at all, it was her parents.

The goddamned hypocrites! he thought. She doesn't want that any more than I do, not Sara, not if anything she's told me is true. . . .

He strode to O'Bragh's lodge, entered, and said, "Bully, I'm leaving for a couple of days. Have to get my head straightened out."

"Why do you wish to leave?" Marsh Flower asked, glancing at her husband.

"Goths layin' the law down to ye, were they?" O'Bragh asked.

"Planning my life for me," Jerry answered. "I need to be away, think things through."

"A medicine vision, that's what ye need, Jerry me boy. Guess it's time ye went to palaver with the Great Coyote."

"Maybe that's it." Soldier Wolf nodded. "Maybe that's it exactly. . . ."

He did not wait for morning. Within a few minutes he had his saddlebags packed, the Starr carbine in its sheath, and he was on his way out of the village. A full moon hung nearly overhead, and the lush meadows glistered before him as he rode, moving upslope now, among the shadows of spruce and pine, picking his way along a tumbling stream that fed from the high snowfields which still lay heavy, as he knew, on the backs of the mountains that formed the very spine of the continent.

Only the cascading water, that sound and no other.

The canyon walls narrowed, and the brush along the stream became too thick for Messiah to work his way through. Soldier Wolf urged the stallion upslope once more, and he reached the crest of a narrow lateral ridge where the undergrowth was not so thick, the trees spaced out, the ground continuing to angle inevitably upward.

An owl called from close by, and the black stallion stopped, whinnied, demanded to be reassured. Then they were moving forward once more, and by the time the orb of the moon had begun to drop westward, they were high above the encampment of the People of the Valley, and miles away. Eastward and southward the great peaks rose, one after another, their white-crowned summits visible and gleaming with moonlight.

The mountain benched off, and Soldier Wolf entered into a meadow through which a small stream meandered, serpentine through the marshy grasses to a low spot in the dark-colored rim of stone and then splashed down the mountainside through a matting of red willow and aspen. Jerry dismounted at the upper end of the meadow, where one of a number of rivulets splashed down over the rocks, removed the saddle and saddlebags from Messiah's back, and turned the big black loose to his own devices.

Jerry gathered together a few handfuls of dry spruce twigs and found a couple of chunks of weathered pitchpine, smashed the larger of the two over a jut of stone, picked up the pieces—the air suddenly rich with the odor of freshly exposed resin. He arranged some loose stones, started a fire—not even certain at the moment why he was doing so.

Hungry, he thought. I'm hungry again. Guess dinner didn't go down so well. . . .

He cut off a thin willow branch, sharpened one end, and used it to spit a large chunk of venison he'd brought along. He put the meat over the fire and sat down, listened to the sounds of falling water, heard the soft wind through the trees, smelled the burning grease that dripped into the fire.

Ate.

Slept.

And dreamed.

Watching myself. I am a boy again, I am climbing up through the mountains. Birds are flying all about me, thousands of birds, so many that I can barely see where I'm going. Their cries are in my ears, but I cannot tell what they are saying.

They are attempting to communicate with me. . . .

Gone now, all of them. And I hear a wolf howling, a terrible, terrible, lonely cry, as if someone has killed his mate.

I am afraid of him. I think of the powerful jaws, I remember a story of wolves coming to steal children, I remember my father telling me that the stories are not true, that wolves do not attack people, and yet I am still afraid.

Silence now.

But someone is watching me. I turn about. A wolf is sitting on the ground a few feet away, the big gray head tilted to one side.

The wolf is wearing a blue uniform, a soldier's uniform.

"I am Soldier Wolf," the animal says. "You are not Soldier Wolf, I am. And I am not afraid of anything, but you are afraid. What are you afraid of?"

I attempt to speak, but I am unable.

"I am not going to be a slave to anyone, Jerry, not ever. The Whitemen are everywhere, and they will hunt me and my people, and after a time there will be almost none of us left. But we will never be their slaves, we will never live as they wish us to live. It is not our way. Always there will be mountains like these, always there will be places for us to go, even though we are very few. Come close to me now and take these blue rags off my back. I do not

know how they got here, but I do not wish to wear them any longer. If you will do this for me, I will let you have your name once again. . . ."

Then the wolf is gone. I have not actually touched him. I have only reached toward him.

Beyond me there are mountain ranges that go on forever. Perhaps I can even see the ocean, far to the west. . . .

Light.

Brilliant light, slanting in through the copse of spruces.

Soldier Wolf blinked his eyes, turned over in his robes—the robes too warm, the sunlight falling full upon him.

Great God, he thought, rubbing at his eyes. The sun's halfway up the sky. . . .

Chapter Ten

In the South, the call to arms caused so many men to volunteer during the early months that perhaps two hundred thousand had to be sent home for lack of training equipment and facilities. When summer came, the Confederacy had in excess of a hundred thousand men under arms, men of every type, and morale was high. Militia units took on names such as "Tallipoosa Thrashers," "Cherokee Lincoln Killers," and "Chickasaw Desperadoes." There were elite units such as the "Richmond Howitzers" and the "Louisiana Zouaves," the latter in exotic uniforms with broad sashes and baggy red pants.

Officers for North and South were graduates of West Point, formerly gentlemen classmates—but now the North stayed North and the South went South.

And all were caught up in a strange, almost carnival atmosphere, almost as though in preparation for some athletic competition.

"Forward to Richmond!"

"On to Washington!"

Smiling and self-righteous, the nation prepared to enter into what was to be an unbelievably bloody internecine conflict.

High on the back of the continent, a mountain goat stood placidly cropping tufts of grass that had begun to burst near the edges of a snowfield, fringes of lichen, twigs of leafless heather.

Eternal fields of snow and small glaciers splashed over the Front Range, the Medicine Bows, the Snowy Range, the Ramparts.

A series of uplifts twenty-five million years ago and continued erosion, shearing the mountains in many places to their granite cores, revealing stumps of old sedimentary strata.

And the mountain goat stared down, gazed through slotted amber eyes, ancient, mysterious. Below it the miners dug away at bank and streambed, and the Cheyennes and Arapahos searched for the great herds of buffalo that no longer existed.

* * *

Past noon Messiah began to snort and prance about. Soldier Wolf reached for his carbine, checked the load, and strode away along the rim of the little basin, kept under the cover of forest.

A rider on a sorrel mare was coming up the long slope.

"Can't be . . ." Soldier Wolf said aloud.

But it was—it was Sara Goth.

"Who goes there?" Jerry called out.

"Jerry? Is that you? Where are you?"

She urged Virgin forward and emerged onto the bench. Soldier Wolf, hurrying down from the rim, caught her in his arms as she leaped from her horse.

"What?" he managed as her lips sought his.

"I came to find you after my parents went to sleep—you weren't at the pine tree. I woke up Bully and Marsh Flower, and they told me where you'd gone. I came after you and got lost—but Bully found me the next morning—then we found your trail, and we saw the campfire smoke an hour ago. . . ."

"Where's Bully?"

"He went back—said we'd want to be alone."

"That meddling old bastard!"

"Don't you want me to be here, Jerry? I'll go back if you don't want me."

"I love you, little Sara. This child loves you for sure. Your parents don't know where you are?"

"Bully will tell them when he gets to the village. . . ."

"But—"

"Jerry, Jerry, I don't want to go away to any school. I want to stay with you, I don't care what they say. I'm old enough to make up my own mind—Indian girls lots younger than I am are already married, the older women laugh at me and tease me. I want to be a woman now. . . ."

They walked together around the edges of the marshy meadow, Virgin trailing behind them, and Jerry unsaddled the mare and turned her loose to graze with Messiah. Then he and Sara sat together next to the smoldering remnant of the campfire—talked about dreams, talked about California, even talked about the kind of log house they would build, a few cattle grazing, a small garden for vegetables.

It's your father's place you're describing, a voice whispered inside Jerry's skull. *Only now it's somewhere in the western mountains, away from the war, away from everything. . . .*

Sara listened, but listened as though she were hearing nothing at all, only watching the man she loved, studying the lines of his face, watching the movements of his mouth as he spoke.

"Jerry . . ." she said.

He ceased speaking in mid-sentence.

She had opened her blouse, had exposed her breasts to his sight. Then she blushed furiously, looked away, covered herself.

"I'm ashamed!" she said.

He knelt before her, reopened the dress, kissed softly at the buds of her small, perfectly formed breasts.

He took her in his arms, lifted her, placed her down on the strewn sleeping robes, and began to remove her clothing. She lay back, relaxed and yet tense at the same time, her head to one side, the sun gleaming in the wave of her black hair, her mouth slightly open, her eyes closed.

Then she opened her eyes slightly, so that he wouldn't know, and watched him as he undressed, stared at his erect maleness, was embarrassed to realize that she had unconsciously pursed her lips.

Is that what I want? No decent woman would. . . .

He lay beside her, touched his fingers over her flesh, kissed her, breathed into her ear, ran his tongue along her throat, buried his face against her.

His fingertips, tickling, and she pressed her thighs together, drew up her knees. He pressed them down again, spread her legs with gentle pressure.

She sat up, murmured a wordless *ooooohh*, and clasped him about the waist. Her eyes were closed, but she felt something brush past her mouth. And yet she lacked the courage to do what she wanted, to take hold of him, to kiss. . . .

"Do it, Sara, please. . . ."

She could feel her face flaming red. Her hands were shaking, but he was trembling too, his entire body was trembling. And she moved her head, placed one hand upon him. She kissed then, nibbled softly, placed her mouth upon him, took the shudder in his loins, the instinctive forward thrusting of his body. But even when he attempted to withdraw, she clung to him. Then he pushed her from him, pressed her shoulders back against the buffalo robe, slid down instantly, and buried his face against her abdomen.

"No, no, no, no!" she whispered, "no, you mustn't do that—it isn't right, Jerry. . . ."

But already the soft sensations of flame were beginning to spread out from her center, were touching her all over, singing over her legs and belly, and she groaned, whined, heard her own voice and did not believe that it was hers at all—some animal, some strange, beautiful wild animal.

"Oh!" she breathed, "Jerry, beloved, oh dearest . . . come into me, please don't make me wait any longer. . . ."

He moved, slid up, and she could feel his maleness against her, touching her. She closed her eyes more tightly and spread her arms out as if in the form of a crucifix, whispered his name over and over.

He was moving into her, into her.

Slow movements, then waiting. Small explosions of pressure, pain—and she could feel her body, her womanhood stretching.

Too big, too big, dearest, please wait, let me get used to you, let me. . . .

Was it thought only, or had she cried out?

The hymen, tearing. Pain and pleasure together. The powerful male body over her, covering her. She moaned, bit at her lips. He was into her, and she was crying, sobbing.

"Sara, am I hurting you? Sara?"

"Yes, no . . . come into me, don't stop . . . my dearest. . . ."

His body working into hers, her own body beginning to respond, moving in rhythm to his, her arms tight about him.

O fire, oh lovely fire, flames all over me, I am dissolving, what has happened to my mind? I can't stand it, oh pleasure, pain, pleasure, will I ever be able to hold him completely?

He shuddered to a stop, and she felt his seed burning into her.

Not over? There's more, I know there's more. . . .

But suddenly a sensation of falling, and she reached out frantically to touch the earth, to steady herself. She felt the rough fur of the buffalo robe, felt the loose soil next to it, then wrapped her arms about him once again, her mouth sought his, sought desperately. He was slumped over her, and she could hardly breathe. It didn't make any difference at all. Even death, she thought, would make no difference now. She had lain with the man she loved.

But was there more?

Yes, and she knew it—didn't know how she knew, but was certain. She would find it with this man, her man.

"Sara, Sara, Sara. . . ."

She heard his voice, wondered how long he had been speaking

to her. It was as if she had returned from some distant place, that they had both returned. Now they were together, here, together, and she opened her eyes and looked past his face, could see the blue sky beyond his ear, beyond his hair, she could see a hawk floating in the sky.

"He is different," Sara thought. "He is not wearing his turban. Have I ever seen him before when he was not wearing it?"

They rode back to the valley by way of a secondary drainage, and, at the bottom of the canyon, they came upon evidence of recent prospecting, some lateral trenches from which a good deal of alluvium had been removed, and in the stream a rough-hewn riffles box.

Soldier Wolf and Sara dismounted, explored the area carefully—but found nothing else. Only the remains of a campfire, a fairly large one, and an area of trampled grass where, as Jerry estimated the matter, perhaps three men had spent a day or two, no more than that.

"They're looking for gold?" Sara asked.

"It appears so. Let's do a bit of mining ourselves and see what they've found. This is land allotted to the Indians, to the People of the Valley, two years ago. Worthless land except for the timber and grasslands down below—worthless until the Whitemen want it for something. . . ."

Soldier Wolf scraped out a quantity of loose gravel and sand, placed it at the head of the riffles, and opened the crude water gate. The current poured through, riling the sand and mud, bubbling down over the slatted riffles. Within a few minutes the water had cleared, and Soldier Wolf removed the larger stones, scraped at one of the riffles with a twig.

"What's that?" Sara asked.

Soldier Wolf bent over, pinched up some sand with his fingers, held it to the light, stirred it on the palm of his hand.

A pea-sized lump of gold—or what looked to be gold.

Jerry picked it up, washed it off, stared at it. Then he placed it into his mouth and bit on it, looked at it again.

"I'm not a miner," he said, "but I think it's gold, all right. Any more in the riffles?"

They examined the sand behind each slat and discovered several more small beads of yellow, as well as a quantity of fines among the particles of black iron-sulfide sand.

"It's gold, all right, I'm certain of it. And a rich little deposit, too, enough to bring a thousand miners in here if the word gets out. You don't suppose . . . ?"

"What, Jerry?"

"Cramdon's men. If they've been over this way poking around, and if they'd found anything, that would explain the raid on the village. . . ."

"But that was two months ago. This is recent, just a few days at most. Someone else, then?"

"Or Cramdon's just getting back here. Might have been working on several creeks in the area. Our attack on his ranch pretty well put him out of business—but he may be back by now, back with a new group of men. I don't know—doesn't really make sense. . . . My God, maybe he was trying to provoke a war with the Indians, maybe he was hoping to get the bluecoats to back him up. No, that doesn't make sense either. Anyway, Sara, this is trouble for everyone. Could be a good deal of money in it for the People of the Valley—if they were interested in digging for gold. But if this gets found, there are going to be miners in here, sure as hell."

"What can we do?"

"Nothing, I'm afraid. Just hope this is a freak, a single deposit, nothing bigger. That way, if it's found, they'll work it out in a short while and be gone."

As they approached the valley, they heard rifle fire.

"An attack, goddammit. Cramdon or somebody's firing on the village. Sara, you stay here—you stay out of it. I'm going down there. . . ."

"I'm coming too," the girl said, her voice utterly steady and determined.

Soldier Wolf stared at her, shook his head. "You're staying here."

"Like hell I am. I've got my own rifle here, and I can shoot as well as anyone."

She urged Virgin forward, and Jerry, cursing under his breath, clapped his heels to Messiah's sides and followed, overtook her, attempted to grab the reins from her hands.

"Don't try to stop me, Jerry! Mom and Dad are down there!"

"All right, then, all right! You do what I say, though. You understand me?"

"Yes—now, let's get over there."

They circled about, approached the village from the north, left their horses tethered in a spruce grove, and moved ahead on foot.

The village was burning, and a number of bodies lay strewn about the big circle. Rifle fire was coming in from the low rise and the thick grove of aspens along the stream.

"We've got to get behind them!" Soldier Wolf hissed. "If you're coming, Sara, come on! If we can open fire on them from the rear, maybe we can discourage them. . . ."

They made it, unobserved, to the far side of the stream, wading across and throwing themselves down on the bank, then crawling forward, clambering up across a shale slide to the crest of a low bluff.

"There they are!" Sara whispered.

"Cramdon! That's him, sure as hell. It is, no question. What? Two dozen men, if this is all of them. You sure you know how to shoot that thing, Sara?"

"Of course I do."

Soldier Wolf took dead aim at Cramdon's broad back, held the bead, and deliberately squeezed the trigger—but Cramdon moved to one side as Jerry pulled off his shot.

The rifle snapped, and the bullet hit a man who had been standing behind Cramdon. The man twisted to one side, clutching his side.

"Someone's back of us!" a voice rang out.

Sara fired then, missed, quickly reloaded her short-barreled Sharps carbine, adjusted the primer tape, and fired again, this time hitting a man who was scrambling for cover. He pitched forward, grabbed his leg, yelled out.

Soldier Wolf's second shot hit him dead center, and the man's arms reached out to either side, and then he did not move again.

"Load this!" Jerry said, handing Sara his carbine.

Using his pistol, he sprayed the clearing below with six fast shots, popped out the cylinder, inserted one of the spares he kept always loaded in his ammunition pouch, and began firing once again.

Cramdon's raiders were struggling onto their horses, were making their escape downstream, beneath the cover of overhanging willow and aspen. Soldier Wolf stood up, grabbed his reloaded rifle, and fired a final shot as the last of the riders passed out of range.

"Drop the guns or I'll kill you where you stand!"

Cramdon's voice.

"What we got here?" Cramdon said. "My old friend Turban Head the federal agent, ehh? Good-lookin' little piece yuh got with yuh, ain't she? Well, well, now. You won't be needin' her anymore, looks like. Drop the gun, Soldier Wolf, or I'll blow 'er head off right now!"

Jerry tossed his pistol onto the rocks and slowly raised his hands.

"Sam!" Cramdon said. "Tie up the filly—we'll find us a use for 'er when we've got down the road a piece. . . ."

The lean, bearded henchman had taken perhaps two steps toward Soldier Wolf and Sara when the girl's Sharps carbine exploded, and a bloody splotch appeared just at the man's collarbone. His gun flew from his grasp, the hands clutched for the throat, and he bent backward from the knees, went over slowly, twisted to one side, his foot kicking, and then lay motionless.

"You goddamn little slut!" Cramdon shouted, his face a mask of hatred, and he fired.

Soldier Wolf, horrified, saw the girl hit, saw her spun about by the force of the slug, saw her topple, crumple, her head striking the rocks, and fall backward over the rim.

"Bastard! Filthy bastard!" Soldier Wolf screamed as he lunged toward Cramdon, was dimly aware of the crushing blow of a pistol barrel across the side of his head, found himself on his hands and knees, attempted to rise. But blows were raining down on him now, repeated jolts to his side, pain shooting through him, a rifle stock breaking across his back as he once again attempted to rise, another smashing blow to his forehead. . . .

He felt his teeth grate against stone as the darkness swirled up about him, darkness streaked with strange yellow and red flashings, and then total darkness.

Extended periods of half-consciousness alternating with total oblivion after that. He knew that he had been moved, did not know how, did not remember what had happened, knew that he was hurt but did not know why. The vision of the big wolf came to him once more, sat watching him, finally spoke to him: *Try to move, try to move if you are worthy of your name, Soldier Wolf.* He tried, and pain shot through him, the wolf swirled into a yellow whirl of small, popping flecks of light, and he knew that he was caught up in a flooding river, the water dark and cold, the current powerful about him; he tried to swim, to reach the surface, but each attempt at movement brought new sheets of pain. Then the face of the wolf filled his mind, he stared into the brown eyes that seemed to have fire in them, fire that seemed to grow in intensity; he felt he was being drawn down into the eyes of the wolf, into the brain of the wolf. Then he could see nothing, he was alone somewhere, it was night, and stars were raining down from the heavens. A voice, the words in some language he did not know, the words that seemed to be asking a question of him. *I can't understand you, speak to me so that I can understand what you're saying!* Laughter, chuckling laughter. Then he knew, even without understanding the strange words, he knew what he was being asked. *What will you do now, Soldier Wolf? Do you wish to sleep forever, or do you wish to awaken? Tell me what it is that you wish to do. Maybe I will help you then, and maybe not. We are wasting time here, I have many others to attend to. . . .* He struggled to speak, but his voice would not come. *I can't hear you, Soldier Wolf.* He gasped for breath, forced the air from his lungs, heard himself growling, growling. *Dumb fuckin' Injun kid, dumb fuckin' half-breed, dumb fuckin'. . . .* He turned about, ignored the pain, forced his hands to his throat, struggled to speak. *All right, goddammit, wake up, then. You'll be back. It's peaceful here in the earth, the grains of the soil are soothing, there is no more pain, there is no more light. . . .*

"Light!" he managed, and his eyes were open.

Where was he? Where was Sara? Was she dead? Sara!

"Sara!" he gasped.

And then the darkness came up around his eyes once again.

A passage of time—how much time, he had no idea.

Then his eyes were open once more, but nothing was clear. He fought to achieve focus; he could tell that people were standing near him, leaning over him.

"Light!" he choked.

"The rock-headed nigger's comin' round. I told ye he would."

"O'Bragh? Bully?"

"It's old Farnsworth, Jerry me boy. Ye comin' out of it now?"

His vision slowly cleared, but his face was swollen, it didn't feel right.

"Bully? How did I get here? Sara, she's down below, she went over the rim."

"Ye're back in the village, Jerry. Me an' Marsh Flower have got ye in the lodge, ye're all right now, goin' to be all right."

"Sara . . . Sara?"

"She's alive, Jerry. She's still alive. I just came from her bedside. Do you recognize me?"

"Frank?"

"Yes, it's Frank. Don't try to talk just now. Rest, Jerry. There's time for talk later."

"She's alive?"

"Yes. We're all praying for her. She lost so much blood. Morning Star Fox is with her also. Between his god and mine, we're doing all we can. It's the Lord's will, it's up to Him now."

"Sara!" he managed once again, and then his vision blurred, and everything turned gray.

When the light came once more, Soldier Wolf sat up slowly and looked about. The lodge was empty, and sunshine was pouring in through the open flap at the front of the tipi.

Pain in his side when he moved, but he rose to his feet, stood there naked for a long moment, trying to gather his thoughts. Where were his clothes? He found them folded neatly on the bench beside his sleeping pallet, and, taking slow breaths between movements, he managed to get into his breeches, shirt, and fringed jacket. He recalled buying the garment new—his trip south from Washington, the ex-soldier with his two stolen horses and his new assignment as an agent for the Bureau of Indian Affairs, a vague notion as to what his mission might actually amount to, the image of a beautiful, frail, black-haired girl fresh in his mind. The coat was well-worn now, sewn-together bullet holes in the side, a number of the leather thongs missing, used for one purpose or another as necessity had demanded, the leather dirty, shiny in places, and stained with the blood of antelope, deer, elk, and buffalo, as well as his own blood.

Sara? he thought. Where is Sara?

And then he remembered it all.

He pulled on his moccasins, started out of the lodge, remembered his turban, found the banding of cloth, and quickly wound it about his head.

Then he was outside.

He remembered the burning lodges, saw that some remained half-charred, saw that others had been recently rebuilt. He remembered the dead he had seen from a distance, saw the skeletonlike tree-hung graves on the rim beyond the village, saw a squaw hobbling across the open space before O'Bragh's lodge, her arm bound in white cloth, her face painted in mourning; he saw the hand from which two fingers had been lopped off.

Her husband was killed.

He placed his fingers to his face. The swelling, he remembered the swelling, realized that his face was still somewhat puffed up. He felt at the half-healed wound across his forehead, and his nose was sensitive to his touch.

Broken.

Cracked ribs.

He breathed deeply and took a step forward, then another. And he walked toward the Goths' lodge. Stooped through the entryway.

Frank was there, and so were O'Bragh and Marsh Flower. Where was Elizabeth?

Sara lay on her pallet, a light deerskin covering over her. She was sleeping.

Soldier Wolf saw the rise and fall of the coverlet.

"Thank God!" he uttered, as the others looked up.

"Tsaragi—what ye doin' up? Jesus, man, ye shouldn't be wanderin' about—ye've got to get back an' lie down."

"I've spent enough time lying down. Is she all right, Frank?"

"Jerry. Yes, I think so. I think she's going to make it."

"Pistol slug went right through 'er," Bully said. "Missed the vitals, though, must of. Thought we'd lost this little gal a dozen times or more, but she's pullin' through."

"Frank . . . where's Elizabeth?" Soldier Wolf asked, but he knew the answer, somehow, even before the words were spoken.

"Dead," Goth answered. "She's dead, Jerry. . . ."

The second week in July a dispatch rider came into the encampment, bringing a message for Goth, Soldier Wolf, and O'Bragh. The young man, his U.S. Army blues neat and clean despite more than a week on the trail, was none other than the former Private Johnson of Boone's brigade—but Sergeant Johnson now, the new stripes freshly sewn onto the sleeves of his uniform. With him were three other soldiers, all privates, as well as a taciturn Arapaho who served as their guide.

Johnson delivered the missive, the contents in a sealed leather pouch, to Frank Goth, saluted smartly even though there was no need for it, got back on his horse, shouted out a brisk "Coluuuumn ho!" and made his way back out of the village, headed toward Denver.

"That youngun's goin' to be a general one day, mark me words," O'Bragh drawled. "An' when the time comes, he'll lead his men against the Siksikas an' get 'em all scalped. You can count on 'er."

"Let's see what we've got, Jerry," Goth said as he opened the pouch.

Inside were federal drafts, written against the Bank of Denver, in favor of Frank Goth, Jerry Soldier Wolf, and Farnsworth O'Bragh, a half-year's pay for each man.

"All we got to do is take 'em in to the bank an' cash 'em," O'Bragh said. "The goddamned fools. Take a little weekend jaunt into Denver . . ."

"A letter from Harriman?" Jerry said. "What's the boss-man got to say to us?"

Frank withdrew the letter:

> Mssrs. Goth, Soldier Wolf, and O'Bragh:
>
> Greetings from the Capital City of a nation that seems irrationally determined to destroy itself. I trust this finds you all in good health and with your mission by now accomplished. We have word, however, that the Cheyenne and Arapaho peoples have not reported to the Sand Creek area. This they must be urged to do, as soon as possible. The major portions of the supplies sent to them, as I understand the matter, will not be distributed until a winter encampment is made. With matters thus settled, half of Colonel Boone's troops will be withdrawn from the frontier and reassigned to the garrison at St. Joseph. We have some worries about the loyalties of the military personnel. If you have reason to suspect anything amiss, do not fail to make a report directly to Governor Gilpin in Denver. If the Cramdon issue is settled, the man in custody, well and good. If not, the matter must be dropped in consideration of larger issues. I have received a report that Cramdon's ranch was burned by unspecified Indian peoples, and certainly this sort of thing must be brought to a halt. It is believed that the Utes are responsible, but no doubt Cramdon will supply the informa-

tion necessary for further action as a result of the inquest into his activities. O'Bragh's assignment is to be considered completed at the end of July, and the warrant provides full compensation. Agent Soldier Wolf's position is to be renewed for another six months, as is Agent Goth's. I write this in haste, hoping to send it along with various orders and dispatches for Colonel Boone, not wishing to trust it to the mails, which are less dependable than ever now that hostilities are well under way. My best to all of you.

Daniel Harriman,
Chief Clerk,
Bureau of Indian Affairs

"We're suffering here," Soldier Wolf said, "from a notable gap in communications."

"Inevitable, inevitable," Goth replied. "What's to be done now, Soldier Wolf?"

"This nigger's thinkin' they's some unfinished business needs tendin' to," O'Bragh suggested.

"Yes." Goth nodded. "God forgive me, but I want revenge—and I'll never rest peaceful until I've had it. Perhaps I'll roast in hell for what I'm feeling, but there are times, I believe, when a man can no longer turn the other cheek. *Judgment is mine, sayeth the Lord.* Unworthy vessel that I am, my mind shattered in the first touch of the flame—and I want to see that man dead."

"Ain't no hell," O'Bragh said simply, shaking his head. "Only this one, right here, the one that we makes up for ourselves. Preacher man, ye got to get ahold of yourself. There be others as have lost their womenfolk. . . ."

"A man can't just sit back and do nothing," Frank said.

"Damn world's flying apart," Soldier Wolf growled. "But I came out here to do two things, and neither of them's done. One's not worth doing. I can see that sure as hell. I'll tell you something, Frank, and you too, Bully. I'm through with playing games for the government. I've been the child of one institution or another all my life because there was a certain degree of security in it, or at least the illusion of security. And that's what it is, illusion. My time as agent is up—this paycheck finishes it."

"What's the other one, coon? Ye said *two*."

"I need a red-haired scalp, except maybe a scalp like that isn't worth having."

"This child's with ye, then. There be three of us an' only one of him, an' it don't make no difference if he does have a few hired guns. Take old Morning Star Fox, now. He's up on the hill over yonder, been there for the last three days waitin' for Old Man Coyote to tell 'im what to do. Hell fire, Saynday's done told him years ago what to do, an' he never listened. Now, me, I've killed mebbe two, three hundred coons in my life, mebbe more, 'cause I never done counted. An' whatever God's around ain't never told me *no*. Ain't never killed no one without a reason, an' that's always seemed like a good rule—animal nor man, ye don't kill without a reason. Ain't sayin' Morning Star Fox's way is wrong, mind ye. Mebbe in the Spirit World it's the right trail to foller. But down here, a coon ends up losin' his ha'r hat that way."

"I have lived a hell in my own mind since Elizabeth was murdered," Goth said. "We're different kinds of men, Bully, you and I. God wanted me to be like Morning Star Fox, one who would teach His wisdom. I've spoken the words, and yet I've always failed, and that's why I've been punished so horribly. . . ."

Goth's voice broke off and he turned away, attempting to regain his composure.

"We will have revenge," Soldier Wolf said, "and the world, this world, will be better off for it. And I'll tell you something else. When I see White Frog again, I'm not going to urge him to go to Sand Creek—not White Frog or Whirlwind or Roman Nose or the others that I haven't even met with yet. They must do what seems best to them, and so must I."

"I was wrong," Goth said, turning to Soldier Wolf. "Jerry, my daughter loves you, just as you love her. We had hoped to send her to school, Elizabeth and I—because we wanted to see her happy. Perhaps we envisioned her as the wife of a minister, a small country church somewhere, east of the Mississippi, a quiet life, a civilized life. But if we had really wanted that, we'd never have brought her with us, would not have watched her grow to womanhood among these Indian people. And so she has chosen her own path, just as she has chosen her own mate. We were fearful, uncertain—it never had anything to do with a lack of belief in you. We have been friends, I think, you and I?"

"That is true." Soldier Wolf nodded.

"Even in the blackness of my own grief, I saw you sitting beside her, hours on end, as she began to recover from the bullet wound. Even though my own mind was numb, I was still able to see a man and a woman who loved each other, who would never choose to be apart. Am I right in this, Soldier Wolf?"

"Frank, Frank," Soldier Wolf said, placing his big hands on the older man's shoulders. "I . . ."

"I will give you my daughter, Jerry. I give her to you. But she's yours already, no matter what I say. Yet I want you to know it—I want to have you for my son. . . ."

Then the three men heard voices outside, the voices of two women, an old and a young. They were laughing and conversing in the Cheyenne tongue.

Marsh Flower and Sara entered the lodge, and Marsh Flower was carrying a woven willow basket full of small pink fruit.

"We have gathered service berries," Sara said. "They're ripe everywhere now."

Chapter Eleven

By 1861 the Pike's Peak area had a population in excess of twenty-five thousand, and the provisional Jefferson Territory had been dissolved, with Congress creating the Territory of Colorado. Lincoln had appointed Colonel William Gilpin as the first official governor, and the latter had arrived in May of '61 and had established himself and his staff in the Executive Chambers, three rooms above a Larimer Street clothing store.

Denver's general run of crime and violence had now become involved with the issue of patriotism, and the city was divided, but with Unionists in the clear majority. Confederate sympathizers, such as gunman/gambling-house-operator Charlie Harrison, Big Phil the Cannibal (reputed to have eaten two men), and Captain McKee, raised the Confederate flag one morning in April, but bloodshed was avoided, and the flag was taken down that evening.

Harrison's Criterion Saloon was the center of sedition, and Gilpin's voluntary militia made raids upon it, but with little success.

McKee and the Southern sympathizers began buying up all the percussion caps in the territory, and Gilpin, alarmed, ordered his militia to disarm the entire populace. As a result, the Confederates quit the town in a body, a hundred strong and well-armed, the postmaster and the mayor among them. McKee and Harrison led the party south to the Santa Fe Trail, where they intended to plunder government wagon trains before continuing on to Texas.

Colonel Leavenworth attempted to pursue the rebels, but first he had to send to the Missouri River for percussion caps.

But the rebels were captured and brought back to Denver and impounded in the stockade as prisoners of war. With help from their jailer, however, they all escaped and fled south once more.

On the high prairies, as summer progressed, Black Kettle, Roman Nose, Whirlwind, and Big Mouth pursued the diminished herds of buffalo. The hunts enjoyed little success, and the people began to speak of wintering at Sand Creek, where Boone had promised assistance.

* * *

White Frog, leading a band of some fifty warriors, rode into the encampment of the People of the Valley.

"Welcome, my friend!" Soldier Wolf hailed him. "Why have you come to the mountains? The buffalo are not here."

"We passed through the Cache La Poudre," White Frog said, "on our way back from the grasslands. Red Face with Red Hair has built a new lodge, but he was not there. I have burned his lodge once more, and we took meat from among his cattle. These are not as good as buffalo, but the flesh is as good as elk meat. Then we followed the tracks the Whitemen had made, and we saw that they were coming this way, across the mountains. I thought my friends might need some help, and so we have followed."

"Where is Cramdon, then?" Soldier Wolf asked as he felt the fury beginning to rise within himself.

"The one with red hair has passed around your village and has gone up the river toward the Never Summer Mountains. Do you wish me to bring my warriors? We will go together to kill this man."

"Not a good idea," Soldier Wolf said, shaking his head. "The bluecoats would come looking for you."

White Frog laughed. "The soldiers are busy elsewhere," he said. "Many have ridden eastward, while others have gone to the south. We are Cheyenne warriors—and we have done what the Whites have wanted for too long a time. Perhaps soon we will have to kill them all. I agree with Leg in the Water now. Soon the time comes when we must fight."

"How many men does Cramdon have with him, White Frog?"

"Not many. Now there are only the number of my fingers and two more. These men intend to dig for the yellow metal, Soldier Wolf. My scouts came close to their encampment two nights ago. They have brought shovels and picks and axes, as well as iron pans and other things the miners use. If Red Hair with Red Face finds gold, then many Whitemen will come into these mountains, and the people of Morning Star Fox will have to leave, unless the Whitemen kill them all. It will not be good if Red Face finds the gold."

"I'm afraid he already has," Soldier Wolf said. "We found where he had been digging—just before he attacked the village this last time."

"We heard of what happened. One of Roman Nose's warriors was up here, perhaps?"

"Yes. He came with the young bluecoat who brought us a message."

"My friend, is Morning Star Fox well? He has grown too old to lead these people, I think. These are times when the people must have strong leaders, for otherwise we will all vanish, just as the buffalo will. Our numbers will become ever fewer, just like the buffalo people have."

"He is well," Soldier Wolf replied. "But he continues to mourn and to seek for a new vision. The young men are uneasy and speak of moving elsewhere. Some wish to join with your people again, and some counsel for crossing the mountains and to live in the lands of the Utes."

"No, that would not be good either. Then the Utes, our enemies, would kill everyone. I will speak with Morning Star Fox now. Where is Irish Vulture? He has not gone to the Spirit World, has he?"

"No, no." Soldier Wolf chuckled. "Just that he spends half his life in the lodge with Marsh Flower now. He's got children in his brain."

"That is good, Soldier Wolf. A man should never grow too old to think of that. But what about you?"

"I will also marry soon."

"The book-man's daughter? She is very good-looking—for a White woman."

A feast was held that evening, with quarters of beef roasting over the coals and kettles as well of prairie turnip, wild artichoke, and calamus roots. Baskets were heaped with chokecherries, service berries, and smoked trout and carp. As the people ate, White Frog's warriors regaled the People of the Valley with tales of their accomplishments at hunting and war, the young men in particular proving rapt listeners.

White Frog, his beaded necklace with dried human fingers and arrowheads attached to it about his throat, sat next to Morning Star Fox, the old chief in full headdress and his face painted white with red about his eyes and nose.

The night was warm and pleasant, and the odors of food spread out and tormented the coyotes, who, from time to time, set up a clamor of yipping and howling at a short distance, their sounds encouraging the camp dogs, as well, to howl and bark.

Soldier Wolf drew Sara away from the festive gathering, kissed her, petted her hair, held her.

"Is something wrong?" Sara asked.

"No, nothing's wrong, little one. But Bully and I are leaving camp tonight while the others are all preoccupied. We'll be gone a few days. The moon is nearly full once more, and it's a good night for riding."

"Where are you going? You didn't tell me anything about going anywhere. . . ."

"That's why I'm telling you now, Sara. This is something O'Bragh and I must do alone. We don't want White Frog or any of the others following us. Tomorrow, when your father wants to know where we are, you must tell him that we have gone hunting. Tell White Frog that if we are not back in three days, then he must come to look for us."

"But where are you going?"

"Up into the Never Summer Mountains—to hunt."

"Why there? White Frog has told you something, hasn't he? Cramdon is up there. . . ."

"There's nothing to worry about, Sara. This is something that has to be done."

"White Frog would take his warriors and go with you—and our young men would go too."

"Then the village would not be guarded."

"Jerry! If anything should happen to you . . ."

"Nothing will happen. Just going wolverine hunting is all. We've heard of a big one up there."

"I'm coming too, I'm not letting you go alone, Jerry!"

"Not alone. Bully and I will be together. You must do as I say, Sara. There are times when a wife must do as her husband says."

"I'm not your wife, not yet."

"But when I return? It is a good time of year for the marriage ceremony. Did you know that your father has given you to me?"

"He told me he's given his blessing, but he didn't say that. I won't let you own me, Jerry Soldier Wolf."

"I know, I know, Sara. But now you must do as I tell you. I will be back in three days, and there will be a marriage feast."

* * *

They rode southeast in the moonlight, O'Bragh on Porcupine the mule, and Jerry on Messiah. The moonlight threw long shadows across the land, giving the spruce groves almost the appearance of the forest after a light snowfall, and crickets and tree frogs sang in the night. Startled deer, sensing them, bounded away in the half-light, thrashing through the dry undergrowth, leaping like jackass rabbits. And the water of the little river was quiet in its bed, flowing black and shining between the clumps of willow and occasional aspens.

Shortly after sunrise they picked up Cramdon's trail, and O'Bragh studied the hoofmarks in the damp earth of the meadow carefully.

"This child counts more'n twenty," O'Bragh said. "Didn't White Frog say they was but a dozen?"

"Packhorses, don't you figure?"

O'Bragh studied the tracks once more, then nodded.

"That's what she is, okay. Some of 'em's not carryin' any weight to speak of. Where do ye figger they're headin'?"

"Upslope, one of the side canyons. Sara and I found a place where they'd been digging gold out of the gravels. I'd guess that's exactly where they've gone."

"Sounds like. How far does she be?"

"Five, six miles from here," Soldier Wolf said. "They might have spread out, of course, and be prospecting along three or four of the drainages."

"The hoof tracks'll tell us, one way or tother."

They rode on for another few minutes, came to the tributary that flowed down from the canyon where Jerry and Sara had found the riffles box, and noted that the hoofmarks, indeed, turned away from the main stream and up toward the mouth of the canyon. At this point they rested their animals, let them drink and graze for a few minutes, and themselves ate portions of cold meat from their saddlebags.

"Mebbe we oughta figger out what it be we're goin' to do when we catch up with 'em?" O'Bragh said.

"A dozen of them," Soldier Wolf responded, grinning. "That makes it just about even, doesn't it?"

"Just what this old nigger was thinkin'. Maybeso we ought to figger what gives us a little edge, huh?"

"Good idea, Farnsworth, good idea."

"Name's Bully." O'Bragh snorted. "Wagh! Coon, how many times I have to tell ye?"

"Right. Okay. Guess we ought to know *exactly* where everybody is before we do anything rash—is that what you're thinking?"

"A dozen of 'em. That include Cramdon, or did White Frog tell ye that Cramdon had a dozen men with 'im?"

"Third-hand information at best. You studied the hoofmarks—could you tell anything?"

"They wasn't exactly spread out, ye damned fool. A man can just tell so much is all."

"Can't remember you ever admitting it before, Bully."

"Anyhow, don't make much difference, do she? We'll figger 'er out when we get a look at 'em."

"Right. Now, this is what I think we should do. . . ."

The midsummer sun poured down as Soldier Wolf and O'Bragh worked their way upslope toward the crest of the ridge above the canyon, a yellow, blinding heat that gleamed back from bare red surfaces of stone and made the duff underfoot dry and brittle.

"Porky's tongue's hangin' out," O'Bragh said. "Figger we better walk 'em the rest of the way up?"

Soldier Wolf drew back on the reins, and Messiah came to an immediate and grateful stop. The big black was sweating heavily as Soldier Wolf slipped down from his saddle.

"Must be a hundred an' ninety-five dee-grees in the shade, an' they ain't no shade," O'Bragh said, wiping at his bearded face with a red bandana. "Might be we should of done this climbin' at night. Not fit for man nor beast, as it is."

Soldier Wolf nodded, looked off to the east—saw the great gray-black towers of thunderheads forming above the peaks of the Never Summer Mountains.

"With a little luck, maybe we'll have a cloudburst in two or three hours. Look at them, Bully. Pregnant clouds, pregnant and waiting to give birth!"

"Full o' lightnin', too. Just our luck, Jerry me boy, an' Old Man Coyote will start throwin' his spears down at Cramdon an' his boys an' end up hittin' us instead. Old bastard ain't got good aim, I tell ye. Never has had."

After a short rest, the two men continued their climb, now leading their mounts behind them. Perspiration was dripping from Soldier Wolf's face, and he was required repeatedly to wipe at his eyes.

"The horses need water," Jerry said. "Won't be any on top—not for several miles on up, where the land tables off."

"Ain't but one horse around here. Ye gonna rile Porky's feelin's. No self-respectin' mule wants to be called *horse*."

"My apologies, Porcupine, old critter." Jerry laughed as he stumbled onward.

They crossed beneath a shelf of red stone, and O'Bragh gestured toward a clump of quaking aspens on the slope ahead, below them a scattering of willow brush.

"I see it," Jerry said. "Some water, if we're lucky—maybe a good place to leave Messiah and Porcupine."

They entered in under the green canopy of the aspens, the light tremulous, inconstant, fleeting, cool. Clusters of sweetgrass, some fern growing just at the base of a large double-trunked aspen.

"Luck's with us," O'Bragh said. "Look at that!"

A basin of moss-covered stones, clear, shallow water. Water skippers gliding across the surface.

"A beautiful spot," Soldier Wolf agreed, leading Messiah forward to the water, allowing the black horse to drink.

"Yep," O'Bragh replied. "Next time I die, I'd like to get planted among some aspens. They's magic trees, for sure. All the years this child's been in the mountains, an' I never get tired of 'em. Always like meetin' new friends, it is."

Soldier Wolf stared at his tall, bony companion and grinned. Another world, another time, and O'Bragh might have been a poet. As it was, the queer combinations of his speech patterns, vestiges of Irish, the rest not exactly English but rather the patois of the mountains—an odd, dissonant species of music. How long had he known Farnsworth O'Bragh, anyway? It seemed like years, like half of his lifetime. But it had been only six months, six months since the shootout at the foot of the Smokies. So much had happened in that relatively short space of time, himself so utterly changed from what he was that any life other than the one he was now leading seemed illusory.

Porcupine drank, fluttered her lips at the surface of the little pool, wagged her head back and forth, her nose dabbling at the water.

Soldier Wolf gazed out from beneath the green canopy of aspens and into the intense sunlight of early midday, into the sweltering heat.

"A good place to leave the animals," he said again. "If we

move downslope at a forty-five degree angle, we should find ourselves just above where Sara and I came upon the riffles box."

"Any reason to think that's where they be, Jerry me boy?"

"Not necessarily. You got a better idea?"

"Cain't say as this coon does. Let's give 'er a try, then."

"Wagh!" Jerry chuckled.

"Now ye're learnin'. Keep sayin' 'er, an' folks won't think ye're a greenh'un no more," O'Bragh muttered, checking the load in his ancient Hawken rifle.

They tethered Messiah and Porcupine and moved off at an angle to the slope of the canyon wall, and within half an hour they had come to the rim of a basalt formation from which they could command a view of perhaps a mile of stream bottom.

"It's them!" O'Bragh said, pointing down. "Look at 'em, busy as beavers, if they *was* any beavers left in the High Shinin'."

"Couldn't be all gone, or you and Beckwourth and Smith wouldn't be planning a trapping expedition to Green River."

"Only flatlanders call 'er the Green," O'Bragh said, shaking his head. "She's Seedskeedee. How many times do I gotta tell ye?"

"Right now we've got some work ahead of us, Bully. We'll think about trapping later."

"She's a good day to die," O'Bragh said—and Soldier Wolf wondered how many times in his life the old man had said those words, wondered how many times he had said them and meant them.

"I count ten from here. That means two, maybe three more somewhere else. Down-canyon, you figure?"

"Lookouts, mebbe yes, mebbe no. Don't seem like that'd take three men, now, do it?"

"Two down-canyon, one up?"

"Who'd be comin' in from up-canyon?"

"Us."

"Ye got a point there, Jerry me boy. Look. Think we can get over to that patch of firs? Put us dee-rectly above 'em."

On hands and knees they moved downslope, through the clumps of buckbrush and stands of spruce, crawling a few feet, then stopping, crawling onward.

"No way for a nigger my age to be travelin'," O'Bragh whispered. "Ye sure this here's worth it? Mebbe we should just of lit fire to the woods downstream, let the wind burn 'em out."

"Isn't any wind," Soldier Wolf whispered back. "Keep moving."

"Just makin' a suggestion is all."

They reached the thick clump of young spruce trees and took cover, studied the men below—men working with pick and shovel, gouging away at the alluvial deposits alongside the tumbling stream. Voices clearly audible now, bits of conversation drifting up to where Soldier Wolf and Bully O'Bragh lay concealed.

"We've got them in range," Jerry whispered.

"Appears like. We just goin' to shoot 'em an' leave 'em?"

"Do they deserve more than that?"

"This nigger don't think so. Where's Cramdon, Jerry? Mebbe my eyesight's failin' me, but I surely don't see 'im."

"He's not here. That means he's somewhere with two other men."

"Or more or less. We don't really know, ye got to remember that, me lad. Ye be havin' a spot of likker with me before we starts the pigeon shoot?"

O'Bragh rolled to one side, produced a nearly full bottle from inside his leathers.

"Where in hell did that come from, Bully, dammit?"

"Got me sources. Ain't ye figgered that out by now?"

O'Bragh removed the stopper with his teeth, took the cork with one hand, and raised the bottle to his lips with the other.

"Wagh!" he snorted. "The ee-lixir of the gods, I'm tellin' ye. Care to try 'er?"

"Why not?" Soldier Wolf said, took the bottle, and drank, blinked his eyes, and handed the container back.

O'Bragh stoppered the bottle and slid it into his jacket.

"Okay, now, this old coon's ready to begin."

O'Bragh and Soldier Wolf were just drawing aim on their respective targets when one of the men standing by the riffles box let out a whoop and called to the others, pointing excitedly.

"Look at that goddamn nugget!" the voice came up from below. "Son of a bitch, we've got a handful of them here!"

The men with shovels and picks dropped their tools and hurried to the riffles box, stood looking down as the one in red shirt and wide suspenders knelt over and scooped something from the box.

"That'un's mine," O'Bragh said. "We got 'em like teals on a pond, Jerry. Let fly."

The carbine and the old Hawken discharged at nearly the same instant, and the man in the red shirt and one other pitched forward across the riffles box.

For a moment the men stood as if thunderstruck, uncertain what had happened. Soldier Wolf took advantage of the momentary confusion and fired off all six shots from his Marston, aiming directly at the cluster of men. Two more fell, and a third grasped at his shoulder, cursed, and flung himself down behind some rocks along the streamside.

The remaining five scrambled for cover, but only four made it—as O'Bragh had finished reloading, had drawn aim, and had fired: half of a man's head exploded, the man taking two more steps before falling face forward and arms out on the gravel bank.

Soldier Wolf snapped a spare cylinder into his pistol, thrust the weapon back into its holster, and drew down on the guard lever of his Starr carbine, jammed in another load, and set the percussion cap.

O'Bragh had his Hawken reloaded already, was tapping the pan to assure firing.

Astounding he can do that so quick, Soldier Wolf thought. Astounding. . . .

"Five down an' one duck winged." O'Bragh chuckled. "Now the odds is lookin' a tad mite better, lookin' better all the time."

Rifle fire from below now, but wild—Cramdon's men still didn't quite know where their assailants were hidden.

"Ain't caught sight of the powder smoke," Bully said, nodding. "Will next time we fire."

The wounded man who had been lying beneath the gravel rim of the creek bed now made a run for it, leaping up, grasping the injured shoulder, and stumbling forward to rejoin those of his companions who were still alive.

O'Bragh squeezed the trigger of the Hawken, and the man flung out his arms, twisted about, and fell.

"Dead center," Soldier Wolf commented.

"Hates to shoot a critter in the back, though," O'Bragh returned as he began to reload the rifle.

Four men now, leaping across the creek, two with rifles in hand, one stumbling, sprawling in the current.

O'Bragh fired again, missed, cursing old age and bad eyesight at the same time. But as the man rose to his feet and plunged forward through the water, Soldier Wolf squeezed off a round from his carbine, and a human form splashed headlong into the current, went under, surfaced, and floated downstream, bumping against boulders like a log during spring flood.

"Three to go," Jerry said.

The others were across the stream, had scrambled up the bank, and had taken cover behind a tangle of brush and driftwood. More shots from below now, the rifle balls thudding into the bare slope below the fir grove.

"Standoff," Bully said. "Ain't no sense in shootin' no more from up here. Those niggers cain't reach us except with blind luck, an' we cain't touch them neither. . . ."

"Think we can make it back to the clump of buckbrush? From there we can get down to the creek, maybe up the other side—come in on top of them."

"Always got to make things difficult, don't ye? What if yer friend's heard the gunfire an's comin' up-crick? Old Red Hair with Red Face."

"Maybe he's not downstream at all. A boss-man doesn't stand guard, does he?"

"Good point, good point. Upstream, then? Lookin' for more places to dig up the dirt?"

"Seems likely, doesn't it? If I were in charge, I sure wouldn't be doing the guard duty."

"Nope," O'Bragh said as he began crawling back toward the buckbrush, "likely ye'd be bustin' your back down there, diggin' dirt."

They made it back to the cover of the brush patch, clearly out of range now, and turned downslope, still on hands and knees, and reached the creek.

"Is too a wind," O'Bragh said. "A current of hot air, movin' right up the crick."

"Might work at that," Soldier Wolf said, nodding.

"Now ye be thinkin', me lad. Stick with old Farnsworth, an' he'll make a *montagnard* of ye yet."

"Name's *Bully*, ye ignorant nigger." Soldier Wolf laughed. "Where do we start her?"

"Fire's temper-mental, lad. A man's got to know how to deal with it. Me, I've always been fond of fire. I'll get the duff right here, you cross the crick an' get 'er goin' on t'other side. Then we just get back an' let the flames do our work for us."

Soldier Wolf waded the stream, the current surprisingly strong, found a tangle of leaves and slough on the far side, and used his striker to ignite a twist of dead spruce twigs, the needles popping and sputtering and flaring out. With this as a torch, he set fire to anything that looked as though it might burn. The flames moved slowly at first, then got into the tangle of dead brush and driftwood from the spring floods, and took off—a sudden yellow torrent of flame, scorching everything around it, hitting the summer-dry willowbrush along the bank, moving upstream and upslope at the same time.

Jerry looked back at O'Bragh, whose fire was also growing nicely.

"Downstream, coon!" he yelled to the old mountain man. "We don't want to be in the way in case the wind shifts!"

He waded the swift-moving stream once again, leaped up the bank, and rejoined O'Bragh.

"Good day for a fire." Bully grinned. "The old dancer's goin' to go right up the canyon, slicker'n green buffler shit."

"Jesus, Bully, I just thought of something. Where the hell are their horses?"

"Down-crick a piece. Cain't ye smell 'em? Worryin' about cookin' some horsemeat, was ye?"

"The horses aren't guilty," Soldier Wolf said.

"True, true it be. Well, they'll get a sniff of the smoke, an' they'll run for ten mile or more."

"Messiah and Porcupine will smell it too, then."

"Ain't no wind up on the ridge, me lad. If it comes down to 'er, though, they'll bust loose and make tracks. Tether rope never kept a mule in place if it wanted loose. An' ye're always tellin' me that horses is smart as mules. . . ."

The fire, aided by the intense heat of midday, ate its way forward, up the canyon, and then exploded, driven by the wind from below. It crowned through the spruces and roared away, a torrent of smoke and flame, moving toward the headwaters of the creek, and leaving a world of ash and smoking black skeletons of trees behind it.

Chapter Twelve

July 21, 1861.

Manassas Junction, Virginia, twenty miles from Washington, on a branch of the Potomac called Bull Run—thirty thousand men each from North and South, the Northerners under McDowell, the Southerners under Beauregard. McDowell's men swept the Confederate left flank, but Thomas J. Jackson rushed his brigade from the Shenandoah Valley by rail and checked the Northern advance by holding a key hill.

"Look, there is Jackson with his Virginians, standing like a stone wall against the enemy. . . ."

The Confederates counterattacked, and the Union retreat turned into a rout, with McDowell's men fleeing toward Washington—throwing down their weapons, overrunning their supply wagons, pouring over bands of sightseers who had gathered to observe the conflict.

Beauregard marching on Washington!

But the Southerners themselves were too disorganized to follow up their great victory, and the war settled down to a conflict of attrition.

The very rivers were to run blood, and by the war's end, the number of lives lost would reach an unbelievable six hundred thousand.

And, perhaps little noticed in the midst of the overall conflagration, would be a huge preacher from Denver, Colonel John M. Chivington, commander of the First Cavalry of Colorado and the hundred days' men of the Third Colorado Cavalry as well, a man who had perceived the solution to the Indian problem to lie in the annihilation of the Indians. Chivington would march on the village at Sand Creek. It would be the morning of November 30, 1864. Chivington and Shoup would move in on Black Kettle's Cheyennes. The officers would reach the summit of a low rise and see below them the ice-crusted stream, its water low, and beyond that more than a hundred lodges gleaming in the morning light. The camp dogs would begin to bark.

The Indians would suspect nothing, would believe themselves to be at peace with the bluecoats. Men, women, and children would be cut down, riddled with bullets, the bodies scalped, mutilated, dragged about over the frozen ground.

"All I can say for officers and men is that they all behaved well, and won for themselves a name that will be remembered for ages to come. . . ."

Sand Creek Massacre.

And to the northwest, a first blanket of snow would have fallen over the Never Summer Mountains, long white vistas of ridges and peaks composed of granites and gneisses. Already the mountains would sleep, would await spring.

The fire, sucking wind behind it, swept up the canyon, leaped ridges, poured a huge plume of blue-gray smoke that drifted away to the southeast, toward the crests of the Never Summer Mountains.

Soldier Wolf and O'Bragh climbed back to where they had left their mounts. The accumulated thunderheads above the peaks had grown remarkably and now presented a massive, bulging back wall, spreading out, moving westward above the basin which lay as a blue-green interval between the Never Summers and the Park Range. And the intense heat of midday was broken everywhere except in the midst of the raging forest fire.

Thunder in the distance, and occasional flashes of lightning visible even by daylight.

Then the first heavy cold drops of rain, hissing on the red rock formations and causing the leaves of undergrowth and quaking aspen to shudder.

"Don't guess she's goin' to burn clear to Denver after all," O'Bragh said, pursing his mouth.

"A downpour coming, Bully. I can feel it. Black bands of rain coming down over there right now."

A blast of lightning close by, splintering a pine on the ridgecrest, and then such a wave of noise that the earth itself seemed to shake. A momentary pause, an utter, waiting silence. Then the clouds broke open, and torrential rain came pouring down over the ridges, sunlight slanting through, and the dry earth soaking up the moisture, drinking greedily.

"So where the hell's Cramdon?" Soldier Wolf asked. "We've killed seven men, and the fire's probably gotten another three. And still no sign of the son of a bitch we're after."

"I'll grant ye, lad, he do have a way of slippin' off."

The rain continued through the remainder of the afternoon and into the evening, and Soldier Wolf and O'Bragh huddled in the aspen grove, the trees providing at least minimal shelter. They managed a small campfire after dark, heated up cold meat from the saddlebags, and slept finally in wet robes.

By morning the clouds were gone, and the day promised to heat up once more. But the big fire was also out, and the canyon below them presented an aspect of blackness and green interspersed.

Soldier Wolf and O'Bragh explored the desolated area where the day before the gunfight had taken place. And they found the charred remains of seven bodies, no sign whatsoever of the remaining three.

"If they got out ahead of the flames, they're halfway across the Never Summers by now," Jerry said.

"I expect so. An' this coon don't figger they's goin' to come back. Mebbe they make 'er back to the Cache La Poudre, mebbe not. Lot of mountains to cross between here an' there."

Downstream they found where the horses had grazed, but the animals were gone, and neither was there any sign of Cramdon and his other man or two men.

O'Bragh studied the horse tracks, concluded that, indeed, three of the animals were carrying riders.

"They've headed back down to the Canadian, Jerry me lad. Three of 'em now, an' two of us. Probably swing west, avoid the village, an' cross back over to Cache La Poudre."

"Think they know someone's after them, Bully?"

"Might. Might not. Could be the gunfire didn't carry this far—just saw the fire an' headed out."

They followed Cramdon's trail, urging their mounts to the fastest pace possible, exited from the mouth of the canyon, and continued down the Canadian.

By midmorning they came to an unexpected meeting with White Frog and his warriors.

"We have come to look for you, my friend," White Frog said. "But we decided to go hunting instead. . . ."

Soldier Wolf noted the two fresh scalps attached to the reins of White Frog's pony. They were the scalps of Whitemen.

"You have killed two men?"

"That is true," White Frog said. "The third is tied up. He is over there."

It was Cramdon.

* * *

Bound hand and foot, Edward Cramdon, former agent with the Bureau of Indian Affairs, was brought into the village of the People of the Valley and was tied with woven leather rope to the base of a scrub cedar close by O'Bragh's lodge. Morning Star Fox and his people stood about in a half-circle and studied the man who had brought sorrow to their village.

"Red Hair with Red Face," Morning Star Fox said, "we were not at war with you, for my people are at war with no one. Yet you have attacked us and have three times attempted to burn our lodges. You and your men have murdered many of my people, including old women and little children. Had these people ever harmed you, Whiteman? Had they cheated you at trading when you came to us and sold us goods that the White Chief had already given to us in exchange for the right to dig for the yellow metal in our lands? Did the young women you raped two winters past ever harm you? Did you steal our young women and take them to the lodges of the Whitemen where they were expected to sleep with strangers—did these young women ever harm you? No, none of these things ever happened, and always we allowed you to live among us and shared our food with you. Perhaps you could speak now and tell all of us your reasons, for we do not know them."

When Morning Star Fox had finished speaking, Cramdon grinned, nodded his head, and spat in the chief's direction.

The old chief stared down at the bound Cramdon, as if from a great distance, as if, for the moment, he could not even see the man bound to the cedar.

"White Frog has brought you to me, Red Hair with Red Face, and he has made you my prisoner. It seems to me now that perhaps I should give you back to him who captured you, for I think he would burn you alive."

"Your Red devils have killed thirty or so of my men," Cramdon said. "And you've burned my buildings on the Cache La Poudre. I don't owe you nothing, old man. Soldier Wolf! You're a government agent, just like I was. I demand my rights as an American. It's your duty to take me in to Denver, and we'll let a jury decide who's in the wrong. There's gold out there, Soldier Wolf. I can show you where it is—there's enough to make both of us rich men."

"There will be no justice if this man is taken to Denver," White Frog said. "For that reason I will not allow it. Soldier Wolf, I wish to burn this man and feed the black remains to the camp dogs. He is not worthy of any other sort of death. In my village, we would turn him over to the women, and they would cut his fingers off, then his nose; then they would gouge out his eyes, then cut him open and feed his intestines to the dogs. This man has no right to live. Those are my words!"

Soldier Wolf stared at Cramdon, the sneering face, the utter hatred in the man's eyes. This was the man he had been sent to capture, had been sent halfway across a continent to capture and bring in. And this was the man who had shot Sara and who had left him, Soldier Wolf, for dead on the rimrock above the village, the man who was responsible for numerous deaths, including Elizabeth Goth's.

"I owe you nothing, Cramdon," Soldier Wolf said. "I think I could watch you burn and take genuine pleasure in it."

"You're like me," Cramdon said. "You play your cards to win, and that's why you'll take me in to Denver, and we both know it. You're a Whiteman, and I'm a Whiteman, and when it comes to that, you won't turn me over to no goddamned Red devils."

Soldier Wolf grinned. "You're wrong about that, my friend," he said. "There was a time when I was half White, but I'm not anymore. That half of me is dead. White Frog is my brother, and the old man here is my father. And he's not White either."

Frank Goth refused to come out of his lodge, and Sara, after falling into Soldier Wolf's arms and clinging to him desperately, said, "Jerry, you must talk with him. I'm afraid he may kill himself—he loaded his pistol when word came that the warriors were returning. He says he's going to kill Cramdon, but he won't, I know him. I'm afraid he's going to kill himself. . . ."

And she turned and walked away quickly to her father's lodge.

When Soldier Wolf had finished speaking to Cramdon, he turned to Bully, nodded, and said, "Goth's got his pistol loaded."

When the two men reached the lodge, Sara was crying, and Frank was praying to the small crucifix attached to the lodgepole away from the entry, his head bowed, himself sobbing and saying over and over: *Forgive me Lord for what I am about to do, forgive me Lord . . .*

"Frank!" Soldier Wolf said. "Get hold of yourself, man. Get hold of yourself!"

Goth, startled, leaped to his feet, pistol in hand.

"I'm going to kill him, Jerry—you won't try to stop me? Even if the price is eternal damnation, I'm going to kill him!"

"Other coons has lost loved ones, ye're not alone," O'Bragh said.

"Father! No, no, it won't bring her back . . ." Sara sobbed.

"Frank's right," Soldier Wolf said slowly. "Let's go do it, Frank. Let's have an execution."

Sara stared at Soldier Wolf, her mouth agape.

O'Bragh raised one eyebrow.

"Will you deliver this man into my hands?" Frank asked.

"I will. He's yours, Frank. But let's get it over with. You ready?"

"Jerry, no! He'll regret it always—you mustn't let this happen."

"It's all right, Sara—let me handle this. You ready, Frank?"

Goth's eyes grew narrow, appeared to be those of a suspicious child. "You're serious, then? I'm ready. He owes me a death. . . ."

"Bully, keep Sara here. I don't want her to see what happens next."

O'Bragh nodded, allowed Frank and Jerry to pass out of the lodge, then blocked the entryway.

Goth and Soldier Wolf walked to where Cramdon was tied, and Goth held the pistol out before him, pointed it at Cramdon.

"BIA man!" Cramdon cried out when he saw Goth's face, "keep that crazy son of a bitch away from me. There's gold up there, I'll share it with you. . . ."

"All right, Frank, there he is—yours. Pull the trigger."

Goth turned toward Soldier Wolf, his eyes wild. "It's a trick, isn't it! You won't let me do it? But I've got the gun, and it's loaded."

"No trick, Frank. *An eye for an eye, a tooth for a tooth*. That's what your Scriptures say, and I believe it too. Your hand's shaking. Let me have the gun, I'll shoot him for you. I've got one or two grudges against him myself."

Goth turned, seemed to come suddenly to his senses. "We can't shoot an unarmed man, a man who's tied hand and foot—we can't do it, Jerry. . . ."

"No, Frank, no—we can't do it. I couldn't do it, and I'm used to killing by now. I have to take him to Denver—or else I have to let him get away, give him something to defend himself with. . . ."

* * *

It was after dark when Soldier Wolf returned to the scrub cedar where Cramdon was bound. The children of the village had come close, and a few had tossed pebbles at him and had run away. Some of the women had come and had hurled insults, had spit at him, and one had lashed him with a branch.

Through it all Cramdon had remained silent.

White Frog's warriors had begun to assemble a large pile of dry wood, branches and logs, and had stacked these into an ever-increasing heap at the center of the fire circle.

Cramdon stared at the activity and began to wonder if the Cheyennes might indeed have in mind to put him to death.

As the shadows lengthened, Soldier Wolf came around from behind the cedar, tossed Cramdon's skinning knife onto the ground in front of the man.

"What's this? That you, *agent*?"

"It's me, Cramdon. You see that pile of wood?"

"I see it."

"All right. I'm giving you a chance to run for your life. No horse, no gun—just a knife."

"Damned *White* of you."

"I'll give you half an hour's start, more or less. Moon's just past full—so you can see where you're going. I've told White Frog what I'm doing."

"Then they all come on horseback, track me down. Is that it, Soldier Wolf?"

"Not quite, Mr. Cramdon. There'll be just one man following you, and he'll be on foot. And he'll have a knife, just like you, nothing more than that."

"You?"

"Now you understand perfectly."

"Ain't a coon alive can keep up with me in this country, not on foot. You just wrote out your own ticket to hell, BIA man."

"We shall see what we shall see," Soldier Wolf said as he cut the bindings.

He watched Cramdon walk slowly, looking back, to the edge of the trees and then begin to run. He heard the splashing of water and knew the man had crossed the stream.

He will head up into the Medicine Bows, that is what I would do, too. He will want to pass north of Clark's Peak, then down to the headwaters of the Laramie, then over to Cache La Poudre. Any other man except O'Bragh would tire himself out in the first couple of miles, but he won't. He's not used to traveling on foot, no matter what he says. But he won't stop, he'll want to put some distance between himself and the village. A man could hide out for years in those mountains, but not without a means of taking game. . . .

Sara, moving as silently as a wild thing, slipped in from behind where he was standing, startling him.

Not a particularly auspicious start.

"You've released him," she said.

"I'll catch up with him. Couldn't let the Cheyennes burn him to death, could I?"

"You're going to take him in to Denver—if you catch him?"

"Don't think he's going to let me do that," Soldier Wolf said, taking the dark-haired girl into his arms and kissing her. "Sara, my little Sara! You going to marry me when I get back from this jaunt?"

"Yes, yes. I'll go anywhere with you, Jerry, do anything you want."

"Careful what you're saying, girl. That covers a lot of possibilities."

"I know. Did you give him a gun? Jerry, why not just let him go? He'll not come back to bother us again."

"He killed your mother, Sara, or his men did."

"Will killing him bring her back?"

"I guess not, and it won't take the scar off your belly, either. Do you think I could live, knowing that he was still out there somewhere?"

"We don't have to stay here—you've said California. There are so many places, Jerry."

"Girl, this half-breed Tsaragi has come to believe in justice. No, he doesn't have a gun. Just a knife. And that's what I'm taking."

"Take your gun, Jerry. . . ."

"No gun, little one. Fate brought me two thousand miles for this chase, ways I can't explain, don't understand. I'll never be free, never be my own man until I've killed him. That doesn't make sense to you? Doesn't make much sense to me, either."

He kissed her one last time, said, "Be back in two days, no

more than that," and turned from her, began running toward the ascending moon.

He did not cross the stream, stayed to the westward bank, moved north at a fast walk, feeling the rhythm of his body, feeling the firm earth beneath his moccasins. The moon was to his right now, climbing higher up the night sky, and the sound of the rippling little river was in his ears.

A pair of owls swooped through the silver light before him, glided above the creek alders, disappeared. A swampy area, and crickets singing, singing, an unbelievable threnody of dissonant music—then quieted as he approached, only a few brave ones continuing to make their noise.

The blood coursed through his body, and he felt good, felt alive, felt real—and he swung into an easy run, moving among shadows, areas of darkness alternating with gray-silver zones of open ground.

He will not take the main trail. That's what he figures I'll do. He'll head for the high pass, north of the mountain. Wait for me at the defile above the meadows in case I do take the trail he takes. He'll wait there until morning, figure to ambush me if I'm following. I know this country better than he thinks—he figures he's away, home free. A man shouldn't underestimate us Tsaragis.

Soldier Wolf finally crossed the little river, swung south of the branch leading down from the mountains, moved for high country, avoiding the canyon bottom.

He felt like whistling but didn't dare take the chance.

O'Bragh, you're either going to be proud of this coon or have to bury him, it's one or the other.

He stopped to catch his breath, rested a few minutes, looked off across the dark canyon below.

He's down there.

The moon was past mid-sky now, perhaps an hour past.

Soldier Wolf got up from the boulder he was sitting on, resumed a fast walk up the ridge spine. When the ground leveled a bit, the ridge rounding out into a plateaulike forest, he began to run once more, moving easily, almost effortlessly, breathing deep, feeling the rhythm of his body, exulting in its strength.

When he came to another outcropping, he stopped, stood tall in the moon-washed night, studied the land below him. He could see the meadows now, remembered the deer he and Sara had shot there two months earlier, smiled at the memory. It had been her first, and her shot had been true, a perfect shot—dropping the animal where it stood, gazing back at her.

What if you're wrong? Probably he's taken the other trail, over the low pass—that way's shortest. All you've done is turn your quarry loose, let him get away from you. . . .

"He'll be there," Soldier Wolf said, startled for a moment by the sound of his own voice.

Some distance away, perhaps a mile or more, across the canyon—a pair of coyotes flung their music to the night air.

Two coyotes, and they sound like twenty or more. . . .

Not time to drop down yet. He would descend to the stream at the head of the narrow canyon with the waterfalls in it—outflank Cramdon despite having climbed to the ridge spine, move back down through the cascades, come out to the open area above the defile where Cramdon would be waiting for him.

The moon hung low in the west now, above the shadowed rims of the great rolling mountains, the moon—pale white, just past the full, distorted from a perfect circle of light only if one studied it carefully. Layerings of cloud, silver-black, trailed just below the lunar orb, and Soldier Wolf watched, intent upon this one thing, as the moon finally touched the clouds, changed shape, slid on down behind the vapors, took on the form of a strange, canted half-moon.

The cry of a single wolf, the wild, lonely voice echoing, echoing. . . .

And his mind drifted eastward, to the land where he had grown up, the forested folds and crags of the Smokies, Grandfather Mountain, Mt. Mitchell, the Blue Ridge, the Newfound Mountains, the thickets of dogwood, redbud, flame azalea, and rhododendron, the forests that burst into flower with springtime, burned crimson and gold with the coming of autumn, the mists that hung perpetually about the humpbacked mountains, the town of Cherokee, his father's farm on Raven's Fork.

Thomas Soldier Wolf. Tamara Soldier Wolf. His brothers, Jed and Mike.

Would the spreading Civil War reach Raven's Fork? His younger brothers be pressed into military service, or would the Whites decide to go it alone, not trusting the motives of Indian people?

That would be better, he thought.

But in his mind's eye, nonetheless, he could see the cities of the North and the South in flame, he could see the armies coming together, could hear the incessant rattle of rifle fire, the booming of cannons, the screams of the wounded and the moans of the dying.

My land, he thought. My country. What is my country?

He remembered the words of his grandfather: *Pass on to the other world, little sister of the woods. I will join you after a time. . . .*

Prayer words spoken to a deer that had been slain.

And he remembered his dream from eight months back, the dream he had had that night with the warm, rainy mist blowing in and himself sleeping under the protection of a government-issue short tarp that he had made a point of not turning in to Supply when he had left the military.

What significance to that fact?

He remembered the dream. *Fires burning across the land, men firing at close range, men with sabers hacking at each other. Black people, their legs sunk down into the earth itself. Himself crying out, telling those who fought to stop, telling them of the insanity of their actions. And the wolf that had appeared that night, would appear again later, the wolf that was surely a projection of himself—but the wolf telling him of other mountains far to the west, these mountains, he realized now, the Medicine Bows, the Never Summers, the entire thrust and sprawl of the range upon range of the Shining Mountains, the Rockies, the High Shining. And the two bears—bears that had spoken to him, had told him—what? That he would remember, that he would look back from the Star Path and remember. It will be all right, all right, all right. . . .*

His people, the Cherokees, the Tsaragis.

Once, perhaps. But who were his people now? The Cheyennes, the Morning Star people? Frank Goth and Bully O'Bragh, Sara Goth, beautiful little Sara, Sara who would be his wife, his woman, his mate—if he were able to return alive from the insane venture that he was now engaged in?

White Frog, the Cheyenne priestly chief who seemed in every way more a war chief, a man his own age, a man who embodied the fierceness and the gentleness that he himself wished to possess?

Soldier Wolf touched his fingers to the turban upon his head, the "funny hat," as one of the Cheyennes had called it. Whirlwind? Or was it Roman Nose, the Arapaho?

Soldier Wolf removed the turban, unwound the cloth, and placed it into the interior pouch of his leather coat. And he felt the night air move about his temples and over his hair.

And he felt free.

I have come home to myself. I am nothing but myself. I will never be more than myself, but I will not be alone. I have found my mate, and one day I will find my place, where will it be? Across the mountains, across the deserts? Somewhere out there. . . .

Soon it would be morning, and the pale moon would drop under the rim of the range.

Mist rose from the small meadow as Soldier Wolf walked down out of the steep ravine where the stream was a white chain of cascades and waterfalls. The sunlight spilled from behind him, and he strode out through the grasses that were heavy with dew, moisture from the torrential rainstorm of two days earlier.

He stood in the center of the small meadow, looked downstream to where the creek passed through the angular crags of gray stone.

He's here somewhere, Soldier Wolf thought. I can sense his presence—a heavy, angry presence.

"Cramdon!" he shouted. "You cannot run any further! It is time for you to face me!"

Silence, and Soldier Wolf scanned the area, thought he detected movement near the base of a pine which grew close to the gray rocks.

"I have come alone, Cramdon! It's just the two of us. Come on out!"

Motion.

Cramdon moved slowly down from his hiding place, crossed the stream, walked out onto the level area of the meadow.

"You surprise me, BIA man. Must have come up one of the ridges, huh? Well, so now it's just two of us."

"Just us," Soldier Wolf agreed.

"What happened to your hat, government man? Fell off along the way?"

"It didn't fit me anymore. You ready, Cramdon?"

"Look, Soldier Wolf—I told you before. Those canyons over there are rotten with gold, enough for a hundred of us. I haven't got anything against you personal, you understand? Might be we'd even like each other, might be we could be partners. You get those

Injuns calmed down, and I'll bring in fifty men with rifles. We'll have those Redskins working our claims for us. . . ."

"You owe somebody a death, Cramdon. I didn't follow you to make deals."

"Have it your own way, then, you dumb son of a bitch! Just remember, I give you your chance."

Soldier Wolf drew his knife and advanced toward Cramdon, who drew his own blade, spit on the steel, wiped it against his pants leg.

The two men were still ten yards apart when a bear cub came scrambling out into the meadow, stopped, looked from one human being to the other. Soldier Wolf stopped his advance, stared at the little animal, perhaps forty pounds of yellow-red fur, its head moving from side to side as if studying these two strange creatures that had, it was certain, absolutely no rights to the meadow.

"Got you an audience," Cramdon growled as he continued to advance, approaching the cub on his way to meet Soldier Wolf.

Grizzly cub—it's not out here alone.

Soldier Wolf turned half about, just in time to see the sow grizzly emerge from the willow brush along the stream—a huge bear, its fur tipped silver-white, in full motion, not bothering to look around, heading straight for its cub.

Son of a bitch! Jerry thought. This is no way for it to end. . . .

But the bear was upon him, and he felt the stunning force of a forepaw. His vision diminished to a point of light, then momentary blackness, then vision once more, but blurred, everything out of focus.

The knife is gone.

He tried to get to his feet, but his sense of balance had vanished, and he fell sideways, his mouth open, the taste of grass in his mouth. His hands were under him, and he pushed at the earth, was on all fours, tried to force his vision to focus but could not.

He could hear the screams.

A great silver-brown creature with a man in its jaws, a man or the form of a man. Shaking it back and forth, shaking it, venting full fury upon it.

The man was screaming, screaming.

And then the screams stopped.

But the bear was still chewing at the thing it held in its jaws, threw it up into the air, lunged toward it once more.

He was not certain how he had managed to get to his feet. But he was running, running—a tree, he had to find a tree! O'Bragh had said that full-grown grizzlies can't climb, too heavy for the limbs. He had to find a tree and get up into it!

He leaped for the fork of a cottonwood, slipped, clung, desperately wrenched himself upward, managed to get his feet solidly onto a limb, reached for a higher limb, pulled himself up.

The grizzly was below him, roaring, snarling, tearing at the cottonwood's bark.

His vision was spinning once more; he was afraid he would fall out of the tree. He grasped the main trunk and held on, fought away the darkness that was threatening to swallow him.

The grizzly, on its hind legs, reaching up at him.

His mind would not clear. Pain in his head, behind his eyes. And the bear, coughing and snarling and chewing on wood, powerful, enraged. . . .

Goddammit, Bully, what am I supposed to do now? he thought, and then his vision went away and he could not think and he clung desperately to the bole of the cottonwood. . . .

How long had he been in the tree? What time was it? Late afternoon, but what day, what had happened? He knew that he didn't dare to climb down, but why not?

Grizzly.

Pain in his head and shoulder, his right shoulder laid open, through the leathers, matted with blood.

He could hardly breathe, and his throat was dry, so dry he could not swallow, tried to speak but could not.

He felt the dizziness swelling up over him once more, fought it off, managed to wedge himself between two limbs, passed into unconsciousness again.

Darkness then, the darkness of night. He could see stars through the leaves of the tree, but they were not points of light, were little white lines, blurs.

"Sara!" he croaked, his throat so dry it was painful—painful like everything else about his body. But the shoulder only throbbed now when he moved his arm too quickly, and the terrible ache inside his skull had lessened.

He slept.

Could see a marriage taking place, a Christian service, with Frank Goth presiding. Sara was getting married, who was the man standing next to her?

"No! Goddammit, no!" he managed, waking himself up.

But the dream continued, and he could see the Cheyenne ceremony as well, the great fire and the feast afterward, O'Bragh standing there, grinning from ear to ear, White Frog standing there also, and Morning Star Fox, him too. Sara, beautiful, wearing a white deerskin dress with porcupine quillwork on the bodice, Sara, her hair long and braided in Indian style.

Who was it? Who was standing there with her?

The man is wearing a turban.

What had happened to his turban? It was gone, had he taken it off? Why would he do that?

Himself.

He was with Sara, they were at the high meadows, making love—no, they were in their own lodge, Sara had made a lodge for them.

No. They were riding westward, toward California.

It was light again. Morning. Soldier Wolf could hear birds singing along the creek, mourning doves, thrushes, somewhere a mockingbird. That came first, and then he was aware of a raging thirst, a thirst so intense that it hardly seemed part of him.

Better to let that bear get me than to die of thirst. . . .

He eased himself down from the cottonwood and crawled toward the sound of water, water he knew had to be close by, but his vision still refused to draw focus.

On his hands and knees now, tangled in berry vines.

Dammit anyway, you stupid, miserable, half-breed son of a bitch!

Your mind is playing tricks. Concussion.

Was he even crawling in the right direction?

Then he was at the stream, and he lowered his lips to the clear, cold water, and he was drinking, drinking.

Voices?

Cheyenne voices? Frank Goth's voice. O'Bragh's!

They had found Cramdon's mutilated body, had stopped, were discussing what had happened. The horses were snorting and stamping their feet.

That other voice, a woman's voice? Sara's voice?

He gathered his strength, pushed himself back away from the water, held his breath for a moment, and then somehow managed to get to his feet. He steadied himself against an alder trunk, then took a step forward, then another, then another. . . .

ABOUT THE AUTHOR

BILL HOTCHKISS was born in New London, Connecticut, in 1936, and is of Scot, English, and Dutch descent. At the conclusion of World War II, the family moved to Griffin Creek, Oregon, and went broke raising chickens. The year 1947 found them in Nevada County, California, where they bought two acres of red dirt and built a house. Soon there were more chicken houses, another four thousand feathered friends, and near bankruptcy once again. Thereafter the elder Hotchkiss worked in the gold mines of the Mother Lode and planted berry vines. Poor times, but always with enough to eat.

Bill Hotchkiss graduated from the high school in Grass Valley, earned a scholarship to the University of California in Berkeley, and worked summers for the U.S. Forest Service. He took his B.A. in 1959, an M.A. from San Francisco State University in 1960, and the M.F.A., D.A., and Ph.D. degrees from the University of Oregon—in 1964, 1971, and 1974, respectively.

Novelist, poet, and critic, Hotchkiss is a man obsessed with the American West—its history, geology, landscape, flora, and fauna. As a boy, he was a ceaseless wanderer of ridge and canyon—to the point where those who knew him had begun to suspect his sanity. For several years he ran traplines—until he came to realize that he wished to catch nothing either larger or smaller than himself. Wild pets have included possums, skunks, ducks, a bluejay, a screech owl, a coyote, and a pair of turkeys, including a magnificent male named Walrus.

After twenty years of teaching (high school, university, and community college), Hotchkiss is now a full-time writer. The author and his wife, Judith Shears, live in Woodpecker Ravine, a few miles from Grass Valley, California. Together they have built their own house, without benefit of any public utilities. An old black bear haunts the ravine, and at night the coyotes sing.